The Poisoned Rose

Also by D. Daniel Judson

The Bone Orchard

The Poisoned Rose

D. Daniel Judson

BANTAM BOOKS

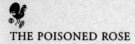

THE POISONED ROSE

A Bantam Book/October 2002

ISBN 0-553-58419-7

Published simultaneously in the United States and Canada

Bantam Books are published by Bantam Books, a division of
Random House, Inc. Its trademark, consisting of the words
"Bantam Books" and the portrayal of a rooster, is Registered in
U.S. Patent and Trademark Office and in other countries.
Marca Registrada. Bantam Books, 1540 Broadway, New York,
New York 10036.

PRINTED IN THE UNITED STATES OF AMERICA

OPM 10 9 8 7 6 5 4 3 2 1

For Tony Outhwaite

The Poisoned Rose

Prologue

I am back at the start again, back on Gin Lane again, a boy of ten with his whole life ahead of him. It is a hot summer morning. Breathing in the barely perceptible ocean breeze is like inhaling the air that rises up from the tip of a flame. The sun is new in the sky but already gives off a warmth that touches my face in the way it should in the hours that follow noon, not dawn. A sound comes from the inland side of the dunes, catching my ear. I turn to face it. The sound punches through the long roar and hiss of the Atlantic crashing in again and again just feet behind me. I hold still, warm sand shifting beneath my bare feet, and listen.

I hear cries, big fear in a voice that sounds tinny. I see nothing, just the dunes and the great houses built upon them. I hear then the sound of a dog barking—this, too, coming from somewhere behind those dunes, from the street beyond. These distinct sounds reach me in waves. They push against the sound of the ocean, fight it, are diminished by it. Still, I can hear them well enough to know something is wrong.

I start toward them, running toward the road that is beyond the dune. I make it over the soft sand to the foot of the dune and hurry to climb it. I drop down to all fours and scramble for the top. Sand disappears below my hands and feet, but I persist and crest it and stumble down the other side to the small blacktop parking lot below, where violence waits.

Asphalt crumbs lay along the broken edges of the lot, where beach grass grows wild. Pale yellow, the grass stands stiff in the August air and brushes my legs as I come through it. Each blade is just moments from combustion, a dry match head aching for the slightest friction.

I see her then. She is a brown-haired eleven-year-old girl, seated on the sun-warmed pavement in the middle of the empty seaside parking lot. She has just fallen from her bike, bare knees scraped, hands shimmering with blood. Stunned, she stares at the source of the barking, which sounds to me like automatic gunfire, short bursts of snarling and grunting that echo sharply off surrounding dunes and the fronts of the nearby houses.

It is, I see now, a mastiff that is charging her, one hundred twenty pounds of rabid viciousness. It is wild and enraged but focused and moves faster than anything should be able to move. But I am nearer to her than it is. I know I can make it to her if I don't let up.

I continue toward her, throwing myself forward, one leg after the other. I feel the sun-warmed pavement shift beneath the balls of my bare feet. I haul it, my lungs burning, my eyes on her, and when I finally reach her, when my out-of-control running turns to barely controllable slowing, the beast is only seconds away.

I drop fast into a crouch beside her and grab her arm and try to pull her up to free the bike around which her legs are tangled. But my touch startles her. She looks at me suddenly, drawing away instinctively. Because she is looking at me she is not paying attention as the mastiff lowers its head like a plow and makes its last wide strides and takes a hold of her right leg with its jaws. It stops on a dime and scoops her up, its barks funneling down to a deep, feral snorting. Long strands of spittle break free from the foam hanging from its mouth and go flying like shrapnel. I feel it hit my face.

The girl panics and grasps at me, looking down in horror at the animal tearing into her. She holds on to me with tremendous strength as it tugs on her. Her fingers dig into my arms. She screams and looks back up at me. I see her eyes so clearly. They are all I can see.

Behind us the ocean collapses on the shore. I hear it.

It seems my only connection to sanity, the world that existed just moments ago, before this burst of violence. I think in a split second that in the mouth of the beast, this girl seems to me less than human.

Over the sound of the waves I hear an approaching siren. Blood and spittle fly in all directions through the air, arcs of milky red. The girl screams again, a desperate shriek, and I cannot take it. I let go of her and grab hold of the dog by the collar and slide between them. I hook my fingers around the tube inside its throat and dig in till the tip of my middle finger and thumb meet.

It takes just a second for the mastiff to gag and release her. But I have not harmed it, merely angered it. When it does release her it wiggles violently, like a game fish on a line, and I lose my grip and it snaps its jaws down on me. Its teeth break my skin and lodge deep into the muscle of my leg, into my thigh bone. It has a solid, crushing hold on. Within a second it begins to shake its head from side to side.

Blood comes out of me fast. I feel myself lifted off the pavement, and then all I see is sky where there should be ground and ground where there should be sky. The dog shakes me like a rag doll more times than I can count. I cannot imagine that it will end. Then out of all this insanity I hear the sound of the siren grow nearer. My ear tunes in on it. It fills my head, then finally stops and all I'm left with is the growling and the tearing of flesh and the crashing waves.

Then I hear the crack of gunfire. I hear it again. Suddenly I am dropped, slick with blood and spit, to the pavement.

The instant I hit the ground I feel two hands grab me by my arm. It is the girl. She is pulling me across the pavement, pulling me toward her, away from the beast dropped by a cop's .38.

I look for her eyes but get only the morning sun, the color of pain and heat, in my eyes...

One

It was in the pale light of what seemed enough to me like morning that I awoke to the sound of someone pounding on my door. Outside my three front windows a steady rain was falling through the few yellow and red leaves that were left hanging on the trees that lined Elm Street, drilling hard into the already saturated lawn two floors below. It had been raining for days and I almost couldn't remember a time when there had been anything else but this. I preferred the sound outside my windows over the pounding on my door, so I let myself hear only that for a time. I was facedown on a bare wood floor, breathing in dust and damp, and thinking how the drops hitting the leaves sounded like rain falling on a hundred tiny umbrellas.

My muscles ached and the left side of my face stung. I

didn't think too much of any of it. Last night's drinking was still in my veins. I could feel waves of intoxicants moving like thickly clustered schools of tiny fish in my blood. A part of me was still asleep, and the part of me that wasn't wanted to join up with it again as soon as possible.

Finally I got up off the floor. It took some doing but I made it to my feet. I wanted more to stop the pounding than to see who was there. When I opened the door I saw George standing in the dark hall outside, his arm poised for another bang. He looked pretty much half in the bag himself. He lived in the apartment below mine and served drinks seven nights a week in the bar one flight below that. The town we lived in was a small resort town that all but shut down between September and May, and the bar we lived above, the Hansom House, catered to the working-class locals who lived there year round, artists and laborers alike. There wasn't much to do at night during the off months out here but drink and gossip, and George was the man to whom most people came when they wanted healthy servings of both.

When he saw me George lowered his arm. He looked a little dumbfounded, and then I realized that his eyes had shifted and were focused on the left side of my face. I felt the stinging again and remembered then the scratches and how they had come to be there.

"Jesus, Mac," George said, staring at my face, "they look worse than they did yesterday." He whispered when he spoke; the dark hallway outside my door seemed to require that somehow.

I ignored George's comment. I felt an urge to touch the scratches but didn't.

"What the hell do you want?" I muttered.

"There's someone here to see you."

"You could have just called me to tell me that."

"I tried, Mac. Your phone's out of order."

"Oh, yeah." Service had been shut off last week because I hadn't paid my bill. Yesterday I received notice that the electricity was next. "What do they want?"

"She didn't say."

"She?"

"Yeah."

"She who?"

"Didn't say."

"Have you ever seen her here before?"

"No, I think I would have remembered her."

"Did she say what she wanted?"

"All she said was that she wanted to talk to you. She said it was important."

I had gotten up too quickly and was a little dizzy. It felt as if gravity were working particularly hard on me this morning. It took pretty much all I had not to just give in to it and lie back down on the floor for as long as it would take for things to lighten up again.

"Just tell her I'm not here. Tell her I left town and you don't know when I'm coming back. Tell her whatever you want. Just make sure she goes away."

"There isn't any harm in talking to her, Mac, is

there? I mean, no harm in hearing what she came to say, right?" He stopped, then added, "She's pretty."

"Just tell her I'm not here. Tell her I'm dead. I don't care."

George nodded. His vision shifted past me and into my apartment. I didn't have to look behind me to know what he saw. My cramped living room was chaos, crowded with furniture that was probably secondhand around the time I was born. I heard then the rain falling past my three front windows. I also heard it landing on the roof above us. I listened to the difference in pitch between the two sounds and said nothing as I waited for George's eyes to shift back to me.

"You should put something on those scratches, Mac. Do you have any ointment or something? If you don't, I could bring you some—"

"I'm going back to sleep, George."

"You coming down later?"

"I don't know."

"Drinks are on the house."

"Maybe, George."

"That guy that keeps bothering the girls is coming back tonight. You know the one I mean. I guess he's been in the city for a while, and from what I hear he's coming back out tonight and'll probably come in. He owes me for a tab he ran out on, and he doesn't seem all that eager to pay it. I was thinking maybe you could talk to him for me."

"If someone owes you money, call the cops."

"I don't want them in the bar. It's bad for business. A lot of people leave if they're around, and those who stay are afraid they'll be waiting outside to bust them for DUI."

"I'm sorry. There's nothing I can do."

"The thing is, the guy's not afraid of me. He's afraid of you. He's said so. Just ask him when he plans on paying me. If he doesn't pay up after you talk to him, then I'll call the cops, I swear. All you have to do is talk to him for me. Anyway, drinks are on the house, like usual."

I was broke, and the idea of continued free drinks appealed to me more than I would ever say. "I'll see what I can do, okay?"

"I appreciate it, Mac. Thanks. Listen, I was just talking to the girls. They'll be in tonight. They'll be glad to see you."

"Isn't it kind of early for them to be up and making calls?"

"What are you talking about?"

"What time is it?"

"It's four, Mac. In the afternoon. What time did you think it was?"

"Shit."

"What?"

I closed the door and went into the bathroom and filled up the iron-stained sink with cold water. As I splashed my face with it I felt as if I were pressing shards of metal into my open skin. I kept my eyes down and avoided the reflection in the streaked and broken hand mirror fixed to the wall above the sink. The scratches on my face were days old now but they were still noticeable enough. I didn't want to see them. Four long marks that began just above my left temple ran down past my eye, ending at my jaw. It would be hard for me to see them and not think of the woman who had made them just hours prior to her death.

I had on only a T-shirt and jeans, so I grabbed an old hooded sweatshirt out of my bureau and pulled it on. It smelled musty but clean and was the last of a wash I had done weeks ago. It was chilly in my rooms, far too chilly for October. I pulled on my work boots and grabbed my denim jacket and started down the two flights of stairs but stopped at the landing above the last flight when I heard George's voice again.

I peeked around and down the stairs and could see him standing in the doorway, talking to someone. It was a woman. I could not see her face, just the shape of her body inside an open overcoat that was sizes too big for her. She was wearing jeans and a thin white sweater. I didn't move, just stayed where I was and listened.

"Do you know when he might be in?" she was saying. The door was open and her voice was nearly lost to the sound of all that rain falling behind her. Even if I couldn't hear her at all I would know pretty much what it was she was saying. I'd heard it before, from those who came looking for my help before her.

"I don't know," George told her. "I'm sorry. He's hard to keep track of."

"It's very important I talk to him." There was a tightness to her voice, which was tonal and low, like a cello. Her jeans were old and faded and baggy. I got the sense by the way they hung off her hips that they had belonged first to a man.

"I don't know what to tell you."

"I've tried to call him but his number's disconnected."

"I can give him a message when I see him. I can't say when that might be. That's the best I can do. Maybe you can leave your name and number with me."

"No. No, that won't work."

"I'm sorry. I don't know what else I can do. If you're in trouble, maybe you should go to the police."

"I can't go to them."

"Why not?"

"I just can't."

"Listen, you're welcome to stay and wait for him and have a drink, if you want."

"I can't do that, either."

"Well, if I see him I'll let him know you're looking for him. What's your name?"

"It's okay. Thanks. I'll try back later on if I can." She backed away from the door then. George watched her go. I waited till he closed the door before I went down to him.

"She's persistent," he said. "She was halfway up the stairs again when I came back down. She must want to talk to you bad."

"You've never seen her before?"

"No. She was a pretty thing, though, don't you think?"

I said nothing to that. I thanked George for his help and left. I pulled the hood of the sweatshirt up over my head and ran through the rain to my ancient LeMans parked across the flooded street. I got in and pulled the door shut, and that was when I saw an old two-door red Saab parked on the other side of the street, a few spots down from the Hansom House. A woman was behind the wheel. I could barely see her through the rain streaming down my windshield and hers. But I could make out the color of the overcoat, and that was how I knew it was probably her. I could see that her head was tilted forward, her forehead resting on the steering wheel. I didn't dare start my engine. I didn't want to risk drawing her attention. I didn't want her lifting her head to the sound of my engine and seeing me. I didn't want her rushing through that rain toward me. I couldn't hear what she had to say. I just couldn't. I was out of the charity business. There was nothing she could say to change that.

So I waited for a few minutes, smelling the damp

must of the old interior, watching her. Finally she leaned back and wiped her eyes with the back of her hands. I looked away from that. Then I heard the engine of her Saab start. Headlights came on. And then she quickly steered away from the curb.

I ducked down a little as her car went past. I didn't think she saw me. I sat up again and looked in the rearview mirror and watched as she turned left and rode past the train station, toward North Main Street. Then she disappeared from my sight.

It was just four in the afternoon but looked like dusk. I had thought just minutes ago that it was dawn. I was close to an hour late for my meeting with Frank Gannon, but there was nothing I could do about that now. If it hadn't been for George pounding on my door, I would have missed the thing altogether. As I drove I thought of all the ways that my going there was a mistake.

I rode over flooded streets into Southampton Village. It was just a little over a mile. I parked at the corner of Main Street and Job's Lane, then ran through the rain to the entrance to Frank's building. I was soaked through by the time I reached it. His office was the only door at the top of thirteen steep steps. Each plank of creaking wood announced my presence as I climbed up.

The office was dimly lit; the only windows were the

ones at the front and the rear, but even when it was a sunny day outside they didn't catch all that much light. Before it was an office, this room had been an attic storage room above a women's clothing store. It still had that feel. The corners were dark and seemed to take up much of the room, particularly toward the back. The furnishings were simple: a desk and chair positioned midway down the long room, two chairs facing it, and a long couch behind those, its back against the opposing brick wall. The rest of the room was just filing cabinets and dark corners and empty space.

Frank was behind the desk when I entered, seated with his back straight in his big leather chair. He was on the phone, a stack of files at one elbow and a lighted reading lamp at the other. Between his elbows was an ink blotter, heavily stained.

His skin was clean-shaven and taut, and he looked like a man who took care of himself, to the point of pampering. No one really knew exactly how well off Frank was. He had his home on Hill Street, his pretty wife, his two daughters, both in nice Ivy League colleges, and his two Cadillacs. He never seemed to want for anything. His exterior appearance was polished, and yet it did little to hide the real man inside from anyone who did business with him, the rough and violent ex-cop who had found a much better life as a private detective maneuvering in and out of the countless cracks that existed between laws.

I closed the door behind me and leaned my back

against it. I didn't want to step any farther into the room. I looked at Frank for a while, then realized there was someone else in the room, standing in the back, by the rear window, in the shadows.

I looked toward him and saw that whoever it was had his back to me and was looking at me over his shoulder. He was holding a folded newspaper under his left arm. He waited for a moment, staring at me, before turning away and looking out the rear window at the cop parking lot below.

There was no getting around the fact that whoever the hell he was he was a big guy with a neck like a hydrant. He wore a gray sweatshirt and jeans, and something about his build reminded me of one of those performers in the circus who bend metal bars around their necks to show their strength. He wasn't muscular like a weight-lifter or a professional athlete, just tremendously solid. He was a giant to my gargoyle, blacksmith to my scarecrow. I didn't have to guess to figure out what kind of work he did for Frank.

Frank waved me in but I stayed by the door. It was a refusal that made my having come this far already a little easier for me to bear. He was listening intently to the person on the other end of the phone, not speaking or even nodding, just sitting with his back straight, the phone in one hand and his other hand spread flat on the blotter. I shook the rain out of my hair and my three-day-old beard and wiped the palms of my hands on my damp jeans. Then I looked again toward the giant at back of the room. He was reading his paper by the weak light that came in through the small window. I looked at him and wondered exactly how he fit behind the wheel of a car.

Then Frank finally hung up the phone and stood. He waved me in again, this time more insistently. He gestured toward one of the two seats facing the desk as he looked through the pile of files. I ignored his gesture and stayed where I was by the door, my hands in the pockets of my jacket. Frank looked up again. He was clearly puzzled that I was still where I was, almost annoyed by it. I took a degree of pleasure from this.

"Jesus, Mac, come in," he said.

I took a few steps forward, then stopped. I turned my head toward the large storefront window that looked out over Main Street. There was nothing beyond it but the shifting, grainy gray of the rain and the half-stripped trees that lined Main. The sound of the rain was so relentless I was starting to feel a little beaten by it. I was spent, a little drunk still, and too tired to think or care about anything.

"You're late," Frank said.

I nodded. "I know."

"I'm running a business here. You work for me, you need to be on time. Do we understand each other?"

The giant was looking at me over his shoulder. His face was in shadow, but I knew his eyes were on me.

"It's enough that I'm here, wouldn't you say?"

Frank was looking at the scratches on my face. He said nothing about them, but then he didn't need to; he knew how I got them, he knew the whole story.

He looked down at the pile of files then and pulled one from the bottom half of the stack. He dropped it on top of the blotter and opened it, flipping through the papers inside. "You know, there's not a lot of work out here for skilled labor, let alone someone like you. You know that."

"I know what's out here, Frank. And I know what's not out here."

"I'm offering you a chance to change that miserable life of yours."

"I'm here for work, not counseling."

"You can make a lot of money in this business. The right man can clean up, buy things, cars, a house maybe, even women. The right man can break old habits and start new ones." He stopped and studied me skeptically. "How long has it been since your last drink? A day? A few hours? Or did you have a little nip on the way over here?"

"Just because I'm going to take your money, Frank, doesn't mean I have to take your shit, does it?"

From the corner of my eye I saw the giant take a few steps away from the back window, moving to join Frank and me. I sensed that if there was going to be a fight, he wanted to be a part of it. I glanced at him again and saw that his hands were empty, hanging at his sides. The folded paper was left on the windowsill.

The floorboards protested loudly under his work boots. He and I stared at each other. The rain slowed then, the sound of it lessening.

Frank closed the folder decisively and placed it back on the top of the pile. He glanced at the giant, then back at me.

"I don't work with drunks," the giant said.

Before I could respond to that Frank said to me, "The men who work for me, Mac, do it because I pay top dollar. I won't bullshit you by saying working for me is an honor, but there are a lot of other men who would be more than grateful to be put on my payroll part time, let alone full time.

"You can go certain places my other men can't. You're part of the scenery out here, which means, for the time being at least, you can poke around and people won't even think twice about it. As long as no one knows you're working for me—and why should they?—then your services can be of some considerable value to me."

"My services?"

"I'm not a big fan of coy, Mac."

"And I'm not a big fan of coincidence. My business goes under and suddenly there you are with an invitation to become part of, how did you say it, 'your team'?"

"From what I heard your business wasn't much of one."

"It paid the bills."

"That's not what I've heard. You've got some debts. You were a housepainter, for Christ's sake. And not a very good one at that. You'd need to work two shit jobs just to catch up, and you'd be lucky this time of year if you found one."

"My point is, Frank, the same day I found myself out of business, there you were suddenly, standing right behind me."

"Your lucky day, that's all. Mine, too."

"Maybe. Or maybe you were just standing there for longer than I realized."

"So I've had my eye on you for a while. You're not exactly a nobody out here. I read the papers."

"Yeah, I read the papers, too."

"So we understand each other."

"What is it exactly you think you understand about me?"

"I think you're sick of getting the short end of the stick and not getting paid for it. You had a partner in your housepainting business. He killed his girlfriend and then himself, right in front of you. That's what put you out of business. Trouble finds you. Some people are just like that. I'd think that at this point in your life you figure if you can't stay out of trouble, then you might as well at least start profiting from it."

"You figured all that out by just looking at me, huh?"

"Figuring things out is what I get paid to do."

"Among other things."

"Listen, I'm running a business, I don't have time for this. Again, in case you haven't noticed, winter is on its way. I'm offering you work, and I'm offering to pay you top dollar. Do you want it or not?"

"I'm here, aren't I?"

"The thing is, I can't use you if you can't see straight. It's as simple as that. I don't know exactly what kind of tidal wave of self-hate you're riding here, I haven't figured that out yet, but you're no good to me like this. You look like shit. Have you seen yourself lately?"

"I'm just tired. I'm just tired."

"I know what you are."

Frank glanced toward the giant again. He offered Frank no reaction at all. Then Frank looked back at me and sighed. He glanced once again down at the file. He opened it. Among the pages inside were photos. It seemed to me he was more thinking all this through than looking for something. He closed the file again before I could see anything more than a few handwritten papers and several black-and-white surveillance photos.

He looked up at me and nodded decisively. "So?"

"Just tell me what you want done, Frank."

"A valued client of mine paid a young man a goodly

sum of money to stay away from his daughter. It was my client's understanding that they had an agreement. He was plain enough when he paid the kid off. But we've recently been made aware that the young man isn't keeping his side of the bargain. He's still very much in contact with the daughter. Our client wants us to pass a message along to this upstart. It's an easy money night, Mac, not a big job at all."

"What kind of message?"

"One the boy'll listen to. On this kind of job I like to send out two men. You'll be working with this gentleman here. Understand so far?"

The giant stepped closer to the desk, moving out of the darkness completely now. I could see him clearly. His eyes were fixed on me, his disapproval of me obvious. He wore his brown hair in a severe military buzz cut, and there were flecks of white around his temples that made him look as if he had just come in out of a snowfall. He was, like Frank, in his mid-fifties, but unlike Frank he looked less well tended, less groomed. A different kind of life from Frank's had left its mark on him.

"He'll get you started, show you what procedures we follow, and so on. Just follow his lead. He's the best I've ever worked with, end of story."

The giant and I were dressed alike, in jeans and sweatshirts and work boots. Beyond that we were as different as two people got.

"If it's all the same to you, I'd rather work alone," I said.

The giant took another step forward. It was a quick one, almost eager. "I can do this better without him tagging along," he said. "Playing nurse maid'll only slow me down."

"Sorry, boys. That's the way it has to be. This is a very prominent family. No room for error here."

In Frank's book every family with money and property south of Sunrise Highway was a prominent family. Every job was an opportunity for him to grab at just a little more power. This and this alone was all that mattered to Frank Gannon.

"I didn't sign on to baby-sit, Frank," the giant said.

"Look, I need someone to show him the ropes, that's all there is to it. And anyway, if it isn't him with you tonight, then it's going to be someone else. I want two men on this. I want it to go right."

"Then anyone but him."

"I need you to do this for me. Okay?"

Neither the giant nor I said anything more. I glanced at him. His eyes were hard but I didn't really care.

Frank said, "The upstart works at a bar in Sag Harbor. On slow nights he usually cuts out around eleven. Traditionally tonight's a slow night. You'll meet up here at ten and ride out together. It's easy money tonight. If all goes well, you should be done before one. Any questions?"

I had only one.

"What exactly is the message we're supposed to send?"

"It's nothing you can't handle, Mac. Just let Augie here do the talking. Watch his back and pay attention, that's all you have to do."

I glanced at the giant, the man Frank called Augie, then back at Frank. The rain picked up again and sounded like something brittle breaking into pieces against the front window.

"I guess I should introduce you two, huh?" Frank said. He smiled then. "Mac, this is Augie. Augie, this is Mac."

No one said a word after that.

That afternoon I shaved and showered, then stretched out on my couch and fell asleep to the sound of the rain. I slept for a few hours, and when I woke up I was thinking a lot about having a drink. But I just sat still and didn't do anything about it. It was easier to do that some times but not others. I was able to do it now, though, no problem. It seemed the fewer moves I made, the better.

It was still raining hard and my head was soaked by the time I got into his truck. The heat was on and I began to dry out a little. Together he and I rode in silence toward Sag Harbor. Once there we parked across from the Sag Harbor Cinema, in sight of the bar where the kid worked, and waited.

We were down maybe fifty feet from the corner of

Main Street and Washington Avenue, parked nose to the curb. The red, blue, and white lights from the neon movie theater marquee bled into the rain-swept street, and farther down the road, where it wasn't touched by the colored lights, the pavement shimmered under the dark sky like a long, taut banner of black silk.

We sat without speaking and listened to the rain drum the steel roof over our heads. It made enough of a racket to distract me from the tangible tension between us. I didn't really want anything to do with Augie. I just wanted to get through the job and hope I would never have to work with him again. The sound of the hard, flattening drops gave me something else to focus on as we sat there and waited.

Augie was wearing a military field jacket over his sweatshirt and jeans. There were no insignia or patches on the jacket, just the name Hartsell stenciled over the left top pocket. His pickup truck was an old rounded Chevy that had seen better days well before I was born. There were holes in the rusted floorboard that I had to cover with the sole of my boot to keep the water from the flooded roads splashing up at me. The rubber around the gear shift had cracked and all but broken off, and the paint on the metal dashboard was faded from almost four decades of sun.

I had caught a glimpse of the Colt .45 that Augie wore under his jacket as I climbed into his truck back in town. It was holstered to his belt, just below his right kidney. It was concealed from my sight now, wedged between him and the seat covered with cracked black vinyl. But I knew it was there. I couldn't help but wonder if this Augie guy was the kind of man who carried his weapon at all times, even at home.

A fairly modern radio was mounted under the old-style dashboard, tuned to a jazz program on the college station. The volume was low but I could hear well enough Charlie Haden singing "Wayfaring Stranger." I listened and felt almost good to be alive. It was a hard song for any man to ignore, and I wondered if Augie was listening. But I couldn't tell. Anyway, when it was done another, lesser song came on after it, and I stopped listening so closely and looked down Main Street toward the bar at the corner where the upstart kid we had come to give a message to worked slinging drinks.

The bar was called the Dead Horse and it sat across from Long Wharf, where twenty-foot sailboats and luxury yachts moored for the summer months. I knew this bar well. It had two large storefront windows and a front door between them that opened onto the corner of Main and Bay streets. Inside there was a short bar, two ceiling fans, two tiny rest rooms, and a dozen tables, nothing more. On weekends ensembles set up in a corner and played, mostly Irish music but sometimes jazz, and the hardwood floors brought the music right to the bottom of your feet. One night, years ago,

I had seen a quartet play radical jazz covers of Jimi Hendrix tunes. I drank dark beer with bourbon backs long after the band broke and stayed there with them and a few other regulars till the sun came up and the streetlights went off one by one down the length of Main Street. To this day I can remember that night vividly—the bass solo during "Little Wing," the joy, the pretty girlfriend of the drummer and how I couldn't take my eyes off her. But I have no memory whatsoever of how I got back to the Hansom House. Even my memory of the days that followed is hazy, full of jagged holes. It was lost time, a span of hours during which I, for all intents and purposes, was not part of this world.

The upstart kid's name was Vogler. I had looked through the folder Frank had given us and studied his photograph. The folder was thinner than the one I had seen on his desk back in his office that afternoon, and almost half the text had been blacked out with a Magic Marker. No names, no addresses, nothing but what little we needed to know about the target. Vogler was in his early twenties and didn't look all that much like trouble to me. He had short brown hair and wire-rimmed glasses and a narrow face that didn't seem to me the kind of face that made people exactly run with fear. There was no mention of the name of Frank's client or the daughter Vogler was suiting anywhere in the file. But I wasn't surprised by that. It was, I was certain, probably the least of what was being withheld from me.

Streams of rainwater ran down both sides of Main Street into a puddle the size of two car lengths. Bay Street was pretty much underwater, like it usually was in the rain. The bridge to North Haven was half lost to a bank of mist that shifted in from the harbor. There were halos around the street lamps and circular pools of grainy light around their bases with stretches of darkness in between. I turned my head and glanced to the south end of the tiny village, and all I could see was a wall of gray in which the stores that lined Main Street began but did not end. Everything looked unfinished, like a movie set or tumbling-down ghost town.

With the motor off, the heater wasn't running, and the air inside grew damp quickly. My hair was nowhere near dry yet. I started to button up my denim jacket against the damp. The metal buttons felt cold to my fingertips. The third button from the top was missing. I had no idea how it came off or where it was.

"You need a different kind of coat," Augie said.

These were the first words either of us had spoken since leaving Frank's office. I had to look past him to see out the driver's door window, which was my only view of the bar. I had done all I could up till then to pretend he wasn't there.

"You need a particular kind of coat for this kind of

work," he added. He didn't look at me, just kept his head turned and his eye on the bar at the end of the street.

"I have an overcoat at home. The seams are torn but it works for the most part."

He shook his head. "An overcoat's not good. Try to find something that doesn't go past your mid-thigh. Field jackets work best, or a pea coat. Long coats and dusters just get in the way, and you don't need that. Besides, if you walk into a place wearing a long coat, you get noticed more. That's a fact. When I see anyone with a long coat I immediately think he's hiding a shotgun or baseball bat or something. I don't take my eyes off him."

I buttoned the last button and then put my hands in my pockets for warmth.

"You can probably get a liner for that jacket, or a down vest to wear over it, something like that. Pocket warmers hunters use are good for long stakeouts like these."

I nodded and looked at the back of his head and saw a thin scar interrupting the hairline near the base of his skull.

"Frank mentioned that you worked for him once before," Augie said.

"Yeah. Sort of."

"What does 'sort of' mean?"

"I did a job but didn't get paid."

"Frank stiffed you?"

"No. He referred me to someone who had a job he couldn't take. They ended up stiffing me."

"And that's how you got the scratches on your face?"

"Yeah."

"They're from a woman, that much I can tell."

"Why do you say that?"

"The width of the cuts, and the depth. Plus men don't scratch lengthwise, not as broadly, anyway. Men gouge, women drag like cats. Anyway, it looks as if the nails that did that had been filed, almost to a point, I'd say, which not only indicates that they were more than likely a woman's but also that she wasn't really the, oh, girl scout type, either. Am I right?"

He was. These scratches had been left by a woman named Callie Weber, a former student from Southampton College, my old college, who had turned addict and hooker. Frank had come to me and offered me quick money if I found her for an interested third party and let him know where she was. The job was, Frank had said, a simple matter of finding the Weber girl, but of course in the end that wasn't the whole story. I learned that she had enemies, wealthy men who were former clients of hers whose lives she could easily ruin, and when I found her and she figured out who I was and what I wanted, she panicked and ran. Like a fool I tried to stop her, and that was when she clawed at my face. The next day her body was found floating almost in the dead center of Peconic Bay.

When I was visited at the Hansom House by Frank

a few days after and called him on his withholding information, he said it was the nature of the job and that I had been told what I needed to know. I wanted to hit him but was too drunk.

Augie said, "You don't like to talk about it, do you?"

"No."

"You can't let this work get to you. It's a part of the order of things, just like everything else. You're not supposed to like it. The minute you start to like it, that's when it's time to get out. But you can't let it get to you."

"So why do it if you don't like it?"

"Like I said, it's part of the order of things."

"I don't like to kid myself into thinking I know what the order of things is. That's the way men like Frank Gannon like to think."

"Don't believe for a moment that because I take his money I'm anything like him."

"So then why work for him?"

Augie looked back out the driver's door window, through all that rain, to the bar on the corner.

"It's personal," he said. "Look, no offense, kid, you don't seem all that bad, but I've got to be honest, I'm not part of the Big Brother program here. I'm not all that comfortable with the idea of you being the guy to watch my back when and if the shit comes down. I've heard some things about you I don't like, mainly that none of Frank's other men want to work with you. When I asked Frank why, he just muttered something about you not being all that popular with the town cops and left it at that. I know a dodge when I see one. I don't like not knowing things. I'm funny that way. I've made some calls to some people in town. I've been away for thirty years but I still have friends here. They told me about you, that you drink too much, that you butt into things you shouldn't. Some even went as far as to say you were a fuckup and that I was stupid to get anywhere near you. How much of that is true?"

"None of it's a lie."

"Yeah, well, I don't much like working with fuckups."

"Not very many people do."

"I want you to understand something very important right now. You are to just sit here and watch, you got that? You don't get out of this truck for anything, you stay and don't do a thing, no matter what happens. You at my back is more of liability than a help. When this is over I'll tell Frank you did fine and that you're ready to work on your own, that you're a natural and that he's lucky to have you. If he wants to keep hiring you, that's between you and him. But I don't want to work with you. You get cautious at my age. It's nothing personal."

It wasn't long after this that the door to the bar opened. We both sat up and watched as a man stepped out onto the sidewalk and stood under the small awning over the door. He was immediately followed by another.

Even across this distance and through the rain I could tell that the one who had exited the bar first was Vogler. The second man out had black hair that hung halfway down his back. Neither of them was a terribly big man. They stood face to face and talked.

"That's him," Augie said. He reached down and turned the ignition. The starter motor cranked twice, then the engine caught with a burst of exhaust tumbling down the dual exhaust below the rusted-out floorboards.

Augie gripped the steering wheel with his left hand and rested his right hand over the knob of the gear shift. I could see it shake from the vibrations of the motor. He sat completely still and waited, watching through his window the scene at the end of the block.

"Someone's not happy."

The kid, Vogler, and the guy with the long black hair were going at it, arguing and yelling at each other, their faces just inches apart. Vogler pointed his finger in the second guy's face, but the second guy swatted it away and pointed back, only at Vogler's chest. He jabbed Vogler hard, and Vogler just took it. He stopped yelling and listened to whatever it was the second guy was telling him. Then Vogler turned and stepped out into the street. The second guy yelled at him as he went, but Vogler just kept going without looking back. He crossed the rain-swept street and got into an old Dodge Rambler. The lights came on and I heard the sound of its motor start, and then the Rambler backed out onto Main Street.

Augie flipped on his headlights and shifted into reverse. He waited till the Rambler was moving forward, then let out the clutch and backed us away from the curb. He shifted into first and we moved slowly forward. I listened to the transmission whine.

But before Augie could shift into second gear an old black Caddy whipped around the corner, turning from Bay Street on to Main, skidding to a sudden stop in front of the Rambler, cutting it off. The Rambler barely stopped in time. It and the Caddy formed a perfect T shape, the driver's door of the Caddy facing the windshield of the Rambler. The instant the Rambler stopped, Augie pushed in the clutch and down on the brake pedal. His truck slowed, twenty-five feet from the other two vehicles at the end of Main.

The brake lights of the Rambler reflecting off the rainy street looked to me like an illustration of fire. I sensed something and my stomach tightened. Just seconds after the near collision the driver's side window of the Caddy rolled down far enough for a hand to extend out. Augie and I saw the gun it held instantly, but there was nothing we could do.

Six shots, one right after another, punched holes in the Rambler's windshield. The first shot sent a jolt through me. My muscles flexed hard. The same jolt tore through me with each successive shot. When it was done, when the revolver was empty and the Caddy began to back away, its tires slipping on the wet pavement, I said, "Jesus," and reached down for the door handle. I jerked it up, and the door swung open and I stepped down to the street, into a good inch of water. I heard Augie call my name, but I ignored him and started toward the Rambler.

The Caddy backed onto Bay Street, the driver cutting the wheel sharply. It spun around, then paused long enough for the driver to shift into drive before it sped forward, heading toward the bridge to North Haven.

I looked for a license plate but the Caddy was moving too fast. The scratches on my face stung in the rain and I felt my legs hollow a little from fear. I kept running, though, toward the Rambler. It was the only thing I knew to do.

By the time I reached the Rambler the driver's door had swung open and Vogler had slumped out from behind the wheel and was lying on the street. The water around his head was dark with blood. The darkness was spreading out fast.

I came to a stop and crouched to see his face. I had to lean around him to do so, and my chest touched his shoulder. His body was lifeless, his limbs falling to a rest at odd angles. I saw his face, or what was left of it. One bullet had creased his temple, the other shattered his cheekbone. Part of his right ear was missing. There was another bullet wound in his chest, and I could hear air being sucked through it. I saw then that his eyes were open, searching. He looked puzzled, shocked. His eyes met mine and there was a cognition. There were bits of shattered windshield glass in his wounds. He tried to move his mouth but the nerve damage to his face was so severe his jaw wouldn't work.

I took off my denim jacket and laid it over his torso. He was on his side. I could see that the bullet that had entered his chest had exited through his back, just below his left shoulder blade. I knew enough to know that he would probably be dead before an ambulance could get to him. The nearest hospital was in Southampton, twenty miles away. The nearest ambulance station was only a little over a mile from here, but in his condition it might as well have been a hundred.

Still, I lifted my head and looked toward the entrance to the Dead Horse, where a handful of people had collected, among them the kid with the long black hair, the one Vogler had been arguing with.

"Call an ambulance," I yelled. The rain was a steady peal in my ears, as heavy as a waterfall. My voice barely cut through it.

Nobody moved at first, they all just stood there and stared at me. I glanced through the storefront window and saw that the bartender was on the phone, her eyes locked on Vogler and me. Gurgling sounds added to the sucking sound coming from his chest wound. I looked down at him. His eyes were fixed on me, but they were becoming glassy and dimming. Any minute they would roll back in their sockets and his lids would half close and the look of dulled surprise that has been worn by every corpse I have ever seen would show itself on his face.

I said, "Hang on," but I knew he couldn't hear me. He was bleeding out of this world, and quickly. I felt his neck for a pulse, but what I found was more of a flicker interrupted by long stretches of nothing.

I looked back up at the people gathered outside the Dead Horse. They continued to stand there dumbfounded, watching me. After a moment, the guy with the long black hair turned away and returned inside the bar. He casually removed a cell phone from his belt, opened it, pressed two buttons, then brought the phone to his face.

I looked back at the people outside the bar and called, "Somebody get a blanket." But before anyone could move, Augie's pickup truck skidded to a stop behind me. I turned and saw that the passenger door was open and that Augie was leaning across the seat, holding the door so it wouldn't kick back and shut. He waved me in.

"C'mon, let's go."

No one by the bar was moving. I looked back down

at the kid. His eyes were vacant. There was no one behind them now.

I heard from behind me, "C'mon, Mac, let's go."

I stood and looked once more at the crowd, then looked down at Volger's body once more before turning and climbing up into the passenger seat of Augie Hartsell's pickup.

We were in motion before I could close the door. I fastened my seat belt as we steered through the stop sign and around the corner. Augie gunned it through to fourth gear as we crossed the bridge and went after the black Caddy.

I sensed him glance at me once we hit the straightaway of Long Beach Road. I felt his stare for a moment but didn't look at him. I kept my eyes fixed straight ahead, looking for the Caddy's taillights on the dark and rainy road ahead.

To our right was Great Peconic Bay, though it was hard to make out in all this rain and dark. It seemed to me like a void in the night, more an absence than a presence. If I wasn't a local I might not have even known it was there. It was hard right then to see things for what they were.

A few hundred feet ahead on the narrow beach road the distinctive rear lights of the Caddy suddenly appeared. Augie flattened the accelerator, and together we raced toward violence.

.   .   .

We pulled in tight behind the speeding Caddy on Noyac Road and followed it closely along the rim of the bay. There was as far as I could see only the driver inside. I looked at the rear license plate but it was blacked out with tape. Several times during that first minute Augie nearly lost control in one of the many sharp and sudden corners in the road. But he always caught it and pulled us out right away. He looked intense, wedged in behind the wheel, and it wasn't long into this confusion before he reached back and removed the .45 from the holster on his belt and laid it on the seat between us.

I looked at it but didn't touch it. He returned his hand to the steering wheel, his eyes fixed on the road ahead. His left foot hovered over the clutch, his right holding the gas pedal to the floor. All I could do was hang on to the frayed door strap with my right hand and grip the dashboard with my left and trust in Augie's skills.

He kept the nose of his truck right there on the tail of the Caddy for several miles, till Noyac Road veered away from the bay and followed a wavering line through the woods. We passed through middle-class neighborhoods, during which I kept an eye out for cars pulling out of driveways and late-night joggers. Then the neighborhoods gave way and we entered a long stretch of barren wood. Here the streets were unlit, and sharp corners came up unannounced. The driver of the Caddy was having as difficult a time keeping his vehicle on the road as Augie was. At one point it fish-tailed sharply and looked about to spin out of control. Augie hit the brakes and backed off so the truck didn't clip the swerving Caddy. But it regained control soon enough and continued on, and once it did Augie pushed the accelerator down to the floorboard again and we surged forward and right back on the Caddy's tail.

The speed limit was thirty-five, and we were easily doing eighty, sometimes more in the brief stretches of straight road. Several times Augie tried to get around the Caddy, but the driver always cut him off. We were only a few miles from the village of North Sea. Beyond that was the town of Southampton. All we needed was to drive the Caddy into either village, where we wouldn't go unnoticed by the local boys who sat in patrol cars on North Sea Road waiting for teenagers and drunk drivers.

But Augie didn't seem content just to push the Caddy toward the authorities. He was determined to run it off the road or get around it and cut it off. I could see his knuckles were white from the force of his grip on the steering wheel. I knew this was foolishness, but there wasn't time to get into it.

About a mile from North Sea we hit a good straight patch of back road, and that was when Augie made his move. He dropped down a gear and pulled into the other lane to cut around the Caddy. His nose was even with the rear door when the driver veered toward the truck to scare Augie away. But it didn't work that way. Augie veered into the Caddy instead, his front bumper denting the rear driver's side door. But the Caddy wouldn't give. They held their lanes, parting only briefly. Whenever they did they only veered back and smashed into each other harder, as if magnetized.

We rode nearly side by side, metal smashing metal. Each jolt rocked the cab of the truck, and Augie and I with it. But he hung on to the wheel and wouldn't budge. He began to move the Caddy toward the shoulder of the road. Then he dropped it down another gear and gunned the gas. I saw the tachometer arc up to the red line. The engine screamed and the truck lurched forward, till my window was almost even with the driver's door. I could see the back left side of the driver's head but nothing more. His window was streaked with rain. The inside of the Caddy was dimly lit by the dashboard lights. Augie jerked the wheel hard, hitting the Caddy with the full length of his pickup. The Caddy swerved away, then swerved back again. Its right-hand tires were off the road and onto the shoulder now, kicking up clumps of grass and mud. This slowed it enough to allow Augie to pull up and then slightly ahead of the Caddy. He was about to cut the wheel one last time and drive the Caddy off the road, but before he could something rammed us hard from behind. It rammed us again before I could turn to look back. But by then it was too late. The distraction had allowed the Caddy to cut back onto the road. It hit the pickup broadside. Augie did what he could to keep control of the wheel, but we took another hit from behind and the truck turned into a fishtail and began a sideways slide. I felt myself pulled down into the seat, and I knew by this that my side of the truck was lifting off the road. The nose of the truck hit the Caddy one last time, in the front fender. It was like a chain reaction. The Caddy lost control then and began to spin. It rode back up onto the shoulder, kicking up earth and grass. The feeling of being lifted increased and I braced myself for a roll. But instead of rolling we slid sideways down a short ditch and stopped dead against the trunk of a tree. We slammed with such force I felt my kidneys shift in their sockets.

Augie's side of the truck had impacted with the tree. The driver's door window had been shattered by the side of his head. The force of the sudden stop had flung me so hard against my seat belt that I thought I might have popped a rib.

Augie was dazed. His eyes looked glassy, and his lids blinked a lot. He looked surprised, and there was blood in the creases in his forehead. I heard a car skid to a stop on the rainy road above. But I couldn't see anything. The windshield had shattered and popped out, and there was rain in my eyes. The car on the road above was certainly the car that had rammed us from behind.

I looked over at Augie. Both his arms were up and out in front of him, like he was trying to find his way in the dark. We didn't have much time.

"Augie," I said. "Augie."

He looked at me but I don't think he saw me.

"Can you move?" I reached down for my belt and undid the buckle. It came free easily. "We have to move."

From the street above I heard a car door open and close. With the windows gone the rain sounded louder. Fine drops bounced up from the dashboard and into my face.

I reached over and fumbled for Augie's seat belt.

"Can you move?" I said.

He looked at me. It took a moment for his eyes to focus on me. He nodded once. I undid the belt and heard voices coming from the street above. We didn't have time.

"Are you hurt?" I whispered.

He said nothing. I reached up and took hold of his large head with both hands and looked at the cut on his forehead. It looked superficial to me. I aimed his face at mine and checked his eyes. He looked at me, and there was a degree of cognition.

"We have to move. We have to move now."

My words seemed to reach him then. I could see it in his eyes. He nodded again. This time there was more certainty in it.

"Let's go."

"My .45."

"What?"

"My .45. Where is it?"

"I don't know."

"It must have fallen off the seat."

"We don't have time to look for. We have to move."

I grabbed the passenger door handle and jerked it up. The door swung open on a creaking hinge. I slid out and grabbed Augie by his jacket and pulled him across the seat. My rib protested sharply. Once he made it through the door, it became clear fast that I wasn't going to be able to hold him. But before either of us could do anything he fell. I went down to the mud with him. He was as heavy as a refrigerator and landed on top of me. Most of his weight was on my legs. I was pinned and couldn't move.

We heard two voices up on the street then and waited where we were, listening. They belonged to the driver of the Caddy and the driver of the car that had rammed us from behind. I could hear only some of their words clearly through the rain.

"It went down this ditch . . . Over here . . . They saw the whole fucking thing . . . No . . . Over here . . ."

I scrambled out from under Augie and got up. I tried to pull him to his feet. He did what he could to help. We fumbled but he finally got up. I got in next to him and wrapped his left arm around the back of my neck. Side by side we stumbled through the mud and around the truck. Augie was still too dazed to walk well, and he was too heavy for me to shoulder and carry. After a few feet we dropped to the ground again behind the tree into which the pickup had crashed. I landed on a root and felt it dig hard into my side. I was out of breath already, my chest heaving. Augie seemed to be struggling toward consciousness, like someone struggling to wake up quickly from a deep sleep. There was nothing we could do but lie there together in the mud by the base of that tree and wait.

I looked around the tree and spotted the first man as he appeared at the top of the bank. He was just a silhouette in the rain. He looked down at the truck, then glanced over his shoulder and waved someone behind him to follow.

"Hurry," he called.

A second man appeared then. He held a flashlight in his hand. The first man took it, switched it on, and shined it down at the wrecked truck.

The drops of rain looked like tiny blurs in the beam of light. The first man shined it on the opened passenger door and into the cab. The inside of the truck seemed evenly divided between bright light and sharp shadows, both of which moved with each motion of the man's hand. He led the second man down the mud bank. They looked inside the cab, then under it. It only took them a minute to spot the footprints. I saw then that the second man had a gun in his hand. I saw small drops of rain bouncing off it. But I couldn't see either of their faces, only the shapes of them in the night, the flashlight, and the gun.

I looked at Augie and held my index finger to my lips. He nodded.

One of the men whispered, "They couldn't have gotten far."

The other said, "Forget about 'em."

"They saw the whole fucking thing."

I was unarmed, and Augie's .45 was somewhere in the truck. For all I knew it may have flown out through the shattered windshield. But either way there was no time to look for it. I felt around the muddy ground for a stone but found nothing but the soft earth. I scrambled up to my hands and knees and searched more. I found nothing. I had no way of knowing which side of the truck the men would come around, the front, the rear, or both. I looked back and forth between the two frantically. I found a few pebbles but nothing that would give me an edge, nothing that would make a difference when thrown at a man. Finally I found something, a stone, its top barely sticking out of the ground. I dug around it with my fingers. It was an act of desperation, and probably a waste of time, but it was all I could do. I kept looking toward the front of the truck, then the rear, all the while digging. But I was getting nowhere and finally gave up. I turned to search elsewhere for a weapon and in the process looked Augie in the face. It was dark but I could see him well enough.

He nodded his head to the right once. I knew right away that he was telling me to go. He looked exhausted, his arms hanging at his sides, like a boxer who had lost twelve out of twelve rounds. I said nothing, just looked back at him. He nodded again, this time with his eyes closed. The blood on his face was watery from the rain. He was covered with mud. I waited till he opened his eyes and was looking at me again. Then I shook my head from side to side. I held up my finger, telling him to wait. Then I turned and went back to the buried rock and began to dig again with my fingers. I didn't think about the pain and just dug, tearing the dirt away. I looked toward the front of the truck, then the rear. Nothing, but I knew they would appear somewhere soon. I felt the under-curve of the rock and wedged my fingers deep beneath it. I hooked my nails against the rough surface and leaned back. The rock gave, but only a little. I readjusted my grip and leaned back again. It broke free and moved a few inches out of the ground, only to stop again. I readjusted the grip one more time and leaned back. The rock pulled free. The sudden give sent me flying backward. I landed on my back next to Augie, the rock on my chest. It was a little bigger than a grapefruit and hit me hard enough when it landed that it knocked the wind out of me. I grabbed the rock with both hands and sat up just as one of the men came around the front of the truck. My eyes searched frantically for a gun but I didn't see one. But that didn't mean it wasn't there. I looked and looked, time ticking off in my head. And then there it was. The bright beam of a flashlight crossed the ground fast and hit me in the eyes. It cast painful shadows inside my head.

"They're here," he called.

I turned just as the second man appeared behind the truck. I didn't wait and with my right hand flung the rock at him with all I had. The throw tore my shoulder and I grunted. My eyes found the gun the instant I let go of the rock. The man saw it, saw something coming and flinched, trying to bob like a boxer. But he wasn't fast enough, and the rock caught him solid on the left side of his face. I heard a good thud followed by a surprised grunt. Then the man's legs buckled and he dropped to the ground.

When I turned back to the first man he was rushing me. The flashlight was in his left hand now, a knife in his right. I rose to my knees to meet him as he took a wide swipe at my face. I slipped it by fractions of an inch. I could hear the blade moving through the air as it passed my eyes. Before he could take a backhand slice at me, I lunged toward him and hugged him around the waist, trapping his knife hand between us. I lunged forward, knocking him back. He landed hard and grunted. I landed on top of him and scrambled to grab hold of his knife hand. I wrenched his wrist till he cried out and dropped the knife. Then I grabbed a handful of his hair and struck his nose three times with my open palm. My heart was bursting in my chest. After the palm strikes I grabbed the flashlight and stood up fast. It was a Maglite, three feet long and heavy as a pipe, as much club as flashlight. I swung it like I was chopping wood into his ribs, reloaded my swing, and swung it down across his right knee.

Then I turned to where the second man, the one with the gun, had fallen. It felt as if too much blood were pumping through my veins. I felt light-headed with fear and fury and rushed to the second man as he tried to stand. The gun was in his hand still. I wasted no time and swung downward like an executioner with the Maglite and smashed his hand with it. He cried out as the gun flew from his grip. I kicked it away and swung with the exact same trajectory a second time and clipped the man's collarbone. But he was still trying to stand, grabbing at me for support, so I laid the Maglite across the side of his head. He was dazed but still grabbing at me, so I laid it again, this time across his face. He dropped then, and I stood over him and rained down blows on his legs. I couldn't stop. My heart was pounding beats ahead of me, and my mind raced. The more anger I felt, the less fear I felt, and somehow each strike I landed on this man made me more angry. I hit him half a dozen times after he had stopped fighting back, after he had passed out, and it wasn't till I sensed someone behind me that I stopped and turned.

I stood face to face with Augie, bloodied and covered with mud. I froze. He could barely stand and looked at me as if he had never seen me before. I lowered my hand and reached out and eased the Maglite from it, then dropped it to the ground.

He just looked at me. The blood that was washed from his face by the rain was replaced almost immediately by even more blood. I looked at him, conscious of my rapid breathing, and listened to the hiss of the rain around us.

It took me a while to come back. He gave me the time I needed. It was a few moments before my heart became anything less than a riot of fear and hate.

Finally I was able to speak. "You need to see a doctor," I said.

He nodded toward the right side of my head. "You, too."

I didn't know what he meant at first. Finally I touched that part of my head and brought away blood.

"You must have knocked your head when we hit the tree."

I looked at the blood on my fingertips. It looked as black as oil in the dark. It shimmered. Without realizing it, I muttered, "So much for the easy night, huh?"

Augie took a quick look around us, at his wrecked

truck and the two men sprawled out on the ground. "We'd better call the cops."

"You know they're not all that fond of me. I've had run-ins with them before."

"It'll be all right. You're with me."

TWO

An ambulance arrived not long after the police. I watched the red and blue lights play hide-and-seek in the treetops. Eventually a few of the town cops recognized me, but Augie stuck to his word and told them I was with him. He showed them something in his wallet and mentioned that we were working for Frank Gannon. They didn't give me shit then. Augie and I rode away from the scene in an ambulance, headed toward Southampton Hospital. I felt light-headed and my limbs were weak. I said nothing about my ribs or shoulder. Augie sat across from me and just stared at me the whole ride. The paramedics cleaned and taped up our cuts and took our stats. Then we were asked our names.

"Hartsell, Augie."

One of the paramedics nodded and wrote it down

on a form attached to a clipboard. Then she looked at me.

"MacManus," I told her. "Declan MacManus."

She wrote that down. As she did, Augie said, "Your last name is MacManus?"

"Yeah. Mac is short for MacManus. Why?"

He shook his head but didn't say anything. It was only a five-minute ride to the hospital from North Sea. We spent it in silence.

Once inside we were taken right in. I knew this was because the other two would be brought in by patrol cars right after us and that Augie and I would have to be kept separate from them. I was led to an emergency room bed by the paramedics and helped up onto it. Then they did the same with Augie, only they took him to a bed on the other end of the room so we couldn't talk. After a few minutes two uniformed cops approached Augie. I watched as he talked to them for a while. Every now and then he nodded toward me, and whenever he did the cops would glance over their shoulders at me, then look back at Augie. Eventually an ER doctor in green scrubs showed up and the cops stepped away. The doctor drew the curtain around him and Augie. The cops just looked at me then, till finally they started toward me. But before they could get to me someone came into my cubicle and closed the curtain around me, cutting them off.

I expected a doctor, but instead it was a nurse named Gale.

She had short dark hair and was taller than I by a few

inches and older by ten years. She had been my night nurse a few years back when a slug from a .45 crushed my collarbone during the last of my foolish favors for people. I'd made the papers then, and Gale kept the reporters away for the month I was laid up in the hospital. She was big on celebrity gossip and visited me often and talked to me about people I had never heard of. It was nice to just listen, to be with someone and not have to talk. She seemed accepting of me, more so than others, and she didn't ask a lot of questions about me or my past. I got the sense that she knew enough.

"Gale," I said.

"I thought I told you I never wanted to see you again," she teased. She stepped directly in front of me to examine the cut on my forehead.

"Yeah, well, I stayed away for as long as I could. What can I say?"

"I'm a magnet, aren't I?" She lifted the bandage, her eyes squinting as she studied the wound. "You play too rough." She removed the bloodied bandage and then tossed it into a garbage can. It landed against the inside with a light slapping sound. "You're going to need some stitches. Are you happy?"

"I don't have any money, Gale. I can't pay."

"You still haven't heard of a little thing called insurance, have you?"

"And I still owe the hospital a shitload for my last visit."

"Actually, your big friend over there says Frank

Gannon is paying for this. Is that true? Are you mixed up with Gannon now? I always thought you were smarter than that."

"I'm not mixed up with anyone, Gale."

"But you're working for him?"

"It was just a one-time thing. I needed the money."

"I can get you a job here, Mac, you know that. We need orderlies, especially in the emergency room on weekend nights."

"I need more than what that kind of job pays. You know what it's like out here. Resort town year-round rents are hard enough to find, let alone cheap ones. And I'm not the roommate type."

"No, you aren't, are you?"

She unwrapped a fresh gauze, then carefully pressed it to my cut. I felt a sharp pinch.

"Just when I stopped worrying myself sick about you, you waltz right back in here and get me started all over again."

"I hardly think I waltzed, Gale."

"They said you saw someone get killed tonight and that you almost got yourself killed, too, in the process. You play too rough, Mac. Have I mentioned that?"

"It was a one-time thing."

"You haven't heard, have you?"

"Heard what?"

"I heard the cops talking. One of their own was killed tonight."

"What are you talking about?"

"Just a little while ago, bringing in one of the men from the accident you were in. The guy had a broken hand or something, his wrist was all swollen, so the cop didn't cuff him. On the way in the guy started convulsing in the back, and the cop pulled over to check him out. He called it in. But it was a trick. Somehow the guy got hold of the cop's gun and shot him with it. They found the patrol car a few minutes ago, empty. Every cop in town is out looking for the killer now. They're going to want to talk to you, to find out what you know about this guy."

"I don't know anything about him. I never even got a good look at him."

"Who's your big friend?"

"His name's Augie Hartsell."

"What do you know about him?"

"Not much. Why?"

"Well, he's got two healed-over gunshot wounds. That's one more than you. In my book that makes him double trouble."

"In my book that makes him lucky."

"Yeah, well, maybe he pushes his luck. You can gauge a man's judgment by the condition of his body. My guess is you might want to stay away from him, find a new friend to play with."

"Thanks for your concern, Gale."

"Somebody's got to look after you. I'm serious, Mac. Stay away from this guy. Do you understand me?"

"Yeah."

"I've got to get back upstairs. Your doctor will be here in a few minutes to stitch you up. You caught us on a bad night. There were two other car wrecks that came in right before you, and some high school girl was raped. They brought her in a half hour ago. So bear with us."

"Thanks."

"And don't play so rough, okay?"

She touched my shoulder with her left hand. I remembered then living for her visits to my room, living for the moments during her shift when she would stop and talk with me about really nothing at all.

I looked up at her face now. It was tanned and finely lined, showing her age. I nodded once. I hated the things in both our lives that made my feelings for her so ridiculous.

"I'll see you, Mac."

She turned then, pulled open the curtain, and took off. There was something about the way she moved that made me think of a person running away. With the curtain open and her gone I was left again in clear view of the two waiting uniforms.

It took an hour for the doctor to make his way to me. He was young, new, and didn't know me. He barely looked at my face. I was stitched up, all the while being questioned by the cops for what was the tenth time. The ER was in chaos. I had to speak in a full voice just to be heard. After the doctor was done and I was questioned a few more times, I was taken back to the Hansom House in a patrol car. The uniformed cop driving kept looking back at me in the rearview mirror. I didn't care about that. I had lost track of Augie in the confusion and didn't know if he was still at the hospital or not. I figured since I hadn't seen him that they had released him and he went to tell Frank what had gone down.

The cop dropped me off outside the Hansom House. I walked up the path through the rain to the porch. The stairs were inside the entranceway, to the left, and I went up them to my rooms. I picked a dry pair of jeans and T-shirt out of the dirty clothes pile at the foot of my bed, then went into the bathroom and peeled back the bandage and looked in the streaked piece of mirror and checked the stitches in my head. My face was hidden behind smudges of dried mud. I reapplied the bandage, washed up and changed, then grabbed a bottle of Beam from the table by my unmade bed. I sat down on my living room couch and poured myself a glass.

The muffled sound of a reggae bass was coming up through the floorboards. Under it somewhere was a trumpet. It was being played by someone who had listened to his share of Chet Baker. I didn't feel up to going downstairs, to facing George and maybe hearing that the woman from this afternoon had come back, or was back, waiting at the bar for me. I wanted nothing to do with anything.

I lay back on the couch and took a long gulp of Beam, feeling it burn my chest as it went down. I needed the warmth. I still felt jittery from the fight, from the moment when I thought maybe Augie and I were going to die. It wasn't long then before I started thinking of the kid, Vogler, bleeding to death on that rainy street.

I drank several glassfuls and then slipped into unconsciousness. It was like being underwater, down deep, the whole workaday world, silent and out of sight, far above me. It was the only peace I knew.

Then some time later I was conscious again. I was still on my couch, still in the dark. I had no idea how much time had passed, and I wasn't certain why I had been awakened. But then I sensed that someone else was there in the room with me. I sat up fast and reached for a nearby lamp and switched it on. I grabbed it as a weapon, the light throwing drastic shadows across the room.

I felt the same riot letting loose inside of me, the same animal instinct to save my life at any cost. It ran through me like a fever. But then my eyes caught something and the fever suddenly ceased in me.

Standing at the foot of my couch, casting the largest shadow of all the shadows in that room, was Augie Hartsell.

"Easy there, partner," he said.

I didn't realize that I was holding my breath till I found myself letting out a sigh. I waited a second, then put the lamp back on the tabletop. The brightness of the sudden light made my eyes ache. I was still lit from the Beam and half asleep. I could barely sit up. I couldn't help but recognize the fact that if it had been anyone other than Augie at the foot of my couch, I would have been deep in some serious shit right now.

"What are you doing?" I muttered.

"I came to check up on you. I thought you might be nose deep in a bottle around now. How are you feeling?"

I shrugged. "You?"

He nodded toward the bottle of Beam on the coffee table. "I might feel a little better if I had some of that."

"Help yourself."

He poured a few inches of amber into my glass, then picked it up by the rim, held between his thick index and middle fingers, and downed its contents in two gulps. He placed the glass back on the table and said, "I assume you heard that a cop bought it tonight."

"Yeah."

He looked around my disheveled living room, then reached into his field jacket and removed an envelope. He dropped it on the coffee table beside the bottle of Beam. It landed with a solid smack.

I looked at it, then up at him. "What's that?"

"It's from Frank. He said to tell you he doesn't normally pay in cash, but he thought you might not have a bank account. And anyway he knows how desperate you are for it."

I didn't take my eyes off the envelope. I said nothing.

"I'll give one thing to Frank," Augie said. "He takes care of his men. He paid both our hospital tabs, and he's over at Village Hall right now telling the Chief to instruct his boys to cut you some slack, that you're working for him now."

Augie was still looking around my living room as he said this. The curtains on my three front windows were ratty and smoke-stained, the hardwood floor was splintered and dusty, and the coffee table on which the money and the Beam sat wobbled like a game horse. He nodded at what he saw, as if it made some sense to him. "You like living like this?" he asked.

"I don't really think about it."

Augie nodded again. "So, tell me, why are the cops not so fond of you? I've heard some talk. But I'd like to hear one or two things from you for a change."

"I guess I made them look bad on occasion."

"How?"

"I found a few people they couldn't."

"You're good at finding people?"

"No. Just lucky. Maybe I looked a little harder than they did. The people I look for are usually on the wrong end of the tax bracket, if you know what I mean."

"Things really like that here? You've got to remember, I left here over thirty years ago. I haven't been back for all that long."

"It depends who you're talking to. It seems like that for some people."

"You think the chief of police is on the take?"

"Yeah, I do. How about you?"

"I don't doubt it. So I've heard a couple of wild stories about how you got those scratches on your face."

I said nothing to that. I looked at the bottle on my table, and the empty glass beside it.

"If you want a drink, pour yourself one," he said. "Don't be shy because I'm here."

"You said you didn't work with drinkers."

"Yeah, well, I say a lot of things."

He leaned down and pushed the glass toward me. I thought about it for a moment, then poured myself a few inches. My hand was shaking but I didn't care about that. I downed the bourbon in slower gulps than Augie had, then placed the emptied glass back by the envelope of money.

"You care to tell me about the scratches?"

"Not really."

"It's amazing what gossip gets around, the things you hear. It's even more amazing what doesn't get around, what secrets some people manage to keep while other people aren't so lucky. There doesn't seem to be that much rhyme or reason to it as far as I can see. It's a random thing. It's like sunken treasure from some ship lost at sea. For every treasure chest found, there's maybe hundreds that go unrecovered." He watched me for a moment, then said, "You know, we stepped into something tonight. You know that, right?"

"Yeah, I sort of figured that out."

"I've known Frank all my life, and if I know one thing about him, it's to never trust him. Maybe he didn't know what we were walking into. But it's also very possible that maybe he did. It might be smart of us to find out for ourselves. Do you feel up to a little moonlighting?"

"Yeah, maybe. What is it exactly we're looking for?"

"Whoever killed that cop, maybe he saw you, maybe he saw me. Maybe he didn't. If he's the one from the Caddy, then he knows we saw him kill Vogler. He's got plenty of reasons not to be very fond of us right now. Maybe he's beat it out of town. But then again, maybe he hasn't. His partner's in custody. He might be of some help, but if they're pros, which I think they are, then I don't think we should count on getting much out of him."

"Pros?"

"The Caddy was the kill car. They probably would have ditched it right way, a few miles out of town. The other guy, the other car, was the shooter's ride home. It was a well-thought-out hit. They knew what they were doing."

I thought about that for a moment, then Augie said, "But if the shooter isn't long gone, if he did see either of us, then I'm not really keen on the idea of sitting around and waiting for him to find us. I'm thinking maybe you might feel the same. You're an easy man to find, Mac. Enough people know you. And I did just waltz in here now and catch you napping."

"What did Frank have to say about tonight?"

"Not much. We didn't really have that much time to talk. But if he is up to something, we can't really rely on anything he says."

"You think he is up to something, though."

"If you're asking me if I think Frank would sell me down the river if it suited him, then my answer is I think he'd do it in a heartbeat."

"So why are you working for him then? Why do you work for a man like Frank?"

"I'm not squeamish about the kind of work he does. I spent twenty-five years in the DEA, in Colombia. Plus I did two tours of duty with the marines in Vietnam. I've seen my share of shit. I don't have the objections you seem to. On top of that, my fifteen-year-old daughter is college-bound in a few years. I want things nice for her. And on top of all that, I told you, I have my reasons for staying close to Frank."

"And they are?"

"It's a long story. Maybe I'll tell you sometime."

"I don't want to get caught in the middle of some old grudge between you two."

Augie said nothing to that. After a moment he glanced at the bottle of Beam. "I could use another belt."

"You know how to pour."

He gave himself a few more inches, then downed it. "You think maybe I could sit?"

I nodded toward the chair by the window. Augie pulled it over and placed it across from me. He sat down on it and looked at me.

"Listen," he said, "I want to thank you for not leaving me there. I guess I was wrong about you."

I could see outside my three front windows behind him to the rim of silver than ran along the horizon, spreading out beyond the bare elm trees. Morning wasn't all that far off. I thought about another sip of Beam, but I was already too drunk.

"I think maybe you and I are a lot alike. We both rush into things without thinking. You ran to the aid of the kid and I got us chasing after a killer. We might not be very good for each other."

"Yeah, probably."

"But my right arm is yours. When you've gone through what I've gone through, you learn fast what men to trust with your life and what men not to trust."

I said, "Thanks," but didn't know what to say after that. Finally I asked, "How long have you been retired from the DEA?"

"A few months. Not long. I moved back out here so my daughter and I could live the quiet life. I grew up out here, but you know that. My best friend growing up was like we are. He had this exaggerated sense of right and wrong. It used to get him nothing but trouble. Eventually he started drinking just to calm it down, just so he didn't fly off the handle at the smallest injustice and land himself head down and neck deep in shit. He was a good man, and I think it's what finally killed him."

"What do you mean?"

"I think he tried to stand up to the wrong person and paid the price for it. He's probably not the only one. It happens. Anyway, that was a long time ago."

"You have a daughter, how about a wife?"

"She died ten years ago. She was killed by a machete gang in Colombia. She was from there. It's just me and my daughter now."

"I'm sorry."

"How about you? Any family?"

I shook my head. "My mother died when I was young. And my father disappeared when I was seven. But you probably know all about me, don't you, from your friends."

Augie shrugged. "Do you remember him at all? Your father, I mean."

"Only vaguely."

"What do you remember?"

"He chain-smoked. He was a cop. We lived in a hotel in Riverhead. I was a boy and as far as I knew he was the whole world."

"Where'd you grow up?"

"On Gin Lane. My father tossed me to a rich guy before he disappeared. It must have been hard for him, a single father, a cop on top of that, trying to raise a kid."

"Tough."

I shrugged. "Your daughter's fifteen?"

"Yeah."

"She must keep you on your toes."

"She's a handful. She's her father's daughter, whether she likes it or not, that's for certain. She saw her mother get murdered. She was left for dead and lived for four days by herself in the jungle till we found her. She didn't speak for almost a year after that. Trauma." He smiled. "Now of course she does nothing but speak. She's a bossy thing, talks her mind, like her mother."

"You two must be close."

"Yeah, we are. Needless to say I'm a little protective of her, considering she's all I have left of her mother. It drives her nuts, but that's the way it is. We take care of the ones we love, right?"

I nodded. "Yeah." I glanced toward my front windows. I could see that the rain was going to end with the night. Morning was still a while off, but sunrise was definitely under way somewhere not far beyond the horizon.

Augie and I drank and talked till daylight was finally everywhere and the birds were singing and the rain had stopped falling through the trees. Together we listened to the church bell half a mile down North Main Street strike seven times. The bottle of Beam was empty and the twittering of the birds was like so much madness outside my windows.

I heard Augie saying, "We've got to find that cop killer before he has a chance to find us.... Yeah, we stepped into it good, didn't we.... I'll probably come back for you when it gets dark.... Thanks for not leaving me there...."

Then the next thing I knew I was alone in my living room and staring up at my ceiling from the dust-covered wood floor. I don't know how I got there. But there was a steady ringing in my ears, and whenever I closed my eyes I saw a floating egg, blue-rimmed with an orange center. I felt as if I were being pulled along on the surface of a foaming river.

When I awoke it was light out and I couldn't move. I was pinned by my own drunkenness. I knew at once where I was and who I was. I knew by the burning in my head and the ache in my chest. I felt spent, exhausted by my own sleep. I was hungry but all I could think about was another belt. I looked at the bottle on my coffee table and saw that it was empty. I felt hollow and weak.

I dreamed most of the night of ways of escape, of back roads out of town and the secondary roads that bypassed the main highways and led off the island. I dreamed of the train tracks running from Montauk to Queens, of mile after mile of metal rails and hardwood ties. I saw myself walking those ties right out of town, counting each one with the morning sun at my back.

But now I was awake and I still couldn't shake all that from my mind. I was still following the course of each way out, rounding their curves, pushing down their stretches of straight road. When I finally got myself up off the floor, I wandered into my kitchen and put on hot water for tea and stood at my window and looked at the train station.

The shutoff notice from the electric company was hanging on the refrigerator behind me. I didn't have to see it to know that it was there. It reminded me of the money on my coffee table, the cash Frank Gannon had given Augie to give me.

I went to it, opened the envelope, and counted through the bills. It was more money than I had seen in a long time. It was almost as much as I had made in my best month last summer, when Jamie Ray and I managed to do three painting jobs in one six-day week of working seven in the morning to eight at night.

I closed the envelope and dropped it back down onto the coffee table. In my head a balloon was expanding past its limits, ready to burst. I waited for it, dreading the noise. But it never came. The teakettle whistled back in the kitchen, and I went to it and took it off the stove and dropped my last bag of ginger tea into a mug and poured the water over it. Then I pulled the chair Augie had sat in most of the night back to its position in front of my living room windows and sat on it backward and looked down on Elm Street. I thought about the chances that I could start a new life here and even made a list of errands to run, followed by a promise to myself to actually get out and run them. But before I could get too far with that I started to think of Vogler bleeding to death on that rainy street. I just couldn't help it. From there it was a short trip to thinking about almost being killed out on Noyac Road the night before. And it wasn't long after that that the scratches on my face came to mind. I touched them with my fingertips, remembering the woman who had left them there.

I had been told by a woman who lived with me for a month years ago that all things have a right to live. I believed her, all evidence to the contrary.

It didn't take much after all this for me to start looking through my place for unfinished bottles of Beam. I found one under my sink that had a few shots left in it. I poured them into a glass and downed them in three long gulps. Then I gathered up all the nearly empty bottles there were till I thought I had enough to get me to sundown. But it wasn't enough. Around nine I finally ran out of what I had scrounged together and headed downstairs for a few on George. I didn't care anymore who was looking for me. I remembered then Augie saying something about coming to get me after sundown. I wasn't sure if I was going downstairs to make it easier for him to find me or more difficult. But I didn't really care about that. The threat of my starting to think again grew with each minute I went without more to drink.

I don't remember her face or much of anything about her. She sits beside me in the dark corner at the end of the bar and we drink together. It is loud, there is a great hum around us, chatter and music. I lose a lot to this noise but it doesn't seem to really matter. She smiles a lot and laughs and I nod at things I don't really hear or understand.

We drink and then we go upstairs to my dark apartment. She opens a window and the curtain lifts and blooms like a ghost. The air coming in fills the room fast, too fast. It is a rush of cold and dark, a rush of outer space. I begin to shiver. She comes to me, presses her body against mine. Then we are lying down. Her body radiates heat. I pull it close to me out of greed. I can see the vague shape of her by the streetlight coming in from outside. Her hair is shoulder length and straight. I smell it, her skin, the Cuervo on her cool breath. She is drunk, too. She laughs. She climbs on top of me and straddles me and leans down so her soft hair brushes my face and makes a cozy little cave for us in which we kiss. She laughs and smiles as we do this. She is almost giddy. There is warmth in her smile.

Afterward she is standing at my bedroom window, wearing nothing but an old army surplus wool blanket around her shoulders. Her feet are bare. The floor must be cold. She stands in that pale light and says something about me being a hard man to find. Then she says something else, says it several times before I finally hear and understand her. I realize she is asking me if I will help her. I hear myself tell her that I can't help anyone. She says something about how he'll think twice about hurting me if he knows we're together. But I don't know who "he" is. I don't ask. I tell her I can't see her face with her back to the light. I ask her who she is. I have asked that before. I know this. She tells me that she is Rose. Don't I remember? I say nothing.

She tells me that I am drunk. I know this but she tells me anyway. There isn't a hint of recrimination in her voice, not that I can hear, anyway. It is just a point of fact that she for some reason needs to make then. I tell her that I wouldn't be of much help. She seems less than reluctant to believe me now. But she goes on to say anyway that he pays men to hurt people. I stop listening. I don't know who he is. I feel the cold again without her near me. I can smell her, us. I remember her face above me, her laughing like we were just two kids at play. I want to be back in that cave, her laughing, my head reaching up to meet hers.

I tell her to come back to bed. But she won't now. I don't remember her, she says. She says she thought I did but that I don't really. She says her face has changed, that he broke some bones, that she had surgery. And anyway it was such a long time ago that she barely recognized me, too.

She is dressing now, suddenly modest. She turns her back to me when she reaches for her clothes and the blanket drops to the floor. I ask her something but I don't even hear my own words. I don't know what I just said. She tells me to go to sleep. Go to sleep, Mac, she says. Go to sleep.

Then she is dressed and standing in my bedroom doorway. She is looking into my living room at something. The light is on in that room. It is dim. She stares at something in there for a long while before looking back at me.

She tells me to take care of myself. Before I can ask her to stay she is gone. I don't hear my apartment door close right away. I wait for it, watching the bedroom doorway, waiting for her to return to it. But she doesn't. I finally hear my apartment door close and follow as best I can the sound of her footsteps as she moves down the stairs. I follow the sound till it is gone. Then it is all darkness and silence and I linger in that till even it is gone.

When I awoke again it was day and somewhere down Elm Street a dog was barking. I got up and tried to shake what was left of that dream from my head. I drank the last of my rice milk and cut up an apple and sat at my kitchen table and ate it. It was the only food left in the house. I was shot and didn't think about anything but shaking off that dream and quieting my hunger. I didn't know what day it was, and I didn't care. But I knew sooner or later someone would let me know.

It was then I remembered that my phone was shut off. I knew that if I went down to the phone company and paid my overdue bill in cash they might restore service today. With all that was going on, a phone would be a good thing to have. I went into the living room to get the envelope Augie had dropped on my table. My legs and back were stiff and sore. It was as if I had run miles in my sleep. I found the envelope there all right on the table, except it looked empty. I picked it up and opened it fast. There was nothing in it. From where I stood I did a quick scan of my apartment. I thought maybe I had dropped it at some point during the night, but the money wasn't anywhere to be seen. I was into the start of an all-out search when I found my old army blanket on the floor by my window and it came to me suddenly. I stopped dead in my tracks.

I remembered her standing in my bedroom doorway, staring back at something in my living room. I remembered the moment's pause between when she left my bedroom doorway and when I heard my apartment door close. I remembered this well enough to know what had happened. But what I didn't know was just who the hell she was.

Not long after this there was a knock on my door. I opened it fast. Augie was standing in the doorway. He easily filled it. He stepped just inside the door and looked into my apartment, as if for someone.

"What's up?" I said.

There was a shopping bag hanging from his left hand.

"I came by last night," he said, "but you looked a little busy, so I didn't bother you."

"I didn't see you."

"I don't think you were seeing much, to be honest. Pretty lady, though."

"I'll have to take your word for that."

"Blackouts are a nice break in the day, aren't they?"

"Something like that." I had a dozen questions I wanted to ask him about the woman I was with, what she looked like, what she was wearing, anything I could think of. But I put that aside. I got the feeling right off that Augie had something bigger on his mind.

"What's up?" I said.

"The town is buzzing with cops. The killer apparently looted the cop car after he dumped it. Shotgun, ammo, computer, everything. He took the cop's hand-cuffs and Mace, even got his wallet and badge. Cool head, whoever the hell he is."

"Any comment from Frank?"

"No. He's been hard to get hold of recently. No big surprise there. He did offer us another job. It was as if nothing happened. Business as usual to him. I think we should take the job, stay as close to him as possible. If we don't he might get suspicious."

"What's the job?"

"It's a tail. Two men, me and you. I told Frank to put you on with me for a few more jobs because you had a lot to learn. He was more than willing to believe that."

I nodded. "Good. Sorry about last night."

Augie shrugged. "It happens. After I left here I went back out to the Dead Horse to poke around. I asked a few questions but no one had anything to say."

"What about the man who hired Frank to scare off Vogler? Maybe we could find out something from him."

"You saw the same file I saw. If I knew the man's name, I would have talked to him already."

"Frank seems to have us pinned in pretty good."

"He knows his stuff."

"So what do we do now?"

"We work for Frank. We stay in close to him. We

keep our eyes and our ears open and wait. Do you think you can do that? Do you think you can handle the job?"

I nodded. "Yeah."

Augie tossed the shopping bag onto the floor near my feet. "Here," he said. "I brought this for you."

I picked up the bag and reached into it.

"It's October now, so it's only going to get colder. You lost your other one, so I thought you might be needing this."

Inside the bag was a brand-new navy surplus pea coat. I pulled it out and held it up. It unfolded. It was slightly oversized and made of heavy wool.

"It's a good winter coat," Augie explained. "Nothing like wool for keeping out the cold."

I looked at the jacket, then at Augie. I wasn't sure what to say. Finally I muttered, "Thanks."

"Listen, we're partners. We take care of each other. Your problems are my problems. My right arm is yours. Got it?"

I dropped the bag and tried on the jacket. It fit nicely. There was enough room under it for a sweatshirt or sweater.

"A jacket like that, it won't slow you down, you know," Augie said.

"Yeah. Yeah, it's good."

"You like it, then?"

"Yeah."

"Good. My daughter helped me pick it out."

"Thanks, Aug."

"Listen, I should go. I've got some things to do. I'll come back for you tonight. I've rented a car, a nice sedan with comfy leather seats. We'll do the tail and keep Frank relaxed and make us some money in the process. Don't worry, sooner or later we'll know what we need to know. We'll find this cop killer, we'll find out exactly what Frank is up to."

Three

Augie and I worked together for Frank Gannon for two weeks, three nights the first week, five nights the second. I made more in those two weeks than I had made in the best two months of my life. I got squared away with the utility companies and paid up front for a six-month insurance policy on the LeMans. I bought half a dozen cases of rice milk and three cases of dried fruit from the whole food store in town. I stocked my cupboards with teas and canned goods. I had enough food to last me a month.

Our first job had Augie and me tailing a cheating husband. We caught him kissing another woman in his car and got it all on videotape. Then we followed another husband to a gay bar in Wainscott, where he met his much-younger male lover. After that we tailed a well-off married woman and mother of two to a strip bar in Patchogue, where she stripped for tips in a blue-collar joint on Montauk Highway. Men were throwing money at her—she knew most of them by name—and she left with a grand, easy. Augie caught it all with a high-tech hidden surveillance video camera that belonged to Frank Gannon. The lens was fitted into the bridge of a pair of black-rimmed glasses, the recorder stowed in the pocket of Augie's field jacket. I stayed by the door and watched Augie's back. I could tell he didn't like the work any more than I did. But compared to what he had been through in Colombia, never mind his two tours in Vietnam, it was all just a walk in the park for him. He had a perspective I didn't, and probably never would. He wasn't affected by suffering the way I was, he didn't pity people as easily. I could understand that. I even envied it. This was just business to him, nothing more. He never commented on the character of the people we caught. He never called them names or made jokes about them. They weren't stupid or greedy in his mind, just people making mistakes. Every tape we made he labeled carefully, logged in a notebook, and then gave to Frank. I could tell as he did so that he was aware of what was going down, of the significance of it, of the lives that would not be the same come morning.

When we weren't working we were drinking, sometimes in bars but most often in his kitchen during the day, when his daughter was at school. We'd sit at his table and drink Beam neat and talk. I always left just before Tina came home, driving back to the Hansom House in the middle of the afternoon in my newly insured car, as lit as a match. Sometimes he and I didn't get home from a job till morning and would start our drinking then. Augie and I were together day and night. Even on the days when there wasn't work we usually met up at some point. On the day his auto loan came through I drove him to Riverhead to buy a new truck. He chose one of those giant Ford rigs with lights everywhere, a cockpit like a fighter, and the biggest motor in production. He drove it home that afternoon, me tailing behind in my rust-bucket LeMans. It was only a twenty-minute drive but we stopped twice along the way for drinks. After the second bar, turning onto his street, Augie nearly took out a neighbor's mailbox.

I liked the money I was getting paid, but the job was getting to me. I began to lose sight of the strategic importance of keeping Frank feeling safe. Frank was on my case about drinking. Augie could hide his battle with the bottle better than I. He did what he could to cover for me, but Frank saw enough despite Augie's efforts and wouldn't let up. It was during the eighth job we did for Frank that the shit finally hit. He had been hired by a suspicious fiancé to tail a young woman on the night before their wedding and sent Augie and me out on the job. We videotaped the woman bar-hopping with girlfriends, drinking too much and dancing with a half-dozen different men. Later on we caught her in a car in a lot behind the bar, rolling around with what turned out to be an ex-boyfriend of hers. When the groom-to-be saw the tape the next morning, he flew into a rage and went to his fiancée and beat her with an antenna he broke off a truck. It cut her face and hands and arms like a whip. She was taken to Southampton Hospital and he got himself hauled off to the Suffolk County Jail, while in the meantime 150 guests were driving to the church where their wedding was supposed to be.

That was all I needed. That was all I could take. I was ready to ditch, and Augie knew it. He could see it in my face. He tried to calm me down but I wouldn't have it. This was just all wrong to me. I went home that morning but couldn't sleep. My phone rang all day but I didn't answer it. Eventually I grabbed it off the coffee table and flung it across the room. The cord tore the jack out of the wall. I didn't care. I bought a bottle of Jim Beam and came back with it and got drunk alone on my couch. I watched shadows move across my living room floor and then up the walls as morning became afternoon. Then I looked out my windows and watched late afternoon gel into evening. Then I watched evening bleed off into night. Some time after it got dark someone knocked on my door. I didn't answer. The knock turned into pounding. Then someone started calling my name. It was Augie. I ignored him. Then the door burst open. Bits of lock and wood flew across the room like shrapnel. I didn't move. I just sat there and stared toward my front windows and the night beyond.

Augie looked at me for a moment, then crossed the room to me. He looked down at me, his hands in the pockets of his field jacket. "I've been worried about you. I've been trying to call all day."

"Something's wrong with my phone."

"Yeah, I can see that. You okay?"

"I can't do this anymore. I just can't . . . do this."

"Try to look at the big picture here, Mac."

"Spare me, Aug."

"Listen, I need you to stick to our plan. Frank's got men on the inside over at the Village Hall. You know there's no better way for us to find out what's going on over there than through him."

"This isn't what I do."

"Our friend the cop killer is still out there."

"I don't care about that."

"You don't care about that?"

"I have to quit. You don't understand. You can't."

"Just try to hold on to your shit a little longer, Mac. I need you to do that. Right now Frank thinks we're all happy as clams. I don't want that to change."

"I'm sorry, Aug. I really am."

"Look, I'm not fucking around here, Mac. I'm concerned about my daughter. Look, this place isn't as safe as I remember it. There are drugs out here, they're being sold to kids. There's shit going down you don't know about. I'm going to need Frank's resources. I'm going to need you. You can go places I can't. I'm going to need your help."

"I'll do whatever you want, Aug. You know that. But I can't work for Frank anymore."

He took a step toward me. "Now's not the time to rock the boat. Just trust me on this. I need you to suck it up and stick it out. Just a few more weeks, that's all. Just hang in there a few more weeks. That's all I ask."

I didn't say anything for a long time after that. I looked toward my windows, toward the dark night beyond the bare elms that lined my street. The way the branches moved in the wind reminded me of the way people breathe when they are asleep.

Finally I nodded. "Okay," I said.

"We need to keep Frank in place right now. We need to keep him happy."

I nodded again. "Okay. Yeah. You're right."

"You going to be okay?"

"Yeah."

"Just a few weeks more."

"Okay."

Augie picked up the bottle of Beam from the coffee table. He shook it. The swishing sound inside was high-pitched, almost tinny.

"This wasn't by any chance full when you started, was it?"

"Probably."

"Mind if I have what's left?"

"Help yourself."

"I think I'll take it with me, if that's okay."

"Suit yourself."

"You should try to get some sleep, Mac. I'm going to need your help tomorrow night. There are some men, some dealers, I want to check up on."

I nodded once more. "I'll be there," I said.

"Good." Augie went into my bedroom and came out with a blanket. He tossed it onto the couch beside me.

"I'm going to go look into something right now. I'll be back later to check up on you, so stick around. You might want to sleep on your stomach, in case you get sick in the night."

"Yeah," I said.

Augie looked at me for a while. It felt like a long time to me. Then he left. After he was gone I stayed where I was. I was too drunk now to sleep. Everything kept moving around me. It was as if I were in the middle of a riot. My surroundings seemed strange. I recognized nothing. Then suddenly I felt as if I had been thrust out into the open night. It was as if I had been speeding down a road that suddenly came to an end and I flew out into stark nothingness. I lingered in midair for a moment like a fucking cartoon character. Then I dropped hard down through the dark. Falling was the last thing I knew for a while.

•   •   •

When I came to later it was still dark. I heard music from the bar downstairs, muffled bass notes that reverberated in the wood planks and beams and high trebles that found their way up through the cracks between. I got up and went to my windows. I stood there with the blanket around my shoulders and looked down at Elm Street and the train station beyond.

The riot wasn't around me any longer, it was in me. It had localized inside my chest. There was a rage in my heart, a tumult. It was like a fire burning and people running. I knew it wouldn't take much to send it out of control again. In the end it took very little at all.

I suddenly felt feverish and rushed into the bathroom. I dropped to the floor and vomited hard into the toilet. I vomited all the heat out of me and became suddenly very cold. Sweat covered every part of me in a second. My gut felt torn up, like it used to when I boxed with my crazy adoptive brother, who worked the body better than anybody I knew and enjoyed every minute of it. I was to be the family bodyguard, that was my role. I was to protect them, my brother and his mother and father, on our many trips abroad. Men were flown in from all over the world to train me in hand-to-hand and weapons, world-class fighters, vale tudo winners, and ex-military men. My adoptive brother went through all my training with me. He was my twenty-four-hour-a-day partner and knew everything I knew.

He loved it more than I did. He had a thing for causing pain.

But I didn't have a thing for pain, back then or now. When I was through vomiting I got up from the cold floor and leaned over the sink and let the water run. I splashed my face with it and rinsed out my mouth. When I was done with that I lifted my eyes and caught my reflection in the dirty piece of broken mirror fixed to the wall above.

I didn't like what I saw. But I didn't look away. I searched my own eyes. I looked over the thick skin. I wiped the excess water from my face and felt the bristles of a five-day-old beard under my palms. My eyes looked sunken, rimmed top and bottom with black smudges. I looked as if I were something rotting from the inside out. I studied myself for as long as I could bear it. Then I grabbed my jacket, and the next thing I knew I was outside, in the cold night, heading for my car.

I drove to Frank's office and climbed the thirteen stairs and pried open the door with a tire iron. Then I went inside and turned the place upside down. All I could think of was how my eyes looked and the pain and rage I felt. I pried open the filing cabinets, all six of them, each and every drawer, and flipped them over. Files went everywhere. I turned over Frank's desk, broke open its drawers, kicking pieces across the floor. When I couldn't do any more damage, when I was spent and there was nothing else left to do, I just dropped to the floor. I had cut myself at some point; there was blood on my hands, on the jacket Augie had given me, on the papers scattered beneath me like a bed. But I didn't care about that. I just lay there, half conscious, panting for breath. I thought maybe I was going to throw up again but didn't. Everything settled into a kind of peace inside me and around me. All I could hear was my own breathing.

Then the next thing I knew it was morning. I heard someone on the stairs but I didn't move. I waited without care till Frank appeared in the open door.

"What the fuck?" he said.

Then I heard his footsteps rushing toward me. Right away I took two kicks to the ribs. I heard more cursing and heavy breathing, mine and his. I tried to move but I was too spent and too drunk. He kicked me a third time in the ribs. Then I heard a second voice from somewhere else in the room, and more rushing footsteps. The two voices argued, there were a few more last kicks, the last of which was followed by the sound of a short scuffle.

Then I heard Frank yell, "Get this son of a bitch out of here right now!" The room seemed to be made smaller somehow by his voice. Then someone lifted me off the ground like I was nothing. I could barely stand. I felt an arm around me and a huge hand firmly cupping each shoulder. Someone was beside me, walking me out the door. I didn't feel the floor beneath my feet.

"Jesus, Mac, you're covered in blood."

I remember recognizing Augie's voice. I don't remember, though, going down the steps to the sidewalk. I don't remember crossing it to the street. The next thing I do remember was being laid down on the torn upholstery of the backseat of my LeMans.

"I've been looking for you all night," Augie said. "I thought we had a deal." He checked the cut on my hand and muttered something about it being superficial. He gave me a rag to wrap around it. I held onto it for a moment, but then my hand fell open and the rag dropped to the floor.

Next we were driving. I looked up and saw trees moving above us, as bare as skeletons. They passed by, one right after the other, like a parade of dead people, the blue morning sky blinking brightly beyond them...

The last thing I knew I was sprawled out on my couch. I lay there and listened to Augie's breathing. Eventually I saw the shape of him in a nearby chair. He was just watching me. After a while, though, he got up and left. He closed the door with the broken lock behind him. Then sometime after that I drifted into unconsciousness and dreamed of some woman named Rosē.

Four

It was months later, on a cool night in early May, that I found myself waiting outside the Hansom House for Augie. The air was still and pale dark clouds roamed the broad black sky in herds. Augie had called me early that morning and said he needed my help with something, that it was urgent, and that he would come by for me when I got home from work that evening. It was a fast call and had ended abruptly. Before that morning I hadn't heard from him in over a week. He was, unlike me, a busy man these days, busy working for Frank, busy keeping him near. He was busy, too, doing something else, something he didn't talk about. That day he called I got home from work exactly at six o'clock and waited upstairs till nine. But there wasn't any sign of him, and it was too beautiful a night to stay inside my cramped apartment, so I went down to the street to wait in the open air and smell the heavy scent of freshly dug earth coming from the potato fields behind the train station.

I was certain that Augie would have called if he had been able. The events of last October were still very much on our minds. The cop killer was still out there somewhere, and we knew nothing more about what it was, if anything, Frank was up to.

With so much still up in the air, I didn't think Augie would have left me hanging like this if he could have helped it. I knew Augie would have called to tell me of any change in plan, as what might appear to be his sudden disappearance, despite our differences, would have certainly caused me concern.

Deep down I knew Augie was up to something. And he knew that I was on to him. He was gone every night of the week, even nights when Frank had no job for him. Augie and I had proceeded over the last six months with a "don't ask, don't tell" policy. I wasn't part of that world, and we both knew it. I didn't want to know, I didn't want to get involved. I suppressed my curiosity, and we steered clear of any mention of that in conversation.

But all that changed when he used the word "urgent." I'd never known him to use that word, or any like it, before. It played in a loop in my head as I drove all day from one end of the East End to the other, delivering truckloads of antique and restored furniture to the affluent.

I had tried to call Augie at his home during my lunch break but got nothing but the same unanswered ringing I got each time I tried his number before going downstairs to take in the rich night.

My back was sore from a long day of sitting, broken only by moments of heavy lifting, and all I wanted was a hot bath and a drink or two and then to turn in early for some sleep. But I was worried and restless.

I hadn't been in the doorway of the Hansom House for very long when I saw an old red-colored taxicab come up Railroad Plaza past the train station and make the right-hand turn onto Elm Street. It was Eddie's cab. It passed the Mexican restaurant on the corner and then slowed and pulled to the curb and stopped across the street from me.

Eddie's arm was hanging out the driver's door window, his white shirt sleeve rolled up, his black skin shiny under the streetlights above. He waved me over. I hesitated, then left the doorway and walked down the pathway to the street and crossed to him.

The motor was running a little rough, the body of the cab trembling slightly. I could hear reggae music coming from inside, drifting out on an invisible cloud of clove oil and Old Spice.

Eddie was a middle-age black man who had come to

America years ago from Jamaica and started a small cab company on the East End. I had helped him out of a jam once, when I was young. He was a thin man with skin like coffee and a narrow, bony face. His smile was pleasant despite his yellowed teeth and shockingly pink gums. His face was unshaven, his bristles white and as thick as quills.

We weren't friends, really. We didn't frequent the same places, we didn't go out of our way to see each other or even say hello. But we knew each other. He was, being a cabbie, sometimes privy to things no one else knew. Sometimes he made a point of seeking me out and telling me things he thought I, for one reason or another, should know.

So I knew by the fact that Eddie drove by my place and stopped that something was going down. My heart raced a little.

"What's up, Eddie?"

His white bloodshot eyes were stark against his dark skin. His face was wrinkled, with deep furrows by his eyes and mouth. Between his teeth, sticking out from the right side of his mouth, was the stub of a cigar, unlit.

"Beautiful night," he said. He hadn't lost his accent even after twenty years. "It's about time, don't you think? I wasn't born for these Long Island winters."

I smiled at that. "So what's up, Eddie?"

"That little girl, that daughter of your friend, I saw

her not long ago in town." Eddie knew pretty much everyone on the East End. He had driven Augie home from my place several times when Augie was too gassed to drive. Augie had even used his cab several times doing surveillance jobs for Frank.

"Tina?" I said. "Augie's kid."

"Yeah, that's her."

"What's going on?"

"I think she could use a friend right now."

"What do you mean?"

"She was with some boys. High school boys in those jackets they wear."

"Where?"

"By the library."

"Is she in trouble?"

"Not yet. But the odds don't seem in her favor, if you know what I mean."

I nodded and looked in the direction of the village. The library was a mile away; I didn't know what I expected to see.

I looked back at Eddie. "I'll check it out. Thanks, Eddie."

"No problem, Mac."

My LeMans was parked just a little ways down on the same side of the street. I took a step toward it, then stopped. I turned back to Eddie. "Hey, you haven't by any chance seen Augie recently, have you?"

"No. Can't find him?"

"It's probably nothing. If you see him, though, let me know, okay?"

"If anyone can take care of himself, Mac, it's your friend. But I'll keep an eye out for him. A man like him would be hard to miss."

I thanked Eddie and continued on to my car. His cab pulled away from the curb as I unlocked my door. I climbed in behind the wheel and pulled the door shut, then cranked the ignition till the engine caught and shifted into gear and pulled into the street. I made a U-turn, turned left at the end of Elm Street onto Railroad Plaza, and then made the left onto North Main Street and followed that for half a mile into the village, heading toward the library.

It was a quiet night in town. The shops were closed, the sidewalks empty. The restaurants I passed weren't all that busy. Unoccupied tables and wait staff with nothing to do were visible behind large storefront windows. The library was around the corner, on Job's Lane, but I parked near the end of Main, close to the corner. I could cut around to the back of the Village Hall and approach the library that way and not be seen on the street by anyone.

My shortcut to the back of town was the alleyway that ran between Frank's office and Village Hall. I hadn't even walked past Frank's place since the night I trashed it and Augie had to pull me out and take me home. The front window to Frank's office was dark now, but I still didn't like being so near it all that much. The sooner I was away from there the better.

I got out of my car and stepped to the curb and listened. It didn't take long for me to pick out the sound of laughter coming from somewhere behind the Village Hall. It sounded distant and thin, and I went after it, walking down the alleyway to the small parking lot used by cops. Once there I heard something other than laughter.

A shriek sounded out and carried briefly, then was cut off, gone.

I tried to place it but it was too brief. Beyond the cop lot was a municipal parking lot the size of two football fields. It was empty now. To the right of that, behind the library, was a small park surrounded by a cluster of fir trees and a cyclone fence. It was a tiny park, not much bigger than my apartment. But I looked toward it intently and waited. It was the only enclosed area around, and anyway I had a feeling about it.

I stopped just outside the alleyway and held still and listened. The shriek had been such a brief sound that a part of me doubted now that I had heard it. But there also was a part of me that didn't doubt it, that heard it well and knew just what it meant.

A car passed down Main Street behind me, and I could hear very little over it till it was gone. Then silence returned to the open parking lot and I waited in it, not making a move, my eyes fixed on the tiny fenced-in park behind the library.

Then my ears found something, a rustling sound from near the center of that small park, the unmistakable sound of a struggle.

I heard murmured words, male voices giving hurried and hushed commands. Then finally I heard it, another shriek, or half a shriek, for it was cut off midway through just like the one before, cut off before it could rise and carry, before it could reach above the dense trees that surrounded that park.

It was all I needed to hear. My heart burst and sent a terrible ache through me, and I broke into an all-out run.

I reached the fence and cleared it quickly, as quietly as I could. Then I moved forward through the border trees. This park was significantly darker than the open lot was, but still I spotted them almost instantly. They were on the other end of the enclosure, in a patch of open ground that was only slightly better lighted than the ground under the crowding trees.

There were three of them, three boys in lettermen jackets. And there was Tina, in the middle of it. I could see her well enough. She was in their arms, not one part of her touching the ground. She was kicking and bucking and trying with all she had to get free of them. It looked like a feeding frenzy.

I could hear her murmuring. One of the boys had his hand over her mouth. They were all talking at once in voices that weren't all that hushed but still quiet. They didn't hear my approach.

The three boys were busy with Tina, busy keeping her still, busy yelling at each other, busy tearing Tina's T-shirt open, pulling at her white bra, trying to peel down her jeans. They had no idea I was even there till I was upon them.

The first boy I reached had shoulder-length hair, thick. I came up beside him and grabbed a handful of that hair and gave a good yank, pulling it like I was ringing a church bell, bending my knees and tugging him almost headfirst to the ground. I used all my body weight and hung onto him till he was flat out on his back. I couldn't have him getting back up right away, the fall he had taken wasn't hard enough to stun him, so the instant he hit the ground I let my legs buckle and dropped down on him, landing my right knee, with all my body weight behind it, onto his ribs. I heard a quick crack and a deep grunt.

I left him there and stood fast. I caught Tina from the corner of my eye. Her T-shirt was torn up the middle, her bra around her neck. Her breasts were exposed. I didn't want to see them but there was nothing I could do about that. Her jeans were unbuttoned and had been pulled almost past her hips, her panties with them.

The other two boys still had her. They were aware of me but hadn't had time to drop her yet. The second boy had one hand over her mouth and the other hand around her waist. The third had his hands hooked under her knees. I saw that Tina's eyes were closed tight, her face contorted with anger and concentration. She was still bucking with all she had.

I moved without hesitation to the boy nearest to me, the one with her legs in his arms. I rushed him, crouching like a peek-a-boo boxer, like Frazier or Tyson, and spiraled with my whole body and being and drove a fast open-handed uppercut between his muscular legs. It landed with a loud slap into his groin. He took all I had and dropped Tina's legs, drawing his arms fast to his crotch as if to catch something about to fall. He fell to a heap on the ground and immediately began to heave his supper.

The third boy had dropped Tina by then and was rushing toward me, moving like a linesman after the quarterback. Tina lay flat out on the ground, her eyes wide open. She had no clue what was happening. The third boy came in for a low tackle. I let him come in. The first blow I landed was a sharp knee thrust. It slowed him a little. A second blow stunned him. I was able then to grab hold of his head with both hands. I hugged it close to me like it was a basketball I didn't want to lose and whaled at it again with my knee. It took two more blows before the third boy caved and lost momentum and stumbled facedown to the ground.

My mind was racing now. I know I should have

grabbed Tina and gotten out of there. I had done what the law allowed and nothing more. This was important to me. But something kept me there. It came to me in this chaos that I had a reason to put a scare into that boy, to say something to him, to let him know I was on to him and I wasn't afraid of him. I didn't want to let him go and then have it come back and cause trouble for me or anyone else.

The third boy rolled out onto his back. I looked down at him. Through the dark I was able to recognize him. I had seen his photograph in the papers, in the local sports pages, there and only there. It appeared nowhere else, not the front page, not in the police blotter, not anywhere. I knew his name. I knew exactly who he was.

Tina wasn't the first girl from the high school to be attacked. Since last October three rapes had been reported by girls who claimed not to know their attackers. The rumor around town was that the investigating cops weren't doing their job. A lot of people had a pretty good reason why nothing was being done.

The first boy, the one whose rib I had cracked, got to his feet fast then and headed toward the park exit. He didn't look back, just bolted clumsily, his arm clutched at his side. The second boy, the one I had clipped in the groin, was on his hands and knees, wiping the vomit from his chin. He looked at me but I wasn't certain he could see much of anything. His eyes were watery. They looked for me in the dark but didn't seem to find me.

"Get out of here," I said to him.

He looked at the third boy, then back up at me. When he didn't move I made a slight step toward him. It was just a bluff. He folded fast and scrambled to his feet and hobbled away as fast as he could.

I approached the third boy then and stood over him. He was out of breath. He looked up at me, his eyes blinking. Since he was a football player I knew he was used to pain, to playing hurt. He was stunned by the shots I had landed but he wasn't broken. I sensed no fear from him at all. He was simply on his back, resting as if between plays.

"Fun time's over," I said to him. "Do you understand me?"

He said nothing, just stared up at me. His jaw was set tight, hatefully.

"I know who you are, kid," I said. "You and your friends, you're out of business. Understand me?"

"My father's the chief of fucking police, asshole."

"I know who your old man is. I don't give a fuck. You're out of business. That's all there is to it. I'm stopping you right now."

"You fucking think you can stop me? I do what I fucking want. You don't understand—"

"—You and your friends don't scare me, Tommy."

"You won't be around long enough to be scared, jackass. You can count on that."

"You're going to come to my house in the middle of the night, tough guy? You're brave enough to come after someone who's waiting for you?"

"You can't touch me."

"You're the one flat out on his back, Tommy boy. I'm still standing. I'm standing here looking down at a pile of shit."

"You're a dead man, that's all you are."

"Your father can't protect you anymore, Tommy. You come near Tina again and you'd better hope I get to you before her old man does."

I turned to get Tina then. I had burned up all the time I had to spare. It was time to go, but I stopped dead in my tracks when Tommy spoke again.

"Your friend's a skank anyway. There are a lot of other sweet little cunts in town. Maybe we won't be so nice to the next one. She'll have you to thank for that. Just a little something for you to think of while my father's got your ass in jail for jumping his son."

"You might want to be careful what you say here, kid," I said over my shoulder.

"She wanted it. They all do. She came with us, she knew what was up. If they want in they have to pass initiation. You don't know shit. This goes on all the time, every weekend, and there isn't a fucking thing you can do about it."

I turned back to look down at him then. I said nothing.

"Your little friend is the biggest tease in school. A skank like her shouldn't play so hard to get. What does she think she is? She can cry rape all she wants. But to be part of the gang, you've got to bang. She knew that when she left the party with us—"

Suddenly Tina lunged forward. I had lost track of her, of where she was, but she came out from behind me, from my left, and bolted toward the fallen boy. She had put her bra back in place and had refastened her jeans and was holding her torn shirt up to her chest. But she was anything but anywhere near put back together.

"You're a liar," she shrieked. "You're a lying pig." She charged Tommy and kicked at his head. It was a powerful and well-controlled kick. She was on him before I could think to move. The tip of her sneaker struck him, and the blow clearly jolted Tommy. She went to throw another kick but the jolt hadn't lasted. Tommy recovered his senses fast and grabbed at her foot and sprang up into a seated position. She fell into him and he pulled her down onto him. He grabbed her close to him and rolled fast, toppling her and landing on top of her.

Though trapped below his weight, Tina wasn't done. She reached up and scratched at his face. She wriggled, trying to get out from under him, screaming at him. I raced toward them and was on him before he could do anything much in the way of retaliation.

I lunged at Tommy then and grabbed the collar of his jacket and pulled him off Tina. I yanked him with everything I had and spun around and flung him to the ground. He landed on his back. The instant he was down I mounted him.

Tommy and I were face to face. His breath smelled foul and felt worse. He barked more than spoke. He struggled against me and I could feel his tremendous strength. I could feel my control over him weakening. He was wild with rage, twisting and squirming below me like a mad dog. I knew I couldn't hold him for long. He was just too strong. It was only a matter of time before he broke free of me, and once he did there would be a nasty fight on my hands. And there just wasn't time for that now. I couldn't get into a wrestling match. I needed to get Tina and get out of there.

I gave up trying to restrain Tommy and slammed the side of my head into his face. He grunted once. But that did nothing to sap his strength. He was on the verge of throwing me, of bucking me like a bad habit. He arched his back, lifting his hips high off the ground, and me with them. My balance was shot. I was too high in the saddle now. He rolled to his left and I fell to the ground. I was on my back now and he was above me.

My legs, though, were around his waist, my knees against his chest. I felt his weight press upon me for a moment and then give. Instead of trying to pin me, Tommy did what a football player would do: he went to stand up.

He was smiling. The reversal had given him confidence. There was hate in his smile. I let him plant his feet solidly on the ground, then reached down and hooked his ankles with my hands and pulled them toward me as I pushed forward with my knees. I moved explosively. Tommy went crashing down to his back again.

I sat up fast. Tommy's feet were right there for me. I leaned back so he couldn't kick my face and slapped an ankle lock on his right foot. He was clueless as to what I was after. He lifted his head and looked down at me but the lock was on. He wasn't going anywhere now. I trapped his right leg between mine. Our eyes met. The smile was gone and there was a puzzled, almost concerned look on his face now.

I could have kicked him in his groin then, done something to stun him, and then grabbed Tina and run out of there. I could have done a lot of things. But I chose to do something else instead. The Chief had gone this far to protect his son. Why would he stop short of that now? I was probably jail-bound as it was. I knew that. The only thing I could think of was that the last thing I wanted was Tommy Miller running free while I was locked away in his daddy's jail.

I would never get a chance like this again. I had it now and had to take it. It was the only order I could find in this chaos swirling around us.

"What the fuck?" Tommy said.

I looked him in the eye once more, then leaned back suddenly, almost laying myself flat on the ground. I moved like a shot, the lock secure around Tommy's ankle. He cried out as I turned the hold ninety degrees and the ligaments in his ankle joint tore from the bone. Without hesitating I turned at the waist with a jerk, one sudden, violent thrust. I heard from Tommy's knee an airy pop and the dull snap. It was a sickening sound. I let go of Tommy then and got up fast. He was screaming now. It was a terrible, high-pitched squeal. It was time to go now.

I rushed over to Tina and took her with my two trembling hands by the shoulders. My touch startled her. Her head lifted quickly, her arms flying up to cover her torn T-shirt. I helped her up. Her body was shaking.

"It's okay," I told her. "You're okay now."

"Who are you?" she demanded. There was a degree of pleading in her voice. She was on the verge of tears.

"It's okay. I'm a friend of your father's. You're okay. C'mon, we've got to get out of here." I glanced at her torn shirt. "Do you have a jacket somewhere around here?"

"No."

I was wearing an unbuttoned denim shirt over a dark T-shirt. I took the denim shirt off and swung it around her shoulders quickly. She held it tight around her, covering herself up. I smelled her sweat and a sweet, citrus perfume.

"Did you have a purse with you, did you drop anything?"

"No."

"You're sure?"

She nodded her head quickly. Her features were a blur in the dark. Her face was blank and her mouth hung open slightly, almost dumbly. "Yes."

"We can't leave behind anything they'd be able to identify us by."

"I didn't have anything."

"Are you hurt?"

"No."

"Can you walk?" She was frozen, her muscles locked tight. She held her shoulders high and was all but rooted to the ground.

"I think so," she said.

"Okay, then, let's get out of here."

"I think I'm going to puke."

"Not now. Suck it up."

Voices were coming from the lot behind the police station. I heard keys jingle and hurried footsteps.

I put my hand over Tina's mouth then. Her eyes went wide. I held my index finger up to my own lips, locked eyes with her to make certain she understood, then took her by the hand and led her along the path that wound around the library to Job's Lane.

We stopped by the front of the building, out of sight, and knelt down. I had her slip her arms into the sleeves of the shirt and button it up. I checked up and down the street, and then we rose and walked as casually as we could up Job's Lane. We rounded the corner onto Main Street and walked to my car. I had my arms on her shoulders and looked around as we went. I saw nobody.

We hurried into my car and I cranked the ignition till the motor caught. Then we backed from the curb onto Main Street. I shifted into gear and eased up to the traffic light, to the corner of Main and Job's Lane.

As we waited for the light to turn green, I looked back in my rearview mirror toward the Village Hall. I searched for signs of commotion. But there were none, not yet, at least. I glanced to my right, down Job's Lane. There was no motion, nothing to be seen but a few cars parked down the block, outside a bar called the Driver's Seat.

Then the light changed and I eased down the accelerator and made the left-hand turn onto Meeting House Lane. We rode the side streets the short distance back to the Hansom House. I obeyed every traffic law there was along the way.

Tina sat still in the passenger seat and stared straight ahead. She said nothing. Her fingers were long and bony, and her hands shook as if from a killing cold.

She sat at my kitchen table with a pint glass of cold green tea in her still-shaking hands. She had yet to take a sip from it. I doubted if she even knew she was holding it. I was behind her, leaning against my kitchen doorway with my arms folded across my chest. I watched her and gave her all the time she needed.

Maybe ten minutes passed before her head moved suddenly, like someone waking up with a start. She looked around the kitchen, startled. Then she turned her head and spotted me.

"You're okay," I told her. She looked over her shoulder at me. Her eyes were gray and a little more focused now. Her mouth hung open slightly. There was still a look of alarm on her face. Her mind was certainly still reeling. I moved from the doorway and sat across the small table from her, leaning toward her.

"You're okay now," I said again.

She stared at me for a while, as if she thought she recognized me. Finally she said, "Your name is Mac, isn't it?"

"How'd you know?"

"You were passed out on our couch once when I came home from school a few months ago."

I didn't remember that. I was almost embarrassed by the thought. "Oh," I said.

"My father said you were his friend."

"I am." I kept my voice low, just above a whisper. She matched my tone.

"Is he here? Is my father here?"

"No, not yet."

"He said he was going to meet you."

"I'm sure he's on his way."

"I want to see him."

"He'll be here soon, Tina. You're okay for now. I'll stay with you till he gets here. Drink your tea. It's good for you. It'll help you calm down."

She looked at the glass in her hand like it was the first time she was aware of it. She stared at it for a moment, then brought it to her lips and took a sip. Her hands were still shaking and she couldn't keep even flow of it to her mouth. She swallowed what she had and put the glass down on the table, wincing.

"It's an acquired taste," I told her. Tears were really welling up in her eyes now, waiting to fall. The shock was passing, her emotions freeing up.

Her eyes pinched then, cutting loose two large tears that bounded down her face. She stiffened, her eyes locked on me, holding the rest back. She muttered, as calmly as she could, "I want my father." Her voice quivered, and for a moment she flashed with anger, anger at her tears, at her breaking voice, at what she had just uttered.

She was her father's daughter, all right, I thought.

"He'll be here soon," I whispered. I didn't know what else to say.

She sniffled and wiped her wet face with the back of her hand. "I'm afraid."

"You don't have to be."

"What if they follow us here?"

"They're not going to be following anyone for a long time," I told her.

"How can you be sure?"

"You don't have to worry. You don't have to be afraid of them. I promise."

More tears sprang free then, rolling down her face. They were followed by even more still. She immediately stiffened against them but it was no good. There was no holding back now. Her shoulders hunched suddenly, as if giving in under weight, and finally she wept.

We moved to my couch, where I put her under my wool blanket. She sat up and curled upon herself like a child. I poured out her tea in the sink and lit a candle to give her something to focus on. Then I pulled up my chair and sat across from her and wondered where Augie was.

A little before midnight she fell asleep, her skinny legs twitching violently now and again under the wool blanket, as if she were still trying to buck herself free of her attackers. I held perfectly still in my chair and waited, listening hard for the sound of footsteps coming down the long hallway outside my door.

Eventually I pretty much gave up on Augie altogether. But it wasn't by choice. I had started to expect the police by now. I doubted that we had gotten away unseen. I doubted that one of the three boys hadn't recognized me. I didn't have the kind of luck that would make that possible. I listened for the sound of multiple footsteps and thought how someone could have seen my ancient LeMans outside Village Hall as we drove away and put the two things together.

Sometime after midnight the candle burned out and I was left sitting in the dark. Then sometime after that I fell asleep sitting up in my chair. I don't know for how long I was out when I awoke again with a start.

I lurched forward in my chair suddenly, startling Tina. She lifted her head quickly and looked around lazily. "What?"

"Shh. Wait," I whispered. I held still and listened hard. The night air was coming through my open windows, lifting my yellowed curtains, filling the apartment with the smells of spring breezes and stale cotton. I could hear the sound that had awakened me diminishing, but I couldn't identify it. I wasn't even sure where it had come from. I looked toward my living room window as if the sound might have come from outside.

Tina whispered, "What is it?"

I held my index finger to my lips. She looked at me but said nothing more.

It took a moment, but then it came again, a heavy creaking sound, the sound of wood compressing under weight. There was no doubt about it now, it had come from behind my door, from the hallway that ran from the top of the stairs to my apartment.

I pointed to Tina and mouthed the word "Stay." Her eyes went down to my lips. She nodded. I got up from the couch and went to my living room window and looked down onto Elm Street.

I saw nothing but the usual number of cars parked across the street. I saw no patrol cars, no flashing blue lights, nothing. I checked my watch. It was close to three in the morning.

I looked out my window again, this time toward the train station at the end of Elm. I thought maybe the cops had parked there so I wouldn't see them coming and escape out my bedroom window. But the lot outside the station was empty, the street still.

I told myself that Augie would have knocked or used the key I kept hidden under a tear in the hallway carpeting.

Then came another creak, heavy, like a wooden sigh. Somebody was outside my door all right, hovering in my hall.

I got up, looked at the door for a second, then walked to it. For the second time today adrenaline was surging through my muscles. I gripped the doorknob and turned it fast, yanked the door open, and took a step out into my hallway.

But then I stopped short. I was standing face to face with Frank Gannon.

The hallway was dim. The only light was behind him, from a bare low-watt bulb hanging from the ceiling at the far end of the hall. But I could see him well enough by it. He was wearing blue jeans and a dark dress shirt and a light jacket made of Argentine leather. His shoes were black cop's shoes.

I pulled the door partially closed behind me. From my doorway the couch where Tina was sitting under my wool blanket was in clear view.

I whispered, "What the fuck are you doing here?"

"We need to talk."

"You could have called."

"Did I come at a bad time?" He glanced at the partially closed door and the firm grip I had on it with my hand.

"There's no good time to find you outside my door. I'm not in the mood for your shit right now."

"We're wasting time. I wouldn't be here if it wasn't important."

"I can't help you, Frank. I don't want whatever it is you're selling."

"You don't understand, kid."

"I thought I made things clear back in your office."

"You might want to hear me out."

"I don't owe you anything."

"It's about Augie, MacManus. I think he might be in trouble. I think he might be in trouble right now, as we speak."

I turned my head and looked past the partly closed door, back into my apartment. It was a reflex. Tina was looking at me. She had stood at some point, maybe to move away from the door. Augie had said how smart she was. Her mouth was hanging open slightly and her eyes locked briefly with mine.

Frank took one step to his right and tilted his head. He looked past me and saw her. It was a casual glance. When he looked back at me he was smiling.

"I'm sorry," he said. "I have caught you at a bad time."

"It's Augie's daughter. She's waiting for him here."

Frank took another look at Tina. Her hands were hanging at her sides. She was staring at us, frozen. The blanket was in a pile around her feet.

"I thought maybe you might know where Augie was," Frank said.

"He was supposed to meet me earlier tonight. He didn't show."

"He called me and asked to borrow some of my equipment. He never showed up."

"Was he working for you tonight?"

"No. He hasn't worked for me all week. He pulled himself off the roster, couldn't tell me for how long. I thought maybe he was freelancing. Maybe it's me, but he hasn't been himself lately. He's been preoccupied. I'm starting to think something's up."

I thought about all that, then nodded. "All right. All right, I'll see if I can find him."

Frank handed me a business card. "Here's my pager number. I'm sure you went out of your way to forget it."

I took the card and stepped back inside my apartment and closed the door. I waited till I heard his footsteps move down the hall. I waited till they were gone before I turned on the small lamp by the door and took my keys from the table on which the lamp sat.

"What's happened to my father?" Tina said.

"That's what I'm going to find out."

"I want to come with you."

"No."

"He's my father."

"It doesn't matter. I'm going to call a cab and have you taken home."

"I don't want to go home."

"I'm sorry."

"I don't want to be alone. I won't feel safe there."

"I know the cab driver. He's a good man. I'll tell him to go inside with you, to check the place out for you, to lock up tight when he leaves."

"Please, can't I stay here?"

"No," I said. "The cops might come looking for me still."

"Why? I don't understand. What for?"

"For what happened with those boys in the park."

"But they were going to hurt me."

"It doesn't matter what they were trying to do. What matters is what I did."

"What did you do?"

"If the cops come looking for me, the last thing I

want them to find in my apartment is a fifteen-year-old girl asleep on my couch like she lives here."

"I'm afraid to leave here."

"Eddie'll take good care of you."

"I could hide if they come."

"Please, we don't have time for this. You have to go home. I'm sorry."

"Will you drive me, then?"

"There isn't time."

She said quickly, "He's been leaving the house a lot at night with his own camera equipment. He's been leaving at sundown and not coming back till dawn. He locks up everything that's important in the gun safe in his study. I'll bet you there are photographs in there. They might tell you something, they might tell you where to start looking for him."

"Do you know the combination?"

"Not by heart. I can never remember it unless the dial is in front of me. Please, Mac. I don't want to be all alone."

I waited a moment, watching her. She held perfectly still, her shoulders tight. There was, I could see, no point in arguing. Time was clicking off in my head.

"All right, you win, let's go."

The late-rising moon was near full and hung just above the treetops. Between it and us rolled a fragmented sky that moved like crowded slabs of ice down a dark river.

It took us less than five minutes to reach their house. It was a small clapboard cottage at the end of Little Neck Road, not far from the college, on the edge of a small peninsula that reached briefly into Shinnecock Bay. Augie's truck was in the driveway, parked outside the closed garage door.

I pulled in behind it and cut the motor and killed the lights. Their house was dark and still, not unlike every other house we had passed along this residential street.

I could hear the lazy lapping of the slight bay waves against the stony shore not a hundred feet away. It seemed the only sound for miles around. I smelled brine through my half-opened window, and wild roses. The sea air was cool against the inside of my lungs.

Tina saw the truck in the driveway and said, "He's home." There was hope in her voice.

"It looks that way, doesn't it?" I said. I watched the cottage through the windshield. I didn't take my eyes off it. Tina was looking at the side of my face.

"What's wrong?" she asked.

"I don't know."

"What is it?" she urged.

"I don't know. Wait a minute. I don't know. Things don't really add up."

"What things?"

"Would he have come home and gone to bed if you weren't home yet?"

She shrugged. "Maybe. He knew I was going to a party. He knew I'd be late." There was a hollowness in her voice, as if she herself weren't too convinced by what she was saying.

"But would he have gone to bed without leaving some lights on for you?"

Tina looked toward the house and thought about that for a moment. "Maybe he forgot."

"Maybe. But if he had come home, don't you think he would have called me? He had to know I'd be concerned."

"It's late. Maybe he just got home. Maybe he tried and we had already left."

"An awful lot of maybes, Tina, don't you think? Too many maybes."

"He could have gone out with someone else, in their car. Maybe he isn't home at all. Just because his truck is there..."

I eyed the cottage, scanning from window to window, looking for something.

"Do me a favor," I said. "Wait here, okay?"

"Where are you going?"

"I just want to check something out."

She said quickly, "I want to come with you."

"I won't be long. Stay here."

I reached up and flipped down my sun visor and removed the Spyderco knife I kept there. I slid it into my right hip pocket and climbed out from behind the wheel. I closed the door quietly, then followed the narrow slate walkway from the street to the front door.

I looked around, then pulled open the outer door. The winter glass was still in place. I leaned close to the front door, listening. I noticed then that the door wasn't closed completely. I nudged it with my shoulder and it swung open a little. I reached down fast and grabbed the brass handle, keeping the door from moving any farther. I listened for something, anything, but all I heard was the broken rhythm of the gentle bay waves coming from around back.

I drew a deep breath and swung the door open enough for me to slip through it and enter. I left the lights off, but I didn't need them to see that the house had been trashed. Furniture was turned over, picture frames pulled from wall and smashed, contents of shelves and drawers flung across the wood floor littered with broken bits of glass.

The television lay on its side on the floor, the VCR beside it. Across the room the stereo lay upside down beside a broken lamp.

I took a few steps into the room and looked toward the kitchen and small dining room. Cupboard doors were opened, food boxes and canned goods all over the countertop and tile floor. Appliances were broken apart, a tray of tableware had been dumped out in the sink. The dining room table had been turned on its side, chairs toppled around it. This wasn't a robbery. It was a hasty search.

I listened for anything, creaking wood, fabric brushing together, matter moving through air, anything. A presence can sometimes be sensed before it is heard or seen. But I could pick nothing up. The house was almost serene, which was odd considering its state.

I took a few more steps deeper into the house. To my right was a narrow hallway that led to the two bedrooms and then Augie's study at the end of the hall. I looked down it and saw that all the doors were open except for the study's.

I moved down the hall carefully, pausing to look into each bedroom before I passed. They, too, had been trashed, searched. In Augie's bedroom his Sharper Image answering machine lay on top of his overturned mattress, unplugged.

I came to his office door and saw that it wasn't shut all the way. It was open by a crack. I pressed the door open with my shoulder and looked inside.

This room had been hit the hardest and, by the looks of it, by a wrecking crew. Augie's desk was torn to pieces, and there were sledgehammer holes in the walls. Even the floorboards had been pulled up in places. The only thing unmolested in that room was Augie's gun safe. It was held securely in place against the wall by two heavy iron brackets bolted into the framework of the cottage. But by the look of the wall immediately surrounding the gun safe, someone had tried unsuccessfully to pry the brackets free with a hammer or wrecking bar.

There was debris all over the floor of the dark room, piles of broken plaster and desk parts and pulled-up floorboards mixed in with the contents of the desk drawers and closet. It was like a scrap heap. It took me a moment of looking at each of these heaps before I detected a shape that didn't belong, before something out of joint caught my eye.

I said, "Shit," and felt along the wall for a light switch. I flicked it on with a panicked hand.

There was Augie, half seated, half slumped against the wall directly across from me, his arms hanging at his sides like an exhausted boxer resting between rounds. His face was battered, little more than raw meat. Blood oozed freely from countless cuts that reminded me of divots in grass. His head was slick with blood and sweat, the scalp beneath his buzz cut dinged and shimmering.

"Christ," I said. I went to him and knelt beside him. I checked the pulse in his neck. It was weak. His skin was cold against my hands.

I stood and started searching through the rubble for a telephone. I began to dig, throwing debris around. I moved quickly, working my way toward the center of the room. After a few seconds I found the handset to the phone. I pulled it out from under a pile, then reeled in the rest of the unit by the coiled cord. I put the handset to my ear fast but there was no dial tone.

I tossed the phone to the floor and bolted through the door, heading down the hallway. My heart was slamming itself against my rib cage and countless chemical reactions buzzed in my head like alarms.

I think I heard their footsteps over the sound of my footsteps. But not in time to eliminate the element of surprise they had over me. One minute I was alone in the house, and the next minute they were there right beside me.

They came out of Augie's bedroom as I passed it, scurrying one right after the other. The first was a big ugly balding guy. The second was a smaller guy, a guy closer to my size. He wore a hooded sweatshirt and jeans and a baseball cap, the bill dipped low. The hood of the sweatshirt was pulled up over that.

The first guy clipped me and sent me into the wall. He threw all his weight against me. I noticed then that he really was no taller than I. But he outweighed me easily by eighty pounds. He was wearing a sweat-stained T-shirt and green fatigues and combat boots. His face and neck were covered with pockmarks, his nose scarred and twisted like a set of rundown stairs.

I only needed one glimpse at his ugly puss to know that he had once been a boxer, and a bad one at that.

He shoulder-butted me twice, driving into me like a bull, forcing me hard into the wall. My body cracked the plaster. I left a deep dent in it. The ugly boxer backed away then, fast, moving as far from me as the hallway allowed. Then he raised a sawed-off double-barrel shotgun to his shoulder, aimed it toward my head, and pulled the trigger without pause.

I had dropped the instant the butt of the gun touched his shoulder. It was the only reason the buckshot took out the wall behind me and not me. I was moving toward him by the time the sound of the blast slapped against my ears like two open hands. Bits of plaster fell on my head and back. I reached the ugly boxer fast and straightened my back, driving my shoulder into the stock of the shotgun as I rose. The barrel was forced upward. I jammed him up against the wall and grabbed onto the gun with both hands. I was face to face with him now, eye to eye. His breath was foul, stale.

His hands hung tight onto the shotgun, and I could see his knuckles clearly. They were thick, like small rocks under his leathery skin. Some were covered with blood. I knew at once it was Augie's blood.

The other one, the smaller one in the cap and hooded sweatshirt, came rushing out of Augie's room right behind the boxer. I saw him coming and stepped to the side of the boxer, moving around and putting him between me and the second guy. Once there I found a better leverage position and forced the gun down fast. I leveled it right at the smaller one's head. His charge stopped suddenly and he stood there, frozen, facing down the remaining live barrel. Without hesitating I threw a head butt with all my weight behind it into the face of the boxer, snapping the top of my head into his nose. It broke clean. The smaller one, out of blind fear more than anything else, dropped just as the bigger one's finger twitched on the trigger and the second barrel blew orange sparks and sweet-smelling smoke and punched a hole the size of a fist into the wall above him.

He hit the floor and sprawled out on his stomach, covering his head with his arms. He waited there for only a second, then lifted his head and looked up at us.

Without a word he scrambled up to his feet and ran toward the living room and burst through the front door.

Blood was running from the nose of the boxer. Still, he held onto the gun, his leathery, bloodstained knuckles whitening from the tension.

For an instant his narrow eyes tried to focus on me through the water that had gathered suddenly in them. Then he lowered his head the way boxers do when they are stunned and want to buy time.

I gave him no rest.

I drove the tip of my knee hard into his right thigh then, tagging him in the sciatic nerve. He flinched and spread his legs slightly in response, opening a clear path to his groin. I took it and thrust my other knee up, landing deep between the legs. He doubled over, and I pried the gun from his hands as he went, holding it by the barrel in one hand like a club. I slammed it down over his right kidney. He twisted and tucked his elbows to protect himself from other such blows. I crouched then and drove the butt hard across his left knee. Then I shot upward as he began to slump and brought the butt down across the back of his head with all I had.

He dropped like dead weight to the hallway floor. I tossed the empty shotgun aside and started after the other one. By the time I reached the door he was tearing down Little Neck Road, heading in the direction of Montauk Highway.

I went back through the living room and down the hallway. I grabbed the boxer by the ankles and pulled him into Augie's bedroom to get him out of the way. Then I rushed into the study and crouched beside Augie.

I knew I shouldn't move him, not in his condition, but Augie was in bad shape, and the two shotgun blasts had probably wakened the whole neighborhood. The cops were probably on their way anyway.

I skimmed my hands over Augie's body, around his neck and down his spine and over his ribs and collarbone, then up and down each arm and leg, looking for breaks. I could feel none. Then I lifted Augie into a more complete seated position against the wall and took his left arm and tucked my head under it. I held his wrist with my left hand, then wrapped my other arm around his thigh. I stood, hoisting him up with me, his stomach across my shoulder.

It took all my strength to lift him. My legs trembled under his weight as I moved step by step down the hallway and through the living room and out to my car.

· · · ·

At the hospital, Tina struggled with the paperwork while I found a pay phone and dialed Frank's pager number. After the beep I entered the number of the pay phone and hung up and waited. Less than two minutes later he called me back.

"I found him," I said. "We're at the hospital now. You might want to check out his house, but bring some help. I left something for you on his bedroom floor. You'd better hurry before it comes to and leaves."

I hung up without waiting for a reply and went back into the crowded waiting room and sat beside Tina.

She was visibly shaken. The clipboard with all the paperwork lay unfinished on her lap, the pencil clutched tightly in her hand. She was staring at the double swinging doors through which her father had been wheeled on a stretcher.

I watched her for a moment, certain that she was no longer aware of me or anything else around her. I reached across and took the clipboard from her lap and pencil from her tight hand. Her hand opened and relaxed once the pencil was removed.

She sat silently, without moving, staring off across the room as I filled out the paperwork. When I was finished, I got up and handed it to the heavyset black woman in white behind the reception desk. Then I sat back down beside Tina. I didn't say anything, just waited with her, watching her closely out of the corner of my eye.

Eventually I left her to her silence and looked through the sliding glass doors that led outside. I could see the sky above the tree line change from black of night to silver, then fade through shades of green as if tarnishing, coming finally to the glassy blue of morning. Despite the activity around me, inside I could sense the stillness that was out there, the quiet moment that came between night and day, that hovered now over the East End like a word unspoken.

The two shotgun blasts that had struck my ears like cupped hands had set off a ringing that was just now beginning to fade. I felt myself emerging from a muted world to a more distinct one, coming out of my own kind of night. I could hear Tina breathing, I could hear conversation around me, I could hear footsteps, shoe soles clicking, sneakers squeaking against tile, dolly wheels rattling as they rolled. I thought about Gale and wondered if she was somewhere in the building.

I heard then the sound of a siren approaching. It grew louder and more insistent as it came nearer. I watched through the sliding glass doors and waited for what I knew by the sound would be a patrol car. The siren grew loader, more urgent, nearer and nearer till finally I saw it pass the doors and then stop just beyond them. I heard car doors open, then close. I glanced at Tina. She sat unaware of this, staring at some point across the room. I heard voices and looked back toward the doors just as they parted automatically and two cops entered with a handcuffed man between them. They held him by the elbows and walked past me without glancing down at me. I didn't realize till after they had passed that the man between them was the boxer. I was too busy looking for recognition in the cops' eyes.

The boxer staggered as they led him to the reception desk. There was blood caked on the back of his head. The cops wore rubber gloves on their hands. The nurse stood up right away and escorted them through the swinging doors and into the emergency room. I watched the doors swing to a close in their wake.

I could hear my heart pounding. Blood rushed in my ears, sounding to me like the echo of a thunderclap out over the ocean. We were all here, in this building, all of us—Augie and Tina, the ugly boxer who had beaten Augie, cops, maybe even the three boys were here somewhere, or at least one of them, maybe still in surgery. Maybe someone who cared about the third boy was there, contemplating a future destroyed and entertaining complex thoughts of revenge.

I had been thrown in the middle of something by Frank Gannon yet again. I had to start piecing things together from what was at hand, I had to catch up or be left behind, possibly even holding the bag.

I wasn't going to get caught up in his world again. I was certain of that. I wasn't going back for anything.

I turned to Tina and said, "I need your help."

At first I didn't think she heard me. She just stared

ahead. But eventually she turned her head a little and looked at me. Her eyes were flat and there was still no color to her face. She stared at me almost as if she didn't recognize me.

"I need to know what your father was up to," I said. "I need you to tell me what you know. And I need you to tell me now."

She looked away, saying nothing. I leaned closer to her and spoke in a whisper. "I'm in trouble, Tina. I'm in trouble and I need your help."

She looked at me then and gave me the same odd stare. Then her eyes lowered, her line of vision coming to rest on my chest. She reminded me of a bird that had stunned itself by flying into a window.

"Anything you can tell me, Tina. Anything."

Her eyes shifted from side to side as if she were trying to decide whether to say something or not. I gave her time, watching her closely.

"There is a boy in my school," she said. Her eyes were still fixed on my chest. "Two weeks ago he died. We were in the same homeroom. He overdosed on heroin. He had bought a bag or whatever of it from someone on school grounds. It wasn't a student, it was a stranger, an adult. My father didn't take the news very well."

"What do you mean?"

"He moved us out here to leave all that behind. I guess he must have thought I was safe from that kind of thing. You know, pushers, gangs. He used to say this was the last safe place on earth. He grew up out here, it was so...safe out here. But when Chris, the boy at school, died, Augie went kind of nuts."

"You said he used to leave the house at sundown with his own camera equipment and not come back till dawn. Was this after he heard about that?"

"It was right after that. That night. He was very angry about it. And then one afternoon I walked into his study and he was cleaning his gun, and his camera equipment was all over his desk. A half hour later he comes into my room and kisses me on the forehead and tells me he's going to work tonight."

"For Frank Gannon?"

"He didn't say. But he used to know in advance when he worked for him, he usually told me so I could sleep over a girlfriend's house. He doesn't like to leave me alone."

"But he left you alone that night?"

"Yeah."

"When did he come back?"

"Dawn. I heard him open his safe and put everything away."

"You think he was trying to find out who was selling shit at your school?"

She nodded again, her eyes still on my chest. "People have seen him out there sometimes during the day, like he was watching the place or something. I never saw him myself. But others did. He'd be sitting in his car, watching the parking lot. It was embarrassing."

"He must have felt like an old enemy had caught up with him," I explained. "It must have hit pretty close to home for him."

"Do you think he found out who the dealer was? Is that why they did what they did to him?"

I realized then that she wasn't aware of the condition their home was in. She had no idea that it had been torn apart. She didn't know about the professional who had tried to kill me with a sawed-off shotgun. All she knew about was the guy she had seen bolt across the front yard in a hooded sweatshirt and baseball cap and the condition of her father.

"I think he stumbled upon something bigger than that, Tina."

"What do you mean?"

"I'm not sure."

Her eyes lifted then, rising from my chest to my mouth. They held there for a moment. I could tell she wanted to say something.

It took her a while but finally she shrugged once and said, "My life would be very different right now if you hadn't shown up like you did. I can't imagine it. Thank you."

"Everything's going to be okay. Don't worry."

"Promise."

"Yeah. I promise."

She stared at my mouth for a moment more, and then she leaned into me, resting the side of her head on my shoulder. I didn't dare move. She stayed that way till a doctor came out of the emergency room and approached us.

His hair was dark and tightly curled. He had an early tan on his face and forearms. Tina and I stood to meet him. He was wearing green hospital scrubs and there were pockets of sweat under his arms.

He spoke to Tina and me equally, alternating eye contact between us. His voice was calm and certain, but there was a graveness to it as well.

"He's unconscious still," he told us. The three of us were together in a tight huddle. "He took a severe beating, particularly to the head. There is some blood clotting that's pushing against the brain, which we can drain, but we'll have to wait till he gets stronger to operate. He's listed as critical, but we're hoping that will change very soon. Our real concern here is in the long term. There may be some brain damage. We won't know anything till he comes around. He's a strong man and he's healthy. It's just too early to know anything for certain. All we can do now is wait and see. If you come back this afternoon maybe you can see him."

He left us alone then. Tina didn't look well at all. Tears welled in her eyes but she refused to let them spring. She seemed as angry by what she heard as she was sad. I wondered then what battles she fought with her father on a regular basis. I wondered if certain aspects of Augie's nature required that this fifteen-year-old girl play the adult. I wondered if she was as much wife as she was daughter, tireless reason to his recklessness.

I knew it was time now to get her out of there, away from this commotion, to get her to a place where nothing else could happen to her for a while. She'd had more than enough. The only place there was for me to take her was my place. And that wasn't exactly the place for a fifteen-year-old girl to be, for a hundred different reasons. It wouldn't be long now before someone in a uniform came knocking on my door.

The police would certainly want to talk to us about what had happened back at Augie's house, about what we knew and what we saw. I didn't want that right now, so I got Tina out of there fast. We walked to my LeMans. I had to hold her with both hands to keep her steady. I was aware of every person who looked at us. The clouds had rolled off with the night, and the morning sky was clear and bright. I squinted against the early sun as we got into my car and made the short drive from the hospital to the Hansom House.

It was before noon when a knock came to my door. Tina was asleep in my bed in the other room, the door closed. I was stretched out under my wool army blanket on the couch and got up quickly and stumbled to the door before whoever it was on the other side had a chance to knock again and awaken Tina.

I was in jeans and a T-shirt, barefoot. I was dog-tired and opened the door in a hurry, forgetting all about the cops, forgetting that at any minute I expected them to come by and haul me away.

But when I opened the door and saw Frank Gannon standing in my hallway, once again all my troubles came rushing back to me in a flash.

I said in a half whisper, "What's going on, Frank?"

Despite the fact that it was high noon outside, it was dark in the hallway. Frank's features were deeply shadowed, his expression, what I could see of it, austere. He didn't make a move to enter and he didn't offer a greeting. He was here on business, that was clear, and I got the feeling somehow that it wasn't going to be a long visit.

"I thought you should know that there isn't going to be any fallout for what you did behind the library last night."

All hint of slumber was gone from my brain now. I wanted to ask him how he knew but I didn't dare say a word.

"Do you even know who those boys were?" he asked.

I nodded, then said, "I'm kind of tired, Frank. I had a busy night. Augie's in the hospital, in case you didn't—"

"I know about Augie. But do you know what kind of shit you're in for because of what you did?"

"Miller and his friends were trying to rape Augie's daughter."

"Hey, you don't have to explain it to me. He's got other kinds of records, too—or would, if his father wasn't the chief of police. Shoplifting, drunk driving, assault, you name it, Tommy Miller's been there. You'd be amazed what a choirboy the Chief thinks his son is. Christ, the walls in the Chief's office at home are covered with dozens of photographs of his pride and joy in action. And now you've put that pride and joy in the hospital. They say he'll be lucky if he can walk right again, let alone run. He was college-bound, you know that. University of Michigan, full scholarship. I'm telling you, you have some bad luck, Mac-Manus."

Frank gave me a minute to think about all that, to let it sink in, then said, "Now, the Chief has two eye-witnesses who picked out a photograph of the man they say attacked them and his son for no reason whatsoever last night. Do I really need to tell you who that person is?"

"That's enough, Frank. I have to go."

"Where are you going to go, MacManus? What are you going to do, jump in that shitbox of yours and hit the Long Island Expressway? They can see you from a mile off in that thing. You wouldn't get past Riverhead. That's the problem with living on this island. There's no real easy way off, is there? This just isn't the place to be if you're a fugitive."

"I've got to go, Frank." Panic was swelling inside me, threatening to burst.

"Don't worry, MacManus. You don't have to go to jail, not if you don't want to. If you'd like, I can get word to the Chief that these two witnesses of his are clearly in error. If you'd like, I can inform him that you were, in fact, with me at the time of the attack, working a case in Montauk. You see, I don't really think it's jail you should be afraid of. I think it's the night you spend in the Chief's custody in the basement of Village Hall. There's a nasty set of cement stairs there. A guy could spend all night falling down those stairs and no one would hear a thing, if you know what I mean. Payback's a bitch, and it's also a reality. But I can remind the Chief, if he needs further convincing, how very dark it is behind the library. I can remind him that the two eyewitnesses were themselves beaten up pretty badly. I can remind him that identifications such as those tend to shatter pretty easily against an alibi as rock-solid as the one I can provide you. I can also remind the Chief that you are something of a local hero around here. Any pending arrest warrant will, I'm certain, be withdrawn once I explain all this to him. Is this something that might be of interest to you, MacManus?"

It took me a moment to nod just once. "Yeah," I said. "It would."

"Good. I'll take care of this right away, then. And

while you're pretty much scot-free on this one for now, you might want to consider lying low for a time. You might want to play it safe. Considering the way cops take care of their own out here, you don't want to get stopped for a broken taillight or running a stop sign or anything like that any time in the near future. You might want to stay right where I can find you. Do you get my meaning?"

Nothing in the world could be clearer than that to me. Nothing was brighter than the circle of light Frank Gannon had caught me in.

"I think so, yeah," I said.

"I don't pretend to know you well, MacManus. I don't pretend to understand you. But I'd be willing to bet you're fostering thoughts of retribution on behalf of Augie. Or that at least you're planning to find out just what happened so you can save him from any future harm. Needless to say, you might want to stay out of the revenge business for a while and let me take care of that. I'll do what I can to find the men responsible for putting Augie in the hospital. I absolve you of that responsibility. Do you understand?"

"Why lie for me, Frank?"

He reached into his jeans pocket for his car keys and pulled them out.

"Let's just say, MacManus," he said in a full voice, "let's just say you now owe me a favor."

I stood like a tagged boxer, too stunned to fall.

Frank turned to go.

"I'll be talking to you, MacManus," he said.

When Tina woke up not long after that, she reminded me that it was a school day and that someone would have to call the high school main office for her. She said it was important. I dialed the number and told a secretary who answered that Tina wouldn't be in today, that her father was in the hospital. The secretary asked who I was and I told them I was Tina's uncle and hung up before she could ask anything more.

Tina didn't want breakfast, which was good because my kitchen was empty. I didn't dare go out for food. I drank two pints of cold green tea and tried to straighten up a little. I wasn't used to having a guest. The last guest I had was last October. Tina just sat there on my secondhand couch for the rest of the morning and bit her nails and stared. I wanted to give her privacy but my apartment was too small. I ended up after a while in my bedroom, flat out on my bed, trying to work out the kinks a night on that couch had caused.

That afternoon we went to the hospital to visit Augie. He was unconscious, his head and face wrapped up in gauze. There were tubes in his arms and mouth. He was breathing with the help of a machine. The doctor tried to be optimistic, but it didn't sound any good to me. If Augie regained consciousness he might not be much more than a vegetable. At best he would have to learn to do the simplest things all over again. Chances were he might not be able to walk again. I thought of Tommy Miller and what Frank had said about him.

After the doctor left I asked a nurse if Gale was working today. I was told that she was on vacation, camping somewhere in New England with her husband, and wouldn't be back till after next week. I think the nurse recognized me. She told me that Gale had recently switched from nights to days.

I decided to leave Tina alone with her father for a while and stepped out into the busy hallway. I found a set of chairs halfway down the hall and sat in one. I looked down at my feet for a long time and thought about nothing. Then I became aware of the sound of footsteps, heavy, booted footsteps. I heard the jingle of keys and the creaking of a leather belt. I didn't look up till after the sound had passed me. When I did look up I saw a man in a cop's uniform walking down the corridor. He was tall, well over six feet, and had long legs and arms. I didn't have to see his face to know it was the Chief.

I didn't move till he turned into a room at the other end of the hall. Then I got up and walked back to Augie's room.

I stepped through the door and stopped short just inside it. I saw that Tina was leaning over her father,

her mouth close to his right ear, whispering something over and over to him and holding his right hand with both of hers. She was squeezing his thick fingers and, though it was barely noticeable, I could tell that he was squeezing back.

Five

It was three months before I finally heard from Frank Gannon. Every day I waited for his call, so much so that every time my phone rang I found myself all but rushing to answer it. When I finally picked up the receiver, it was with a degree of caution and dread. But one morning in early July I awoke shortly before dawn to the sound of my phone clanging on the coffee table near my couch and quickly answered it, without for once thinking about Frank. My only concern was not waking Tina, who was asleep in my bedroom.

"I need to meet with you," he said. His voice sounded thin and far away. I could hear commotion in the background but I couldn't identify exactly what kind. I knew, though, that he was on a pay phone somewhere.

And I knew because of that caution of his that bordered on paranoia not to expect much in the way of conversation. "I have something I want to discuss with you," he added.

"When?" I said.

"Right away."

"Jesus, Frank. Where?"

"It's a nice morning for a walk on the beach, don't you think?"

"It's your show," I muttered.

"The public beach at the end of Halsey Neck Lane. Your old stomping grounds. Ten minutes." He hung up.

I returned the receiver to the cradle, then rubbed my eyes with the back of both hands and checked my wristwatch. It was a little after six. I wasn't built for this time of day.

I got up from the couch, my joints stiff, my back sore, and picked my jeans and T-shirt up off the floor and put them on. I glanced in on Tina; she was still asleep in my bedroom. The door was open and I could see her tangled in the sheets. I saw bare legs and arms. Her limbs were lanky and tanned. I knew by her breathing, by its rhythm and depth, that she was still sound asleep. But it might as well have been the sound of a ticking bomb instead that she was making.

I moved carefully and tried to make no noise as I reached under the kitchen table for my sneakers. I pulled them on over bare feet and took my keys from the table near the door and left. I pulled the door shut behind me as softly as I could.

It was there in the dim hallway that I became aware for the first time that day of the terrible heat that had descended upon Long Island. I had forgotten somehow that we were in the middle of a heat wave, a literal killer with days of near hundred-degree temperatures and air so humid your lungs felt like they were wrapped in shrunken leather when you breathed in. But one step out into the trapped hallway air, which wasn't unlike the air that rushes out at you from an oven when you open the door, brought it all back to me quickly enough. It was worse in the stairwells, where climbing down was like descending into the rising exhaust and heat of some fire. The air was better on the street but not by much.

I still wasn't completely awake as I pulled open the heavy door of my aging Pontiac and got in behind the wheel. I had left the windows down overnight to keep the interior cool. My car was too gone with rust to be worth stealing, and any kids looking for a joy-ride wouldn't get very far—the gas gauge was busted, and I never kept more than a gallon or so of gas in the tank at any given time. I was broke and paid filling station attendants with change from the bottom of my pocket. These days I needed every cent I could spare.

Halsey Neck Lane was on the other side of the village, south of Montauk Highway. I'd make it there and back with the gas I had. I had grown up not far from Halsey Neck, on Gin Lane. The big-time rich lived there, old families who were among the first to build homes out here. But there were a lot of newly rich there now. The East End wasn't like it was when I grew up. It wasn't the quiet resort town where famous families summered in their grand homes. It was more than just New Yorkers who came there for the beaches and quaint villages. Europeans looking for a new Riviera came there now. Hollywood types flew into East Hampton Airport on private jets. I hated this part of town more and more with each year that passed and made it a point not to go there for any reason. I was certain that Frank somehow knew this. That was why he picked it as our meeting place. Frank was the kind of man who wanted, and found at all costs, every advantage.

My limbs felt heavy as I drove south toward the ocean. My vision blurred now and again. The heat was like an unwanted blanket. It pressed down heavy on me. Sleep lingered in my body like a mood I couldn't shake. But I knew I had to wake up. I knew I had to be on my toes. I had to listen to what Frank had to say. Most important, I had to try to hear what it was he really meant.

I made it to the parking lot at the end of Halsey Neck in less than five minutes. Frank was already there, waiting beside his silver Seville. He was dressed for the heat in white summer slacks, a blue linen shirt, and loafers. His Seville and my LeMans were the only cars in the lot.

I steered toward him slowly, broken bits of asphalt popping beneath my balding tires. There wasn't a part of me that was asleep now.

The first thing Frank said to me after I got out was "You look tired, MacManus."

"What is it you want, Frank?"

He started walking and nodded for me to follow. We stepped off the parking lot and onto the sand and walked over the primary dune and down the other side of it to the beach. I didn't see anybody but us there. The sand was soft beneath my feet, hard for walking. I recalled running on this beach as a youth twenty years ago to build my endurance and legs for fighting, running from where I lived with my adoptive family on Gin Lane, all the way to Road D at the end of Dune Road, just before the Shinnecock Bay inlet.

Frank veered right, heading west down the beach. Gin Lane was to our backs. I liked it that way. I followed him and looked ahead down the long beach and wondered if I could make that same run now, at my age. My toes sank deep into the soft sand, my calves working hard, harder than they'd had to work in a long time.

Frank glanced at me as we walked across the sand. "I like this time of the morning," he said. "You can speak your mind and no one will hear it. It's the safest time of the day for conversation."

My lungs ached from breathing in the stale air. I felt a look of strain on my face.

"Late night last night?" he asked.

"It's this heat."

"Get air conditioning."

"Can't afford it."

"You mean you can't afford to buy it or you can't afford to run it?"

"Both."

He looked ahead, then to his left, out over the ocean. Then he looked back at me. He seemed to me to be enjoying himself a little too much. I thought of the Seville and its air conditioning, of the tranquil and comfortable ride down Halsey Neck Lane he had just made in it, passing great homes owned by people many of whom were probably in one way or another indebted like me to Frank.

He veered us closer to the shoreline, where the sand was packed harder and was easier to walk on. Waves roared, then broke, collapsed, and retreated lazily, white foam hissing in their wake. The seagulls above beat their wings, trying to ride the windless sky.

"I couldn't imagine having to live on what you make," Frank said.

"I couldn't imagine living on what you make, either."

"You're still working for that restoration company, driving that delivery truck, sweeping the floors, right?"

I nodded.

"It's almost a record for you, isn't it?"

I glanced out over the gray Atlantic. A slight mist hit the air every time a wave crashed in, but it wasn't cool.

"You bring home, what, two hundred a week. That'd be hard to live off anywhere in the country. Doubly hard out here. You're off the books, right? No benefits, no unemployment if you get laid off, no sick pay. You miss a day of work and you, what, go without eating for a week?"

I didn't look at him, just kept my eyes straight ahead, the way I did when I used to run this beach, heat, rain, snow.

"Pretty much," I said.

"It's a real shame, you know, a guy with your talents, your education, your smarts. It's a waste."

"I know my résumé, Frank. I don't have a lot of time. You might want to get to it."

"I've got some good news for you and Augie, and I've got some bad news, too. The good news is a few days ago the FBI picked up a man in New Jersey, a known leg breaker out of Atlantic City. He's got a record for assault, attempted murder, the whole thing. Plus he's the suspect in several Atlantic City area hits. They found in his possession the badge of the cop who was killed last October, along with his piece. The serial numbers were filed down but the lab was able to recover them. They're extraditing him back here, where he'll be charged with the murder of the cop and the Vogler kid. I thought you and Augie would want to know that. It's been a while, but I thought maybe it might still be on your minds. I figure you'd probably still be looking for him, as well as the guy who sacked Augie and got away, if I hadn't grounded you."

I felt a lifting sensation in my gut. I felt I had just slipped out from under a tremendous weight. "Does Augie know?"

"Not yet. I'm sure it'll be a big relief to him when he finds out."

"I'll tell him when I see him tonight."

Frank nodded.

"So what's the bad news, Frank?"

"People tell me you're downstairs a lot, that you've seemed to hit your stride and are drinking more than ever."

It was too early for this shit. I looked at Frank but I didn't say anything. Anyway, what really could I say?

"Is that true?"

My apartment was small, and no matter where I went in the past three months, there was Tina. She had begun recently to demand a lot of attention, more than I was willing to give. More than I could give. Eventually every night I took to going downstairs, where she couldn't follow me, to kill time till she fell asleep and it was safe for me to go back home. I had been doing well for a while laying off the booze. But now it seemed I had to be numb. Going down and drinking free on George had become yet again a ritual I didn't dare skip.

"You obviously have your sources, Frank. Why bother coming to me for confirmation?"

"They can tell me what they see, but only you can tell me what's really important: if it's under control or not. So, be straight with me, MacManus, is it under control?"

I knew all he wanted was for me to tell him that it was. I knew if I told him it wasn't that he would put off repayment of the favor to another time. He was that cautious. But I wanted out from under his thumb badly, I wanted this over with finally and once and for all. I didn't want to spend another three long months waiting for him to call.

I said, "It's under control, Frank. Nothing to worry about. I can stop any time, you know that. I'm one hundred percent."

"I'll have to take your word for it, won't I?"

"You don't have to do anything you don't want to, Frank. You're lucky that way."

He didn't say anything to that, just regarded the beach and the working gulls and the gray Atlantic to his left.

"I'm going to be needing you for a job," he said after a while.

"What kind of job?"

"A family wants their daughter found. It's a prominent family."

"Aren't they all?"

"I'd like to make an impression on them. This job

could go a long way to making certain things happen for me."

"Running for mayor again?"

"Not exactly."

"I don't suppose you can tell me who this family is."

"I'll get to that. Right now I just want to be assured that you'll be available to me over the next few days."

It was Friday morning. The Fourth of July, Independence Day, was Monday. I had no plans that would take me too far from my phone.

"I'm not going anywhere," I said.

"Which brings me to another point. You have an exposure and you need to take care of it before I can let you do me this favor. This isn't open for negotiation. Do you understand me?"

"What are you talking about, Frank?"

"It's all about appearances, MacManus. We live in a small town, you know this better than anyone. I told you that you had to keep your nose clean for a while, that you had to lay low. Playing house with a fifteen-year-old girl wasn't exactly what I had in mind."

"Where else was she going to go?"

"You can play the fool on your own time, Mac. Not mine."

"I'm not playing anything, Frank. Her father's due home from the hospital after the weekend. She'll be going home with him then."

"That's not good enough, and you know it."

"It's the best I can do."

"The phony alibi may have protected you from prosecution, MacManus, but don't think for a minute that the Chief doesn't know what really happened. Hell, everybody knows. He's just waiting for his chance. I'll give the Chief one thing, he's a patient man. When he moves against you, it won't be for littering. He's waiting for something juicy, and statutory rape is about as juicy as it comes."

"You've got a dirty fucking mind, Frank."

"You'd be lucky if I was the only one around who did. There's talk all over town already. Christ, the Chief doesn't need to make the charges stick. He just needs to get into the paper the simple fact that you were arrested and charged. He just has to feed the talk that's already going on. And the fact that you allegedly took advantage of your best friend's daughter while he was in the hospital learning to walk again is just the cherry on the top, so to speak. I'll tell you one thing right now, if the people in this town had to choose between labeling you 'local hero' or 'pedophile,' they'd chose pedophile in a heartbeat. It's the way people are. You know this as well as I do."

"So, what are you suggesting I do about this 'exposure,' Frank?"

"I can't have you vulnerable to the Chief like that while you're working for me. You have to get rid of the girl."

"I'm just supposed to kick her out on her ass?"

"Put her into a motel."

"She's a kid, Frank."

"Doesn't she have a girlfriend she can stay with? A schoolmate? Augie said she did that when he worked nights."

"She won't go. She only feels safe around me."

"I'm sure she does. You beat the shit out of the three strapping football players who tried to rape her. And you took down the man who put her big bad daddy in the hospital. I'm sure in her mind you're something out of mythology. But her feelings about you shouldn't be your concern right now, Mac. If you don't know what to say to her, then talk to Augie. He's her goddamned father. Disciplining her is his job."

He lost me suddenly. "What are you talking about, Frank?" I said. "What do you mean, disciplining her? What the hell are you talking about?"

"Jesus, MacManus. How do you think all this talk about you two got started? It came from her. She's told all her little friends at school that you two are hot and heavy lovers living together in your crappy apartment. That's where it all began. It was the fucking girl."

I was a fool for not seeing this coming. I was a fool for choosing not to see it coming. I chose to turn a blind eye to the way she behaved around me, to the way she looked at me, for letting certain things she said fall on deaf ears. Maybe I had hoped to ride it out. Her return home was so near. I was a fool.

"Shit," I muttered.

"I can talk to Augie, if you want me to," Frank said.

I shook my head. "No. I'll talk to him. I'll go see him this morning."

"What about your job? Don't you have to work?"

"I'll call in."

"How can you afford that?"

"I'll figure something out."

"Look, I'll compensate you, if you want. Put you on payroll for a few days. I don't want you starving."

"Let's just keep this simple, Frank. I do this job as a favor to you and we're even. I cover my own expenses, everything. I do this job and I never hear from you again. We're clear on this?"

He nodded. "Very."

"So what exactly is it you want me to do?"

"I need you to find a woman named Marie Welles. Last her family knew of her she was living in Flanders with a guy named Tim Carter. Then two weeks ago she disappeared, and no one has heard a word from her since."

"What do they think happened?"

"Her trail ends very neatly, very deliberately. It's almost as if she wanted to disappear, like she planned it out carefully and then went underground. There's not one loose end leading to her."

"Except this Carter guy."

Frank nodded. "It turns out he's something of a petty crook. He has a record. Possession to sell, that kind of thing. He was fired from his most recent job for stealing from the register. From what I know of him, he strikes me as one of those people who can't decide whether they're a crook or straight, so they kind of muddle along the in-between, doing a generally half-assed job in both worlds. But he has no record of violent crime. And there is no evidence that anything happened to the girl. She's just gone."

"There's a difference between missing and gone, Frank."

"Maybe. Carter is still in the cottage they shared in Flanders. I need you to go there tonight and find out from him where she is."

I knew what he meant by that.

"Why hasn't her family gone to the police?" I said.

"They want this handled privately. They had their own people working on this, but when they came up with nothing the family called me."

I looked out over the ocean and thought about all this. Several waves came in and tumbled over before either of us spoke again. I didn't like any of what I was hearing from Frank.

"How old is this Welles woman?"

"Your age. Early thirties."

"Old enough to know what she wants, wouldn't you say?"

"She has a history of mental illness. That's why her

family kept such close tabs on her when she moved out."

He took a slip of paper from his shirt pocket and handed it to me.

"Carter's address," he said.

I didn't take the paper at first, just looked at it. Then finally I reached out and took it. It was damp from sweat. I slipped it into the pocket of my T-shirt without reading it.

"Any questions?" Frank asked.

"What if he doesn't want to tell me what I want to know?"

"I'm sure you'll come up with something persuasive. You're not without your skills, Mac. I'll call you tonight when it's time to go. Meet me back here tomorrow morning at eight and tell me what you've got."

"And if I don't have anything?"

"Just find where the girl went, Mac. That's all."

I drove to Southampton Hospital and caught up with Augie as he was coming out of his morning physical therapy. He had already traded in his crutches for a cane, though by the way he walked I couldn't help but wonder if he had done so prematurely. Of course I knew that was just the way he did things. The beating had done enough brain damage that he had to relearn pretty much everything. Some things didn't come as easily as others. Walking was one of them.

We headed down a long hallway to a large plate-glass window that overlooked Old Towne Pond. We stood there, shoulder to shoulder, and looked out over the lawn below and the patients who roamed over it in all that heat. They were wearing hospital bathrobes and slippers. Augie had on shorts and a T-shirt and running shoes. He refused to dress like an invalid, in gowns or even pajamas. The doctors had given up fighting with him a long time ago. These were the same doctors who told Augie that the chances that he would walk again were slim.

Augie and I chatted for a while about his recovery, his impending release, about the idiot doctors and how they don't even dare to stick their heads into his room anymore. He said that Gale was around here somewhere but I didn't see her. I had other things on my mind.

"So what is it? What's bothering you, Mac?"

"They picked up a man in Jersey," I said. "He had a cop's badge and gun. They belonged to the cop that got killed last October. He's a known leg breaker and suspected killer-for-hire. They're bringing him here so he can be charged."

"That's great news. Where did you hear it?"

"Frank told me."

"When did you see him?"

"This morning. He called me, asked me to meet him."

"We knew this was going to happen, sooner or later. He didn't call just to tell you about our friend, did he?"

"No."

"What else did he have to say?"

I didn't know where to start. I clammed up.

"What's going on, Mac? You've got that look on your face. What did Frank say to you?"

"He told me something. It's something I should have seen coming, but I just didn't. I should have, though."

"What did he tell you?"

"He said that Tina's been telling her friends around town things about us, about her and me. Things that aren't true."

"What exactly is she saying?" His voice was even.

"She's saying that she and I are lovers."

Augie shrugged once. "That was bound to happen."

"What do you mean?"

"You saved her from a horrible thing, Mac. Two horrible things, really. A crush was bound to happen."

"Maybe. But now people are talking, and things with the Chief being what they are, well..."

"It's definitely the last thing you need right now."

"I don't want to give a damn...I mean, it's no one's business...but..."

"You don't have to explain yourself to me, Mac. You've been a good friend. Better than any friend I've ever known. I've put you out long enough as it is already. You've come through for me. I'll take care of this. Don't worry about it. I'll set this straight."

"I don't want to bail on you."

"You're not bailing, Mac. You couldn't bail if you wanted to. It's not who you are. I'll see what I can do about getting Tina a motel room or something."

"It's July Fourth weekend, Aug. Everything's all booked up. Even if you find a vacancy, you'll pay through the nose for it."

"It's only for a few days. I'm out of here soon, remember? Besides, I know a woman who owns a motel in the Shinnecock Hills. She might be able to help me out. Eddie can pick Tina up and take her to work and take her home. Don't worry about it, Mac. You've done more than enough."

"Ah, fuck it, Augie. Fuck 'em all. Let her stay, if only just to spite them."

"No. You and I, we both want our lives back. I'm sure if you could have somehow gotten me out of this hospital sooner, you would have, right? Well, I can get your life back to you sooner, and that's just what I'm going to do."

"It really hasn't been that bad. Having her around. She's not a bad kid, Aug. She was decent company, up till recently."

I looked at him closely then. His face was healed now but it wasn't unchanged. His features were uneven, and just a little unfamiliar. Looking at him was like entering a room you know well after the furniture has been moved around. Things weren't exactly where you expected them to be.

"I don't think I've said this before, Mac. I should have

said it a long time ago. I want to say it now, though. Thanks for my life. Thanks for the life of my daughter, and for taking her in like you did without my even asking. She's my daughter, but I'm not blind to things. I know how she can be. I've had to chase more than one boy away from her bedroom window. It was easier for me in here knowing that she was with you."

I said nothing to that, just stared out at the hazy summer sky and enjoyed the cool air against my face.

"Anyway," he said, "I owe you, man. I owe you big time."

"I'm not keeping track, Aug."

"When Tina comes by after work today I'll talk to her. Don't worry about anything. We'll get everything straightened out."

"Thanks."

"We should have a party when I get out of here. I'll throw myself one. A cookout. There's probably a veggie burger of yours still in our freezer."

"Sounds good."

"We'll get tanked and toast to our sobriety."

"I'm there."

"Good. Everything's going to be fine, you know. I'm going to kick this cane, I'm going to be one hundred percent again, everything's going to get back to normal. Just wait and see. I've done a lot of thinking in here. There's not much else to do when you're flat out on your back, right? I've got a lot of great ideas, ideas for the both of us. Things are going to turn around. You don't almost lose everything that matters to you in this world and not be changed by it."

I waited a while, let his words sink in, and then I said, "I've got to get going, Aug." I realized that if I went back to work after lunch I would be short only twenty dollars come payday, not forty. I could certainly use the twenty.

"You take care of yourself, Mac. You do what you have to do, and don't ever think twice about it. Remember that."

He extended his hand and I took it. We shook and then I left him in the cool hallway and went outside into air so hot it brushed my skin like a flame. My lungs felt tight, wrapped still in that damp leather, and my eyeballs dried fast. Two weeks ago I had misplaced my only pair of sunglasses somewhere in the bar. I just didn't have the five bucks to spare to buy a new pair at the drugstore on Main Street.

I went into work after lunch, made four deliveries, and got back home a little before five. My back was shot and I was dead from the heat. I turned on each of the three tabletop fans I had and lay down on my couch to rest. When I woke up there was twilight outside my windows. My apartment was dim, a single, dull light burning in my bedroom. I sat up. My clothes clung to my back and legs. I saw Tina tiptoe past the open bedroom door then. On the bed just inside the bedroom door was an oversized canvas shoulder bag. As Tina passed the bed she tossed a folded shirt into the bag, then disappeared from my sight again. When she reappeared she tossed something else into the bag, then disappeared from my sight once more.

My skin was radiating heat, my forearms hot to the touch. I had napped too deeply and for too long. Coming to was more like sobering up than waking.

Over the humming of my fans I could hear voices coming up from Elm Street below. I checked my watch. It was just after eight. People were coming to the Hansom House early. I realized then that it was Friday, that there would be a reggae band, that there would be good times, or at least something close to it.

I thought about Tina being gone, of myself being free to come and go again as I pleased. It was a nice thought. Once I felt that I was awake enough to deal with her, I got up off the couch and walked to the bedroom doorway and stood in it.

Tina looked up from her packing and clutched at her heart suddenly with one hand. Her mouth dropped open and she jumped dramatically. I had come up on her by surprise without meaning to.

"Shit, Mac. Don't do that. You scared me."

I tried not to laugh. "Sorry." My voice was scratchy, low.

The small reading lamp beside my bed was the only light on in the entire apartment. Tina had last week covered the lampshade with a handkerchief to hold back the heat it gave off. It held back a great deal of the light, too.

Behind me my fans sounded like airplane engines when heard from a distance. Air moved around me like a commotion.

"You were asleep when I came in," she said. She had gone back to folding her shirt and tucking it into the bag. She didn't look at me and gave much more attention than necessary to the task.

"What time did you get back?"

"A little while ago."

My eyes shifted to the bag in the center of my bed. I already knew the answer to my next question but asked it anyway. "You saw Augie today?"

She nodded and managed then to look at me.

"He signed out of the hospital this afternoon," she said.

"What?"

"Augie signed himself out of the hospital today. I rode home with him. Eddie drove us in his cab."

"They released him?"

"Not exactly. He insisted on leaving and made a stink about it. They didn't put up much of a fight, to be honest. I think they were just glad to get him out of there. He gave the doctors such a hard time."

"Where is he now?"

"He's home."

"You left him alone?"

"He insisted that I come back here and get all my stuff. Eddie's coming back for me in a little while."

I wasn't pleased by this. This wasn't what was supposed to happen. Anger moved through me quickly. I heard it in my voice. "He can't just check out like that. What the hell is he doing?"

"He wants to be home. He's been away from his life too long. That's what he says, anyway."

"Shit," I muttered. I was pissed. It wasn't supposed to go like this. I wasn't sure if I would have been so ticked really if Frank Gannon wasn't the reason that this was happening. But that didn't seem to matter now.

"Augie told me to tell you to remember what you talked about this morning."

At that moment I couldn't think about much except how badly I wanted to wring Frank Gannon's neck. I felt the urge to pay another visit to his office for some redecorating.

"You saw Augie this morning?" Tina said. "You weren't here when I got up."

She waited for me to explain where I had gone and why I had seen her father. But when I didn't offer an explanation she shrugged and said, "Anyway, he wants you to come over tomorrow for a welcome-home cookout. We don't have much in the house. I was thinking maybe you and I could go shopping tomorrow sometime. You could pick me up and we could get some things. It would be fun."

I didn't say anything to that. I was still pissed.

"He's a big boy, Mac, in case you haven't noticed."

"He shouldn't be out. I know it's only a few days early, but he keeps rushing things and he's going to fall flat on his face one of these days."

"I'll take good care of him, Mac. Don't worry. Just like you did for me."

She was standing beside the unmade bed, wearing cut-off shorts and a pink T-shirt that kept few secrets. I could smell her skin. Her arms and legs were branches that ran too long for her trunk. She was lanky, awkward, and, though she wasn't by most standards a beautiful girl, there were things to her that I just couldn't allow myself to see.

It seemed to me that there was something brave in the way she stood there, by my bed; in the way she held perfectly still and the way she met and held my gaze boldly, without blinking. She was typically a shy girl, and to see her do this, to see her put herself before me like this for me to just reach out and take if I wanted, was alarming in ways too numerous to count.

She was offering herself to me. I could see this. This was her way of letting me know her feelings for me. I did what I always did lately, what I always did when she did this. I pretended not to notice, to not have a clue.

"Do you have everything?" I said. I could taste my freedom and wanted her out the door.

She nodded. It was the only move she made. She was frozen, waiting for me to catch on.

"I think so," she added.

"You should get going then."

We had become friends long before the offerings began. It wasn't always like this. It wasn't always unbearably uncomfortable. We used to be able to sit in my kitchen and drink cold tea and listen to the music that came up from downstairs. In school she was taking Spanish, her original tongue, which she hadn't spoken since her mother was killed. We sometimes spoke it in conversation to test her. Now that she was going I had hopes that she would become once again the teenage daughter of my best friend and just drop all this other nonsense.

"I could stay for a little while," she suggested. "If you wanted me to I could stay."

"You shouldn't leave him alone for too long, Tina."

She smiled bravely then and placed the strap of the bag over her shoulder. "Okay," she said. She moved toward me, and I stepped aside to let her pass through the door. But instead of moving through it she stopped in it suddenly. We were standing face to face.

She was inches from me. She looked at me but said nothing. Then, suddenly, she leaned forward and kissed me on the cheek. I smelled her breath and her sweat as she came in close to me. I smelled the fabric of her shirt. Her breasts brushed across my chest and her right kneecap knocked with my left. She took the crook of my left elbow in her right hand.

Her lips grazed my rough skin. It was an inexperienced kiss, rushed and almost panicked. Though it was a fast kiss she withdrew slowly, leaning back with her eyes open. Her hand dropped from my elbow.

I didn't move a muscle in any direction. I didn't offer any response. But that didn't seem to faze her a bit. She smiled at me, once. It was a tiny, fond smile, wan. She said in a girl's voice, "Call me tomorrow, Mac."

Then she crossed my living room and left my apartment without looking back. I kept my mind clear as she went. And then, suddenly, finally, just like that, it came to me that I was alone in my place for the first time in a season.

I tried to go to sleep but the heat was too much. My fans ran on high but it did nothing but stir around hot air. My bed felt strange after having slept on the couch for so long. The minute I lay down in it I smelled Tina. But there was nothing I could do about that. After a while I slipped into a shallow sleep. I dreamed of making love with a woman I didn't know. I dreamed of the sound of winter thunder at night, of snow falling on an ocean the color of ball bearings.

Then I awoke a few hours later to the clanging of my telephone. I knew even before I answered it who would be on the other end.

"Yeah."

"It's me," Frank said. He was on a pay phone, as usual. I heard the hissing of cars passing in the background, and the line crackled several times, sharply. I thought at one point I might have lost him. But I wasn't that lucky.

"Yeah," I said. "I know."

"You're on."

In my mind the snow was still falling. Frank's voice and Tina's smell were the only things I sensed.

"I'll do what I can," I said.

"Just find the girl, Mac. Just find the girl."

He hung up.

Six

The street name on the slip of paper Frank had given me was a right-hand turn off Flanders Road, which ran from Hampton Bays into Riverhead. I found the side street easy enough and started down it. It was narrow, poorly lit, the homes small working-class cottages. It came to a dead end a few hundred yards from the main road on the shore of Flanders Bay.

A mailbox on a post was at the end of a long dirt driveway that led up a slight grade to a cottage set on a bank overlooking the bay. The numbers on the mailbox matched the numbers on the slip of paper in my hand. I could see that the windows of the cottage were dark and that there were no cars in the dirt driveway. I killed the motor and headlights and sat there behind the wheel and looked the place over.

After a while I opened my glove compartment and took out my flashlight and Spyderco knife. I clipped the knife inside my hip pocket as I got out of my car. I looked back up the street, toward Flanders Road. There was nothing to see but darkness. I listened carefully and heard only the lapping of waves on the shore of the bay behind me. I turned on the light to test it. The beam was weak, but it would have to do. I switched the light off again and started up toward the cottage. I walked on the grass, not wanting to leave the imprint of my sneakers in the dirt.

The cottage was set maybe a hundred feet back from the road and fifty feet from the bay. It was in an open lot surrounded on three sides by rows of trees. I walked close to the shore, close to the tall reeds that grew along it. I waited till I was directly in front of the cottage before I cut to my right and climbed the inclined lawn toward the front door.

There were wraparound windows on three sides of the cottage. As I approached it I could see the reflection of the smoky night sky in the wide panes. I moved quietly to the front door, then I stopped and listened hard. I heard nothing but my own breathing.

I started up the short steps to the front door. I noticed at once that it was ajar by a few inches. I eased the door open with the back of my hand. I moved it just enough so I could pass through, then took one last look behind me and slipped inside.

It was dark inside the cottage but I didn't take out

my flashlight. I stood there inside the door for a while, trying to make out what I could without it. The front half of the cottage was an open room, part living room, part office. The back half was divided into two rooms, a kitchen and a bedroom. The bedroom door was open. Eventually, when my eyes adjusted, there was enough light for me to see part of an unmade bed in the back room and a bare wall beyond it.

I took a few steps into that front room. The planks beneath my feet were wide and sturdy, but still they creaked. The entire cottage seemed well built, tight like a ship. The wraparound windows offered a nice view of the bay. But they gave me the feeling of being exposed, a feeling even all this dark around me couldn't put away.

Eventually I made my way deeper into the cottage. I went to the bedroom door and peered in to make certain that no one was there. Then I looked into the kitchen. It was empty. There were dirty dishes in the sink, though, and the lingering smell of cooking.

There was a back door in the kitchen. I went to it and opened it a few inches, just in case I needed to go through it quickly for one reason or another.

I went back into the front room. Since there was no one for me to ask the whereabouts of the Welles woman, I decided not to waste the trip and took a look around to see what I could find. Maybe I could get lucky and come across an address or phone number or something and get out of there and get Frank off my back for good.

On the office side of the front room there was a desk. I went to it and took out my flashlight and carefully searched through the drawers. I stayed down low, under the windows, out of sight. I found mainly bank statements and bills and notices of payment overdue from the Bank of the Hamptons. I found a payment book with the tear slips for April, May, and June still attached.

On top of the desk was an electric typewriter with a piece of paper in the roller. I aimed my dying light at it and saw what looked like prose, part of a story of some kind. I read a few lines. It was a first-person narrative that seemed concerned with the look of a rose in a vase on a windowsill at first light. I didn't read any more.

I opened the desk drawer directly under the typewriter and searched through it. There was nothing but paper clips and disposable pens and tubes of correcting fluid. There was a filing cabinet near the desk, but its drawers were locked. I took a look then around the room, making a sweep with my dull light, searching for something, anything that might help me. In the other half of the room, the living room half, there was a bookcase with a few dozen paperback books spread out on the shelves. I started to cross toward it, passing a door I hadn't seen before, a door set between the kitchen and the bedroom. It was cut into the wall panels, invisible except for its black hinges and door han-

dle. It must have been a closet door. I stopped at it and
waited a moment and listened, then reached for the
handle. But before I could touch it the door flung suddenly open. I jumped back, the swinging door missing
me by an inch, the rush of air its motion created brushing past my face. Suddenly there was movement, footsteps, and a lot of rushing around. A man with a
chrome-plated .357 revolver lunged out at me, the gun
aimed at my head. I took a few steps back, out of blind
reflex, and raised my hands. He took as many steps forward. He pulled the hammer back with his thumb.
There was maybe three feet between us. I thought
about moving, about what I could do. But before I
could do anything, another man came rushing in from
the kitchen. He held a smaller revolver with a dark fin-
ish in his outstretched hand. It, too, was aimed directly
at my head.

He came in closer than the first one and pressed
the barrel of his revolver against my temple like an
amateur.

"Don't make a fucking move," he said.

The other one stepped toward a table near the door,
reached down, and switched on a lamp. He kept his
eyes on me as he went, his gun up and aimed at me.

Above and below the lamp a circle of white light
shone, but the rest of the room caught only the soft
yellow light cast through the heavy lampshade. The
wraparound windows went dark then, the night

beyond them now invisible. The windows became like mirrors, reflecting from three sides distorted images of everything inside that small room.

The man by the lamp stood up slowly. His eyes were fixed on my face. He looked deeply puzzled, almost surprised. The barrel of his gun lowered then, drifting down. He seemed preoccupied, troubled.

The one directly beside me was a kid, maybe twenty, maybe less. He was still caught up in the excitement, still riding the commotion. His breathing was fast and shallow. He ordered me to hand over my flashlight. I let it slip from my hand instead. It fell to the floor with a thud. He stooped down to pick it up.

The one by the lamp had a shaved head and Fu Manchu beard. Dark tribal tattoos covered his forearms. He seemed to me almost concerned by the sight of me, uncertain maybe just what my presence here meant.

"I know you," he muttered.

The kid beside me had the flashlight in his left hand now. He went to press the barrel of his revolver once again against my temple.

"Is this the guy?" the kid asked.

"No. It's someone else. It's another guy. How the hell did you find me?" he said to me. "What the fuck do you want?"

"Listen, I'm just looking for money. That's all."

"Bullshit," the one with the shaved head said. "I've seen you before. You don't remember me."

"Look, I don't want any trouble." I held my hands up at shoulder level. "I didn't take anything. Let me walk out of here now and you'll never see me again."

"Let's just fucking waste him and get out of here," the kid said. His voice was increasing in pitch. He was getting wild with fear. "Let's just take him out back and pop him."

The one with the shaved head was calmer. He looked at me curiously and said, "He sent you, didn't he?"

"Who?"

"The brother. The brother sent you, didn't he?"

"I don't know what you're talking about. Whose brother?"

"Let's just fucking pop him and go. They know where to find us. Let's just take him out back and pop him."

"Are you working with someone else or alone? Was that you outside?"

"What?"

"We heard someone outside, coming through the woods."

"No, that wasn't me, man. I told you, I was just robbing the place."

"You're no thief. How did the bastard know where to find me?"

"Who?"

"The rat bastard brother. How did he know where I was?"

"Let's just fucking pop him and get out of here," the kid insisted. His knees were drawn together, as if he had to piss badly.

"First I want some answers from our friend here."

"I've told you, I don't know what you asking. I don't know any brother. I'm just after money. The house looked empty."

The one with the shaved head lost his temper then and snapped. "Bullshit! Bullshit! Tell me, how did you find us?"

"Let's just fucking pop him, man. Let's go. There's someone else. He's out back. I can fucking hear him moving around."

Before I or anyone else could say anything more there came a cracking sound from outside, a hard, brittle snap, followed immediately by the sound of a window shattering and scattering broken glass across the floor.

My knees buckled and I dropped quickly to the floor. The kid beside me did the same, but he landed hard. The one with the shaved head, the one who looked puzzled by my presence, came down last.

I expected more gunshots from outside but heard nothing except the labored and panicked breathing coming from me and those around me. After a minute the guy with the shaved head got up into a crouch, ready to stand, ready to fight. He held his gun with both hands, the barrel pointing up.

"Stay down," I whispered.

He shot me a look as if to tell me to shut up. He was wired.

The kid was still on the floor beside me. He hadn't moved since he took his hard fall. I was about to reach down and take his .38 away from him when I felt something warm under my hand. I lifted it fast and saw that there was blood on my palms.

I scrambled up into a crouch. There was blood spreading all around the kid. He was flat out on his back, his eyes open and blinking, his mouth working as if he were trying to speak.

Only he wasn't trying to speak. He was trying to breathe. I heard small gurgling sounds come from him then, and deep wheezing. Fine streams of blood were spurting into the air. They rose, arched, and then fell in long drops down to the floor.

I could see that a bullet had sliced his throat open. Where blood wasn't gushing, it flowed, running fast like hot motor oil.

"Fucking shit," I said. I went to him and knelt beside him and pressed both of my hands against the open wound in his neck, trying to stop the flow. I felt warm blood spray against my palms and spread between my fingers. But I stayed there, leaning with my weight down on the wound.

But the blood wouldn't stop flowing. I was kneeling in it, it was everywhere now, it just kept coming.

I said to the one with the shaved head, "Get me something to stop the bleeding."

But he didn't move. I turned my head and looked at him. He was frozen, breathing fast, sweat like a glaze on his face.

"I need something to stop the bleeding," I told him. "Fast. A towel, something, anything. C'mon, don't just sit there, do something. You want your friend to die?"

It took him a moment, but then he crawled to the couch, pulled off a blanket, and brought it to me.

I told him to fold it up. He did, then handed it to me. I grabbed it and applied it to the kid's throat, then pressed my bloodied hands on it and leaned forward, my elbows locked.

"Call an ambulance," I said.

Again he didn't move. He just looked at me.

"Call an ambulance."

He watched my face and shook his head from side to side and said to me, "I can't be here when the police come. Neither can you, right?"

I said nothing. He was not at all familiar to me. I was thinking that when he said the strangest thing to me.

"I think this makes us even. Take care of yourself, Mac."

He looked toward the broken window, then rose

and moved bent at the waist to the front door. He paused there, his .357 held in both hands, the barrel pointed up, and looked back at me. Then he broke into a run, bolting out the door.

I listened to his hard run across the grass till I could hear it no more. I braced myself for more gunshots then but none came. All I could hear was the sound of the bay tapping the shore fifty feet down the sloping lawn and the last few feeble breaths of the kid.

His face was expressionless, his mouth hanging open dumbly, his eyelids half closed. His skin was white, his forehead already waxy. I eased back on the compress and removed my hands. Whoever he was, he was dead, and whoever the guy with the shaved head was, he was long gone. It was time for me to go, too.

I pulled off my T-shirt and wiped down the desk and the filing cabinet. Then I used the shirt to wipe my hands. I got them as clean as they would get for now. I picked my flashlight up off the floor, then grabbed the bloody blanket and went to the front door and paused to listen.

The yard was still, quiet. The torn haze above the bay shifted slowly. I listened for a good minute, listening for the sound of someone in the woods, for the sound of sirens approaching. But I heard neither of these things, just a night so quiet I couldn't tell whether to feel at ease or rise to my toes.

Eventually, I did like the guy with the shaved head and bolted out the door and out into the night. I ran down the lawn toward the street. Before I got into my car I took off my blood-covered sneakers, wrapped my shirt around them, then folded the blanket over that. I set the bundle on the floor beneath the passenger seat and flung my flashlight over the high grass and out into the bay. The water caught and swallowed it with a gulp.

Back in my apartment, I tossed the blanket and its contents into a garbage bag, then removed my jeans and tossed them in, too. I took a quick shower, scrubbing the blood off my hands and from under my nails. Then I dried off and put on clean jeans, another T-shirt, and my work boots.

It wasn't even eleven o'clock and the Hansom House was just coming into swing. People were arriving. I waited till it was as clear out front as it would get and left with my garbage bag and walked to where I had parked my car far down Elm Street, in a patch untouched by streetlights.

I got in behind the wheel, cranked the ignition, and headed west on Sunrise Highway. I rode out of town, over the Shinnecock Canal and past Hampton Bays, into the pine barrens of Quogue. On a long stretch of deserted highway I pulled over and got out with the garbage bag. I walked into the pines to where the dirt was soft and dug a hole deep enough to take the bag. Then I covered it with dirt and pine needles and ran back to the edge of the woods. There I took a good look around. The highway was a long stretch of emptiness and dark. I was sweating from the heat. I ran back to my car and got in and took off for home.

Back in my apartment again, I was too riled to sleep. My heart was still racing. It was only midnight. I had eight hours to wait till I would see Frank and maybe get some things answered. I could hear the lazy reggae rhythm rising up from the bar two floors below, the steady thumping of the drums and the bass. I didn't feel their call now, though. What I needed right now I couldn't find in a bar.

I was still awake at closing time and listened as everyone left. I heard voices rise up from the street outside my window. I heard car doors shut and engines start. I was awake, too, at dawn, when night drained off into morning. At seven-thirty I left my apartment and drove down Halsey Neck Lane to the lot and waited there by the hissing waves and bickering gulls for Frank, just like we had planned.

I waited almost an hour but he didn't show. I went home through town but couldn't spot his Seville anywhere. I called his pager from a pay phone outside the camera shop on Cameron Street and waited for a call back. But none ever came.

I decided that maybe it would be better for me to get off the streets. Something was going on that I didn't understand. There were too many things unanswered. I needed to lie low and maybe figure some of them out. I drove back to my apartment and sat at my window for hours and waited. I ran through everything in my head, over and over. But I was getting nowhere.

I realized that today was July Fourth. I checked my watch. It was after four. Southampton Village I knew would be crowded now, as summer people came in off the beaches to eat and shop. Elm Street itself was quiet, except for when a train from the city pulled in and late-arriving guests would be met by their hosts and driven off to the waiting party.

Around five I thought about calling Augie, but I resisted. He had problems of his own. Evening was coming, and I wasn't any closer to any answers than I had been in the morning. I smelled charcoal burning somewhere down Elm. I heard the voices of excited children as they played. I heard the whistle and pop of a few early bottle rockets.

At 6:55 another train from the city pulled in. Six people got off and met waiting friends and hurried into cars. Eddie's cab was there, waiting. He drove away with two passengers. Everything happened so fast. The station was empty of passengers even before the train pulled out again.

Then the next thing I knew it was dark outside my window. I must have dozed off. Fireworks were whistling and snapping somewhere out in the distant night. I sat up and listened and knew it was probably the big display over Lake Agawan, in the park off Job's Lane, not too far from the library.

The bursts sounded a little like gunfire. I looked

toward the sounds but could see only a black sky shifting lazily past the tops of dark trees. I considered that there was a chance that these were maybe my last moments as a free man. If I had money, I would have fled. But I was broke, and where anyway would I go? I decided to savor these moments, the sound of the fireworks, my view. I decided to wait where I felt safest for them, whoever they would turn out to be, to make their move against me.

It was somewhere around this time, during the fireworks, that my phone rang. I went to it and answered it on the second ring.

"Yeah," I said.

I expected Augie or Tina or maybe Frank on the other end, but the voice I heard wasn't immediately familiar.

"MacManus?" It was a man's voice.

"Who is this?"

"This is MacManus, right?"

"Who is this?"

"I have a friend who wants to meet with you."

"Who is this?" I demanded.

"She wants to talk to you. You know Long Beach Road in Sag Harbor."

I didn't say anything.

"Get there as soon as you can," he said. "Come alone."

"Who the fuck is this?"

"It's your new best friend, from last night. I could have killed you but I didn't. I hope you're smart enough to appreciate that. I hope for both our sakes you remember that."

"Do you have a name?"

"Some people call me Skull."

"What exactly is it you're up to, Skull?"

"Just meet my friend at eleven. I think you might have heard of her. She's heard of you. Her name is Marie Welles."

Before I could get a word out, the line went dead.

Seven

It was just after ten when I left the Hansom House. I stopped at a filling station on North Sea Road and bought all the gasoline I could with the change from my pocket. It wasn't much, but it was enough to get me to Sag Harbor and, I hoped, back.

I took the back roads through Noyac, along the rim of Peconic Bay, and made it to Long Beach Road a few minutes before eleven.

Long Beach was on a strip of land one hundred yards wide and maybe three hundred yards long that ran between Peconic Bay and Sag Harbor Cove. It was here, last October, that Augie and I caught up with and gave pursuit to the Caddy when that kid Vogler was killed. On the cove side of the road, beach grass grew in clumps, and on the bay side, a small beach marked with white stones and shells ran from a blacktop parking lot to the water.

I pulled into that lot and killed the motor and lights. The night was stagnant, the surface of the dark water smooth, creaseless. It was like someone had taken an iron to it. I heard nothing but the steady ringing of crickets and frogs coming from the cove side of the road as I got out of my car.

Across the lot a woman was standing a few feet from the water's edge, alone. I walked toward her. It took me a minute to reach her. I noticed as I walked two cars parked side by side on the opposite end of the lot, an old black Saab and a small dark blue pickup truck. The Saab was empty, but someone was in the pickup, behind the wheel, smoking a cigarette. It was too far off and too dark in that part of the lot for me to see who it was. But I was fairly certain that I knew anyway.

I wondered if he was still in possession of both his chrome-plated .357 and his sense that all was even, whatever that meant, between us.

The stones and shells that cluttered the beach made sounds under my feet. They announced my approach. The woman was facing the water, but when she heard me coming she turned to look at me.

She was wearing tan pleated slacks and a white mannish shirt, the cuffs folded over twice. She stood with her hands in her pockets, her chin held up slightly, her shoulders back, like a cadet. Her hair was dark and thick and fell all one length to a blunt cut just past the collar of her shirt. She had an athletic build, a good tan, and offered me a pleasant smile as I approached her. I didn't recognize her.

I didn't really know what to expect, but I knew I hadn't expected this. She acted as if we were friends meeting for cocktails, not strangers on a dark beach off a lonely strip of road meeting under less than cordial circumstances.

She stood with ease and poise, her hands deep in her pockets. She smiled warmly at me, and yet she seemed to be waiting for something, watching me closely. I got the sense that she was waiting for what I would say, as if this would somehow determine how things were going to go for us.

We were just a few feet apart. I could hear little over the peal of frogs and crickets across the street.

"You're Marie?" I said.

She laughed once, as if from relief or maybe surprise, her smile widening even more.

"Yes," she said. Her voice was faint and raspy, barely above a whisper.

"Are you sick?" I asked.

"Laryngitis. From the air conditioning. I don't like the heat."

I nodded.

"Thanks for meeting me," she said.

I glanced toward the pickup truck. The figure was still behind the wheel. I saw the glow of the cigarette. I looked back at Marie.

"What is it you want?" I said.

"If I'm straight with you, will you be straight with me?"

"It might be easier for both of us if we were."

"Good."

"So what is it you want from me?"

"I assume you're working for my brother." It was an obvious strain for her to talk. Her voice sounded whiskeyed.

"No, I don't work for him. I don't work for anyone."

"But you were sent to find me, right? That's why you were at the cottage last night. You weren't there looking for money, like you said."

"Right."

"But you weren't sent by my brother?"

"I don't even know who your brother is. I was sent by a man who was hired by your family. I don't know who exactly in your family hired him."

She considered all this carefully, then said, "So you don't know who I am?"

"Just that your name is Marie Welles."

"That's all you know?"

"Yes."

"And you've never seen me before?"

"No. Not that I can remember. Why?"

"Have you ever heard of my family?"

"I don't really run with that part of town anymore."

She thought about that, then said, "Do you find people for a living? Is that what you do?"

"Not really. I'm just trying to get someone off my back."

"I know what that's like. Listen, I wanted to meet you because I would like to ask a favor of you."

I said nothing to that.

"I know about you," she said. "I've heard about you. I know you've helped people before." She nodded toward the truck. Her voice was giving out but she continued nonetheless. "Our friend back there told me what happened last night, what you did. It was the act of a reasonable and compassionate man. So I thought if we met face to face that maybe I could appeal to your reason and humanity. I thought maybe between you and me we could maybe work something out."

"Like what?"

"I come from a very powerful family. I don't know if you know that. I don't know what you know, how much you've been told. My family is dangerous, and I don't want anything to do with them anymore. I've decided to start my life over again, and I don't want them or anyone to know how to find me. You can understand that, can't you?"

I nodded. "Yeah. But why exactly don't you want to have anything to do with them anymore?"

"I have my reasons. They're my business. I'd like to keep it that way if I can."

"Fair enough. But from what I understand they're worried about you, they'd like to know you're okay."

"They're only worried about themselves. My well-being has never been a chief concern of theirs. There is nothing compassionate about my family. I don't think you'd understand them. I have a hard time, and I'm, as they like to say, one of them. I know they've probably told you that I'm crazy. But it's not me, it's them. They're crazy and they're dangerous and I want to be free of them once and for all. And if that means living my life like a criminal on the run, if that means going into hiding, then that's what I'll do."

She took a step toward me then. "Do I seem crazy to you?"

I shrugged. "No."

"It's easy to believe what you hear, isn't it? They tell you I'm crazy and you have no reason to doubt them. It's called faith, and I'm not a big fan of it. But you know all about that, don't you? People believe what they hear about you. They come to you for help, not knowing or caring you just want to be left alone."

I suddenly felt a little uncomfortable. Marie was watching my face closely. I don't think I hid my discomfort from her.

"You still haven't told me what you want, Marie."

"I'll live like a criminal if I have to. I'm prepared to

do that. But if I don't have to do that, if I can find someplace to settle where no one knows me, where no one can find me, and live a relatively normal life out in the open and free of fear, then I'll do that, if I can. I don't deserve to live my life in fear, afraid to leave the house, hiding from shadows. No one does."

I thought about all that, about my life these last few months, these last few years—hiding from people in need, from Frank, from the Chief, from Tina. I thought about all this but said nothing.

"You know how the rich are, Mac," she said. "You know them as well as I do. You grew up one of them."

"How do you know me?" I said bluntly.

"I know all about you. I didn't have to do much homework. People talk out here. You know that. And I know you can't possibly have any loyalty to my family. You don't even know who they are. They're just another rich family in town to you. You can't want to help them. I know this."

She took another step toward me then. If I wanted to I could have reached out and touched her.

"I want to offer you a deal," she said. "A deal between just you and me. Do you think you might be interested in that?"

I watched her face closely. Her features made me for some reason think of Augie. Her face seemed somehow unnatural, somehow constructed. Up close there were several thin, intricate scars, old ones.

She said, "You could tell whoever sent you that you looked but didn't find me. You can tell him that you found a friend of mine at the cottage, that he told you that I had moved, that I went to New Haven and no one knows exactly where."

"Why New Haven?"

"I went to Yale. It makes sense that I'd hide in a city I knew well, wouldn't you agree?"

"Yeah. Yeah, that would make sense."

"I'm thinking maybe my family will see my living there as a kind of self-imposed exile and decide to leave it at that and not try to find me. They're dangerous and they're crazy, but they're also businessmen. Why waste time trying to lock me up if I've sent myself away?"

I wanted to ask her why they wanted to lock her up but didn't. It was her business, not mine. Instead I said, "People with resources tend to be very willing to exhaust them, Marie. If finding you is important to them, I can't imagine they'd see you living free just across Long Island Sound too much of an obstacle. They'd hire men to go to New Haven and find you."

"Then that means they won't be looking for me here, and that's all I really want. I don't want to leave here. The East End is my home. So all I'd have to do is stay out of sight."

"That's easier said than done. Trust me."

"Scully knows a few things about staying hidden. He's my protector—"

"Who?"

"Scully. Skull."

"That's him in the pickup, smoking a cigarette, right?" I said.

She didn't move, just stood there, her hands still deep in her pockets, her shoulders tight. She was uncertain suddenly as to how much she should admit. Finally she relaxed her shoulders, dropping them a bit, and said, "Yeah."

"I'd like to talk to him, if I could. I have a few questions about last night I'd like to ask him."

"He says it'd be for the best if you two avoided each other for now."

"Why is that, do you think?"

"I really don't know."

"You started to say that he's your protector?"

"He is."

"And the dead kid at the cottage. What was he?"

"His name was Tim Carter. He took care of me, too, for a while, anyway."

I said, "You know that Scully ran out on Carter without even calling an ambulance. He just left him to die."

"He told me all about it. He also told me that you tried to save Tim's life. Like I said, that's why you're here. Compassion."

"Carter and you used to lived together, right?"

"Yes."

"You don't seem all that broken up over his murder. Or even surprised, for that matter."

"We were over a while ago. We meant nothing to

each other now. Anyway, what happened to him he brought upon himself."

"How so?"

"He wasn't anywhere as clever as he needed to be. And for what he had gotten himself into, he needed to be very clever."

"What was it he had gotten himself into?"

"Let's just say he was in way over his head."

"I don't suppose you want to tell me any more than that."

"The less you know, the better it will be for you."

"And you."

She nodded. "And me."

"Are all your friends like those two?"

"What do you mean?"

"Well, they both carry guns, for starters. Carter had a record. Scully certainly looks like he should. Shaved head, tattoos, jailhouse stare. What's a rich girl from Halsey Neck Lane doing mixed up with guys like them?"

"What's a boy from Gin Lane doing hiding himself away from the world above a bar?"

"This isn't about me."

"I'm sure you want to keep it that way."

"I just don't want trouble."

"It seems we have that in common, too."

"Then what are you doing with a man like Scully?"

"Staying alive, that's what I'm doing. I choose my

friends carefully, Mac. If a man can help me keep my brother from getting his hands on me, then I do what I have to do to keep that man around. It's as simple as that."

I looked at her for a long time then. She stared back at me. Her posture didn't change once.

"I could pay you," she offered. "It wouldn't be much. But it would be something."

"This isn't about money."

"Then what is it about?"

We both had secrets we wanted to keep. This was clear. I thought about what Augie had said, how some secrets break through to the surface while others remain buried, and how random it all seemed. I didn't want to play dice with my secrets.

I glanced toward the pickup again, at the figure behind the wheel, then back at Marie. Suddenly I didn't care if I owed Frank anything. This wasn't any of my business. This was family shit, rich family shit. And I didn't want anything to do with that.

"Keep your money," I said.

"So you'll help me?"

I nodded. "It wouldn't look very good for me if someone happened to spot you any time in the near future. You'll have to be very careful. The man who sent me to find you is crazy and dangerous in his own way. I don't want him coming back to me and saying someone saw you buying groceries in the IGA. Do you understand?"

"I think it's pretty obvious that our mutual best interests lie in me not being found. My own sense of self-preservation guarantees your preservation. This appears to be one of those few times in life when it just works out like that."

"How do you survive?" I asked. "How do you make money?"

"I waitress, off the books."

"Where?"

"A little place out in—" She caught herself and stopped short. She held still for a moment, looking at me squarely. Her mouth was sealed tightly.

"You have to be careful of things like that," I said. "Little slips like that can lead to trouble for both of us."

"Maybe I'm not as clever as I think I am," she said.

"Very few of us are."

"So we have a deal? You'll do this for me?"

The sound of the crickets and the frogs swelled then, filling up the hollow of the open night, ringing like countless bells. It was alarming, almost deafening.

"Yeah," I said. "Yeah."

I left Marie there on the beach and managed to make it back to the Hansom House without running out of gas. I craved being there deeply. I thought about what I would tell Frank and how I saw this as a way of escape, a perfect back door out of my situation. I had done what he asked. I had found her. The other part of it, the lie about where she was, I didn't care about that.

I was out from under him now. I had my life back. Tina was out of my place, Augie was home, my debt to Frank was paid. All I had to worry about now was making a living and staying out of the Chief's way. Making a living was one thing, but dodging the Chief, that was easy enough. I would just remain up in my rooms whenever I wasn't working. And that didn't really sound all that bad to me.

It was a little past midnight when I got back. There wasn't much activity in the bar; tomorrow was a workday and everybody with a job was at home, enjoying the sleep of the just. I had to be at my job by eight. I was beat and looked forward to stretching out on my own bed. I looked forward to that little extra room. And I looked forward to sleeping straight through till morning, but when I reached the top of the second flight of stairs I realized at once just how gravely misplaced all this newfound optimism was. I froze, dead in my tracks.

Standing in my dim hallway was the Chief.

He was a physically imposing man, tall, long legged, wide through the shoulders. He was in uniform, complete with leather belt and gun and tall boots. His hair was thinning, gray, but his face held the ruggedness of an outdoorsman. It was deeply lined, gaunt and grim, colorless now, though I knew his complexion to be usually ruddy. When I was a young child and he was just a cop all the children feared him and told wild stories about him. Back then he had reminded me of one of those mountain men from the movies. As I grew he didn't seem to diminish in size at all. He held his stature, his prominence. I could only assume that today's children held him in the same regard and spread their own half-truths about his meanness and cruelty.

He stared at me in that hard way of his from the end of the hallway. A uniformed cop was standing behind him. The Chief gestured toward my door.

"I think we'd both rather do this inside," he said. "C'mon, let's go, I don't have all night."

Inside I turned on a light as the uniformed cop made a quick sweep of all my rooms. When he was done he said, "All clear, Chief." And it was only then that the Chief stepped inside. He closed the door.

I had crossed paths with the uniformed cop years ago. He was one of three cops who found me on the kitchen floor of an unrented house in the Shinnecock Hills, a .45 caliber slug in my collarbone and a dead girl in the basement. I remember his face above me. I remember his look of uncertainty, as if he weren't sure what to make of me. That was the last time I saw him. It had been, I think, two years.

His name was Long, and I could tell by the stripes on his sleeves that he was a sergeant now. His face was flattened some, his jaw square like a box. His hair was dark and tightly curled, cut close to the scalp. He was from what I heard a decent guy. He stood behind the Chief as the Chief and I faced off. There was something about the way Long looked at me, and the way he stood just behind and to the right of the Chief, that gave me the impression that he wasn't necessarily one of the Chief's boys.

The Chief hadn't moved. He stood just inside my living room, the shut door behind him. It was as if someone had planted a tree there. He eyed me hard for a while and said nothing. I had to look up to meet his flinty eyes. His jaw muscles flexed under his thick skin like hard springs. After a while of staring, as if in disgust, he moved past me, stepping farther into my living room.

The Chief, like Long had, made a survey of the room then. But his was a quick, perfunctory one, more curiosity than security. When he was done he looked at me again. A single, heavy drop of sweat sprang down my ribs, rolling over one bone at a time. Then it ran down my waist before collecting in my cotton T-shirt.

"So this is where you hide from me," he said. "So this is the rat hole you won't leave. It suits you."

I said nothing to that.

"I won't take up too much of your time, Mac-Manus," he said. By his look I expected that at any minute he might grab me by the throat and squeeze. His lips were pursed tightly, and there was sweat under his nose, small transparent beads that trembled just a little with the rage he labored to contain.

"I understand that Frank Gannon hired you to find a woman who calls herself Marie Welles."

I kept still. I didn't move from where I was. I didn't want to offer him or Long the opportunity to misunderstand even the slightest move on my part.

"I also understand," he continued, "that you just had a meeting with her."

I kept still and watched him closely. He took several shallow, tight breaths through his nose, as if he were trying to breathe but not take in some horrible odor. He made another sweep around my living room, then shifted his weight from one foot to the other, his leather belt squeaking in protest.

"What do you want, Chief?" I said. I let my impatience show.

The Chief took a step toward me. It was a sudden move. Then he thought better of it and stopped short. As much as he certainly wanted to let fly on me after all this time of waiting, he held himself back fairly well.

It took him a while to speak again. I could feel his hate. It felt like cold coming through a window pane on a winter night.

"A young man was killed last night in Flanders," he said. "His name was Tim Carter. You were there when he got killed. Don't bother to deny it. You were sent there by Frank Gannon to find out where this Marie Welles had gone to. At some point during that visit a bullet zipped open his throat and he drowned in his own blood."

"I really don't know what you're talking about, Chief."

"Carter was a nothing, a small-timer. I don't care about what happened to him. I don't care who did him. What I do want to know is why would a family as powerful as the family this woman comes from want to have a nothing like him killed."

"What makes you think her family had anything to do with it?"

"You don't ask the questions here, you answer them. Got that?"

"I have nothing to say to you, Chief."

"I don't have time to fuck around with you, MacManus."

"So don't."

"You don't even realize the shit you're in right now, do you?"

"What shit?"

"You don't listen well, do you, kid? You're not all that bright, are you?"

"What do you want from me, Chief?"

"I want to know why this woman's family is so desperate to find this girl."

"Why?"

"Because I'd like to know. I like to know what goes on in my town. It's my job. I take it seriously."

"Wouldn't you want to know where your kid was if he was missing?" I said.

"If my kid was missing and I wanted to find him, I wouldn't send the man they're using to look for her."

"I told you, I wasn't looking for anybody for anyone."

"I'm not talking about you. I'm talking about the man who shot that kid. The man who shot Carter in that cottage you've never been to."

"If you know who he is, then why are you here busting my ass?"

"Sweat about it, MacManus. Fear becomes you."

"I'm a little tired for games, Chief."

"Don't worry, kid, I'm almost done with you. The man who shot Carter, he's also the man who was hired by the girl's family, allegedly to find her. But he's not a particularly nice man. Like I said, he's not the kind of person you send to bring home a loved one. You've crossed paths with him before."

"What are you talking about?"

"I like to see you sweat, MacManus. Work it out in that little rat brain of yours, if you can."

"So this is it, Chief? Nothing good on TV tonight, thought you'd come over and play with my head?"

"That's part of it. That's the fun part. The other part isn't so fun for me."

"And that is?"

"I want you to find the girl, and I want you to bring her to me. I want to talk with her before her family gets their hands on her. 'Cause I think once they do there won't be much she'll be able to say, if you know what I mean."

"Why do you care about this girl so much, Chief?"

"There's only one thing I hate more than you, MacManus, and that's rich people trying to get away with murder."

"Why should I think this is anything less than some kind of sucker setup?"

"When I get you, MacManus, believe me, you won't see it coming."

"You still haven't answered my question. Why should I help you?"

"Because there's something in it for you, too."

"What?"

"You look for her, you'll find out soon enough."

"That doesn't tell me much."

"Live with it. Or don't. I don't care. I have business with the girl. You have unfinished business with the man her family sent to find her. It seems for this rare, brief moment in time, we can help each other out. Which means for now you are free to come and go as you please. Your name, for now, anyway, is off my wanted list. You won't even get pulled over for speeding in this town, as long as you're looking for her."

"It doesn't matter anyway, Chief, because I have no idea where she is. I don't know where to find her."

"Bad news for you if you don't. The funny thing about it is, you don't even know how bad yet. But you will."

I could barely breathe. I needed air.

"Why me, Chief? Why me?" I could hear sadness in my voice. I was tired.

"You send a rat to get a rat. You find the girl. In the process, if you cross paths with this man, you do what you have to. When it's over give Long here a call and he'll pick up the mess. Do you understand?"

Long offered me a business card. I didn't take it. He let it drop on the floor and then stepped back. He was watching me closely. My eyes met his for a moment, then I looked back at the Chief.

"Are you sending me to kill a man, Chief?"

"Hear what you want to hear, kid. You live in this town, too."

"What does that mean?"

"Think about it. You've got forty-eight hours. After that it's open season on you all over again. And believe me, MacManus, when the opportunity presents itself, I will send you straight to hell. For right now, though, your miserable shitty life belongs to me. There but for the grace of me. Do we understand each other?"

"I'm not killing anybody, Chief, not for you, not for anyone."

"I wouldn't worry about that, either, MacManus. He won't give you a choice. I can promise you that."

He turned toward the door then.

"I won't help you, Chief. This isn't what I do."

He turned back and looked at me. "You just don't get it, do you, MacManus? You need it spelled out for you, in big bright letters. Fine. They want her *dead*, not found. Her family wants her dead. If you find her, then maybe you can save her life. You did it once before. I know you do that kind of thing."

"What do you mean, I did it before?"

"Figure it out. Just find her before he does, if he hasn't already. Chances are you led him right to her tonight, in which case we're already too late."

I watched from my front windows as the Chief and Long drove off in an unmarked police car. Then I ran down to the street and got into my car. I cranked the ignition till the engine caught and then followed Montauk Highway past the Shinnecock Indian Reservation. There I turned left onto Little Neck Lane, then right into Augie's driveway.

He greeted me at the door as I came up the walk. He must have seen me pull up. He was wearing a bathrobe over knee-length baggy shorts and a jersey. He leaned on his cane. His hand gripped the handle so tightly that his knuckles were white. I could tell by the way his bathrobe hung off him that there was something heavy in the right pocket.

"What's up?" he said.

It was a little after two in the morning but Augie looked awake enough. Rain clouds, steel gray and massive, like giant warships in the sky, had begun to gather in the northeast, obscuring the low moon. The terrible heat remained still, but maybe its end was near now. Air was moving a little, the leaves in the scrub oaks across the road from Augie's yard hissing lightly in a slight breeze.

Augie saw the look on my face and said, "What happened?"

"Where's Tina?"

"At Lizzie's. Why?"

"The Chief just paid a visit at my place."

"Come on," Augie said, ushering me in. He looked past me to his street and made a quick survey. "We'll talk inside."

We sat across from each other at his kitchen table. I told him about the Chief, what the Chief had said, and about Frank. Then I started to tell him about Marie Welles.

"I don't know of any family named Welles on Halsey Neck Lane," Augie said.

"Maybe they just moved there."

"Maybe."

I told him then everything I knew about her. He listened carefully, but the instant I mentioned Scully's name a look came across his face that made me stop.

"What?" I said. "What is it?"

"Hang on a second," Augie said. He got up and left the room. He went down the hall to his study and came back a minute later with a manila envelope in his hand. I could tell there were photos inside it. Augie sat back down and opened the envelope and spread the photos out on the table. Then he searched through them and finally picked one out and handed it to me.

It was a surveillance shot of a man walking out of a bar. It was taken at night, from a distance, but it was good enough of a shot for me to see that the man was Scully.

"Is this him?" Augie said.

"Yeah."

"That's Will Scully. He deals drugs out of that bar in Sag Harbor, the Dead Horse, the one that kid Vogler was shot in front of. The Horse was on the top of my list of places to stake out last spring. A lot of heroin moves through there. Most of what comes out to the East End is headed there. Which makes you wonder about the name, doesn't it? The Dead Horse. Anyway, Scully is a major player in the local trade. That's all I really know about him, except that he doesn't much like having his photo taken."

Augie showed me another photo. In this one Scully was looking straight at the camera. He was on the side-walk outside the Dead Horse. I recognized it behind him now. It was obvious that he was aware of the cam-era. It was obvious, too, by the look on his face that he was pissed off. The next photo showed Scully turning away from the camera and waving someone over. In the photo after that a blur was entering the frame. It was a man, or part of one. You could barely see him, let alone who he was. That was the last photo.

"I got out of there after that," Augie explained. "I didn't much like the look of his friend."

"When did you take these?"

"Last spring, when I found out that shit was being sold at Tina's school. It was the night before my ambush."

"You think maybe these were what your attackers were after?"

"I don't know. I sure would like the chance to talk to this guy Scully, though."

"What else can you tell me about him?"

"Like I said, not much. He's good at keeping out of sight and underground. Actually, he's a fucking ghost. Very, very hard to find. Very cautious. But if you want to find him, I'd say the Dead Horse is the place to start looking."

I took another look at the photos. I looked closely at the one of Scully looking angrily into the camera. If he was the man who had sacked Augie, it was a face and an expression I wanted to see in person now more than ever.

I handed the photo back to Augie and said, "Thanks."

He shuffled the photos together then and returned them to their envelope. He seemed a little lost in thought. I thought I knew by the expression on his face what it was he was thinking about. I remembered Frank forbidding me to look for the men who had almost killed Augie. It was hard to believe I was possibly so close to one of them. It was hard to believe I had looked him in the eye.

Augie was quiet for a while. I left him to his thoughts and followed my own. When he spoke finally his voice was low, his eyes focused on his hands.

"Remember the other day in the hospital when I told you that everything was going to be fine, that I'd been doing a lot of thinking, that change was coming?"

"Yeah, I remember."

"It's easy to think that way when you're in a hospital room, all safe and sterile. But it isn't so easy when you're back out in the world. I wasn't prepared for how hard it was to come back into this house. I thought that in the three months away from it I had come to terms with what had happened here. But it isn't that easy. It took me a whole day before I could go down the hall and into my study. I sleep with a loaded .45 by my bed. That is, when I sleep. Mainly I just lie awake at night, listening for sounds. I was so convinced that last night was the night they were coming back for me that I sat up in a chair with my .45 on my lap and stared at my front door. I didn't dare fall asleep. I've come to realize that all the happy horseshit I said to you back in the hospital was just that, happy horseshit. Nothing is going to be fine till I find the bastards who did this to me. My life can't start again till I do that. I know this now."

"Come and stay at my apartment for a while," I said. "You and Tina. We can make room."

Augie shook his head. "I wouldn't make it up and down all those stairs. Besides, being scared in my own house is one thing. Running away from it is another thing altogether." He watched my face for a moment. I held his hard eyes and thought of the night we had first met. "Look, Mac, if this Scully guy is the one, then I want him. Do you understand? I want him."

I nodded.

"Your enemy is my enemy, Mac. Remember that."

On my way to Sag Harbor, it started to rain. Things weren't any cooler for it, though, just all that more humid. Inside the Dead Horse I sat in a corner and waited for Scully. I didn't have a thing to drink, not even a soda. People stared at me all night but I didn't care. I waited till the bartender called last call. It was early, just past one. My eyes were fixed on the door the whole time. But Scully was nowhere to be seen. I waited outside in my car for a while, till the bar was all closed up and the bartender was gone. Still nothing. Finally, a little before two, I drove home through the rain.

I went back up to my apartment. I paused at the top of my stairs to look down my hallway before proceeding. No one was there.

I unlocked my door and went inside. Before I could close the door behind me Tina came tearing out of the

kitchen. I half expected by the way she moved someone to be behind her.

She was crying. She ran into my arms, almost
knocking me down. I'd never seen anyone so scared in
my life. Her hands were trembling but the rest of her
young body was rigid.

"What?" I demanded. "What's wrong?"

Her hair and clothes were soaked from the rain.
Even though she was in my arms she seemed uncertain
where to go or what to do with herself. The urge to
flight was like a current rushing through her.

I asked her again what was wrong. There was rain
on her face. I hadn't seen her this shaken up since that
night behind the library. Even this seemed worse.

"Tina, what's going on?" I said again.

Her breathing was uneven. Had she been running?
Rain was still beaded on her face.

"What, Tina? What?"

Her voice was jittery. She didn't seem to know
whether to cry or not.

"I was walking over here from Lizzie's house. I
wanted to talk to you. Someone started following me."

"What do you mean?"

"A man started following me."

"It was probably some guy coming to the Hansom
House, that's all."

"It wasn't like that."

"Did he say anything to you?"

"It was him," she said then, her voice sharp, hostile.

"It was who?"

"It was him. I know it was." Her eyes locked onto mine. She was shaking with terrible force.

"It was who, Tina?"

"He was following me, he was right behind me. I started to run, and then he was gone. But when I got here, he was right outside, he was right here, standing across the street. He must have gone back and got his car and beat me here—"

"How long ago was this?"

"Just a few minutes." She looked at me. She was starting to cry. "It was him, Mac."

"It was who, Tina?"

"It was him." She snapped, impatient with my slowness.

"Who?"

"It was him. The man who hurt Augie. It was him, he was right outside. I know it was him. I remember his picture in the paper. It's the same ugly face. It's the same man."

I went to my front windows and looked down through the branches to Elm Street. My car was parked directly across from the Hansom House and, standing beside it, on the curb, was a man.

The streetlamp nearest to him was out. I saw what I thought was broken glass scattered around its base. But I could see well enough with what little light there was. I could see what I needed to see.

He was wearing a raincoat and his hands were deep in the pockets. He was looking up at me, the same ugly, battered face I had seen in Augie's hall, the same buzz haircut, the same bull of a man who had nearly driven me through a wall.

In one horrible moment things started to make sense.

I tore from the window without thinking and bolted out my door and downstairs. I moved faster than I had ever moved before. But by the time I reached the curb the man wasn't anywhere to be seen, and I was left alone on the quiet, unlit street.

Back upstairs, I called Eddie and told him to come pick Tina up and to take her to her father. Then I called Augie and told him what I had seen and that he should take Tina and get out of town.

"I'm not going anywhere," he said. "Tell Eddie to take Tina back to Lizzie's house. Tell him to make sure he's not being followed. I'm not leaving my home."

"This guy's a professional, Augie."

"So am I."

"What the fuck is he doing out of jail?"

"I think maybe that's something that we should try to find out. I'll make a few phone calls, ask a few questions."

"I don't want to leave you alone, Aug."

"Don't worry about me. What are you going to do?"

"I don't know. Something."

"Call as soon as you know anything."

"Take care of yourself."

"You, too."

After we hung up I called Eddie. I watched for him from one of my living room windows. Tina and I said nothing to each other as we waited. When Eddie's cab pulled up, I walked Tina downstairs. The bar was closed. I put Tina into Eddie's cab and told him where to take her. There wasn't time to explain anything. Eddie knew better than to ask. After they drove off I went back upstairs. I called Frank's pager and punched in my number. I waited for him to call back. But the phone never rang.

Finally, around four, in that darkest hour of the night, I realized there was only one place I could go.

Eight

It was less than a hunch. It was raw instinct. And it was a long shot, but it was all I had.

I had his card but I didn't want to call. I knew where he lived, that was if he still lived in the same place he was living in when he was one of the three cops who found me flat out and bleeding buckets on the kitchen floor of that unrented house by the canal.

It was dawn when I reached his house. The rain had stopped and the air seemed cool. But I barely noticed. He lived in a small middle-class home on Moses Lane, off Hill Street. His unmarked cop car was in the driveway as I rode past.

I parked at the curb one yard down and made my way around back, to his kitchen door. I saw him through the window. He was at his kitchen counter, his back to the door. He was in his uniform and making his lunch. I knocked on the windowpane. He turned quickly and saw me. He didn't move at first, then finally he put down what he was doing, wiped his hands on a dishrag, and started toward the door.

His gun belt was on. I saw the Glock 9mm in his left-hand holster.

He opened the door only partway.

I said, "I need some answers."

"Not here," Long said abruptly.

"You know your boss is a criminal, don't you?"

"Not here, not now."

"I need your help."

"Not here."

"Where then?"

"Give me a few hours. I'll pick you up behind the movie theater."

"I need to know what's going on."

"You'll get answers. Just meet me there."

"When?"

"Nine. That's the earliest I can get there."

"You're not a fan of the Chief. I can tell."

"I'll see you at nine, MacManus."

He closed the door on me. My heart was racing. I could barely breathe as I walked back to my car.

At nine exactly Long pulled in behind the Southampton Cinema in his unmarked car. I could see right off that he was in street clothes. He pulled up beside my

LeMans and stopped. I got into the backseat of his car and we drove off.

"I took a sick day for this," Long said.

"I need to know what the hell is going on," I blurted.

"This'll make twice now I've saved your life."

"How did the guy who jumped Augie get out of jail?"

"Just sit tight, okay?"

"Where are we going?"

"It's just five minutes up the street."

The car smelled clean, new. I sat back and watched the trees that lined Montauk Highway pass by the rain-streaked window. After a few minutes Long made a left hand turn, onto Halsey Neck Lane. I looked at his eyes in the rearview mirror.

We were headed into that part of town I did my best to avoid, that part called "south of the highway" where I had spent my youth living with my cruel adoptive father, self-absorbed adoptive mother, and their unbalanced son.

"Where are you taking me?" I said.

He didn't answer me. We followed Halsey close to where it ended on Meadow Lane, then turned into a driveway, passing through a wrought-iron gate attached to two stone columns. I knew where we were going then. I'd been to this home before, long, long ago, when I was boy. But what I didn't know was why we were here now.

I hadn't thought of this place in years, but the estate was just as I remembered. The grounds were lined with twelve-foot hedges, as was the driveway, which curved like a sickle till the hedges ended suddenly and the driveway spilled into a circle at the front of a century-old mansion.

This house was gray stone and ivy covered, three storeys high with white marble pillars at the entrance. It was giant in that way ships are when you see them out of water.

Long parked the unmarked car halfway around the circle. There were no door handles on the back door. He had to open it from the outside to let me out. Together he and I walked to a front door made of heavy oak. It was framed by intricate scrollwork and rose up to a rounded point, like a church door, which was, if I remembered, where it was from. It had been taken, I think, from a ruined church somewhere in Europe at the end of one war or another.

An old black woman in a gray maid's uniform answered the door and led us through a marble entrance hall to a dark hallway lined with wood paneling. She looked at me closely before leaving us. At the end of this hallway was a door that led out to the backyard. It was there that a man near my age was waiting for us.

He was standing under an awning that was extended over a stone patio at the back of the house. The manicured lawn beyond him was tree-lined and sloped gently down to Taylor Creek fifty or so yards away. Across the narrow body of water was the Dupont Sanctuary, above which clouds to the west of us were beginning to fragment and let through the angled late-afternoon light.

There was harshness to his handsome face, which for some reason then I thought I had seen recently. But if he was who I thought he was, that couldn't be. If he was who I thought he was, then I hadn't seen him in decades. I looked in his face for something that I would recognize from all those years ago.

We didn't shake hands, only nodded to each other as we came face to face on the stone patio.

"I don't think I would have recognized you if I saw you, Mac," he said flatly. "It has been a long time."

I recognized his voice, the way his mouth moved when he spoke, the way his eyes looked at me.

"Jean-Marc," I said.

"You have a good memory."

"Not really. If we weren't here at the house I don't think I would have made the connection."

Beside us was a wrought-iron table with a glass top and four chairs around it. On it was a leather knapsack and a pair of binoculars and a tall glass half filled with a clear liquid. It was over ice cubes that had melted down to their white cores.

The three of us sat at the table in a way that allowed each of us a clear view of the sloping lawn and the water beyond. Beams of sunlight were punching through the clouds almost everywhere you looked now. The rain was moving on, and the drops it left behind sparkled in the reopening light.

Jean-Marc sat across from me, Long to my right, his back to the house. I saw Long shift several times in his seat till he was comfortable. Holstered behind him, to his belt, was his gun.

Jean-Marc leaned back in his chair and stared at me, sizing me up. "How long has it been? Twenty years?"

"Longer than that, I think." His friendliness made me cautious. I had never liked Jean-Marc much, even as a boy.

He was part of the Bishop family, old money, a real fixture in town. I had grown up not far from here, and we had played together, Jean-Marc, his twin sister, and I, for a few summers around when I was ten.

"I hear you still live in town," he said. Even when he smiled his eyes were harsh. "Above that bar by the train station. With your girlfriend, or something like that?"

"I live alone," I said. I looked at Long, then back at Jean-Marc. His dark face was cleanly shaven. His brown eyes were still and alert. They pierced like eyes of a hunting bird. He wore a polo jersey tucked neatly into jeans and tennis sneakers. His hair was black and short, parted low on the left side. On his right wrist was a gold watch that did all kinds of tricks in the emerging sunlight.

"Listen, I don't have much time to play catchup with you, Mac," he said. "Things are kind of hectic here right now. Family stuff. You know. So I'm just going to get down to it, to why I had you brought here. I don't mean to be rude, but the clock's ticking."

He paused a moment, then said, "I need to ask you, as a favor to our family, to cease your attempts at contacting my sister. I understand the pressure on you, but I can't let you continue to interfere with family matters. Do you understand?"

"No."

"You don't understand?"

"I don't have a clue what you're talking about."

"I can understand your wanting to help her, considering what you two went through as kids and all. But I need—we need you to just leave her be."

"Jean-Marc, I—"

I stopped suddenly and looked at Long.

"Marie," I said. "Oh my God. Marie Welles is your sister. Marie Welles is Marie *Bishop*."

"She started going by that name several months ago. Part of her refusal of her own family. The doctors say it's a common thing for someone with her problems to do." He smiled. "You know, I'm not surprised you didn't recognize her. It's been a long time. Plus, she's had her share of reconstructive surgery over the years. She was never all that fond of her nose and chin. And her hair was blonder back then, from all that sun."

"I just saw her the other night," I muttered. "She

acted a little like we knew each other but didn't say anything."

"Our family troubles are really nobody's business but our own. I think you can understand that. I mean, you and she go way back, right? My father and I have never forgotten what you did for her. You were a brave kid. You saved her life. We remember that, we remember what you went through because of it. That's why we'd like to do you a favor, a favor in exchange for doing us the courtesy of respecting our privacy."

I didn't say anything to that. In my mind it was the other night and I was face to face with Marie Bishop again, searching her face for any hint of the girl I had known that hot summer so long ago.

When I came back to the dangerous present I felt as if I had just missed something. Jean-Marc nodded toward the leather bag on the glass tabletop. Long reached across and took it, then placed it in his lap and opened it. He reached inside and pulled out a clear plastic zip-lock bag.

Inside it was a small automatic handgun with a long barrel. He held up the bag for me to see, then placed it on the table between us. I could tell just by glancing at the size of the barrel that it was a .32 caliber.

"Long here tells me that you're in trouble with the Chief," Jean-Marc said. "Something to do with his son. I don't care about any of that. Family matters are family matters, as far as I'm concerned. But I'd like to help you if I can. The Chief has been a friend of my family for almost as long as you have. We told him we needed a man to work for us and he sent us a man named Searls, a real animal. Now, we don't know why he would do a thing like that. He's sent us men before when we needed them, and they've all been highly professional. We've always been satisfied with their work. We asked for a man to help us find my sister, and he sends us a butcher instead."

I glanced at Long. He held my stare. I knew then that he was here with Bishop and me behind the Chief's back.

"You see," Jean-Marc continued, "it's time to clean up. This whole mess with this thing named Searls gets put away tonight, once and for all. I think you'd agree that we're all better off with this animal back in jail. And it won't be long before we find my sister. We're negotiating with someone right now who can bring us to her. So all that leaves us is you. I don't want any harm to come to my sister. I'm sure you feel the same. She's not a well woman, and it's my responsibility to look after her. We understand that this Searls man may be following you because of some grudge, and if he is, you might inadvertently lead him to her. There's no telling what an animal like that might do. I'm told he's quite brutal. So we obviously want to be as careful as we can. As I've said, I realize that you have something of an interest at stake here. The Chief wants you to find my sister and is holding the murder of Tim Carter over your head. I believe your biggest concern is that a certain weapon might turn up in your apartment and make you connectable to the crime. I'd like, if I may, to put you at ease on that matter right this very moment. So please, as my gift of thanks to you for being a loyal friend to my family, I want you to take this and do with it what you will."

He nodded toward the gun in the plastic bag on the table. I looked at it but didn't make a move to take it. After a while I looked at Jean-Marc. Then finally I looked at Long.

"When you catch Searls, won't you need that to charge him with Tim Carter's murder?" I said.

"We feel it's more important," Jean-Marc said, "that you have no reason whatsoever to seek out my sister."

"We'll have enough on Searls to get him back to jail," Long said. "Don't worry about that. He's been having a lot more fun than you know about, Mac. He won't be getting out of jail again for a long time."

"Just how did he get out to begin with?"

"Does that really matter now?"

"Maybe."

"Let's just say the Chief has his ways. It came suddenly to someone's attention that Searls hadn't been duly processed. Not a very difficult thing to do, really. Lawyers did the rest."

Jean-Marc said, "The Chief must be getting old. He's slipping. He not only let this animal loose on his own streets, but he sent him to work for us. Maybe he's distracted by whatever it is that's between you two. Maybe it's something else. Maybe he knows just what he's doing. Whatever the reason, that's why he isn't here today. He's on his way out. He's made too many mistakes to be any use to us any longer."

I looked away from both of them then. The water looked lead-colored under the broken clouds and many gasps of light. I didn't really care for local politics so I had stopped listening. It didn't matter to me who ran what, as long as I was left alone. Long couldn't be any worse of a chief than the Chief was.

The handgun in the zip-lock bag was still on the table before me. No one was talking. I didn't make a move toward it, I didn't even allow myself to think of taking it. I had learned long ago to shrink away from the things that looked too good to pass up. But how could I do that now? How could I not grab at this shiny thing? What if it was, for once in my life, gold?

"How do I know that's even the murder weapon?"

Long took a folder from the leather bag and dropped it on the table.

"It's the ballistics on the bullet that killed Tim Carter," Jean-Marc said. "There's also a lab report there confirming that that bullet was fired by this gun. The cops found it at the scene. It has a partial print matching Searls'. The Chief had it locked up in his office. It wasn't in the evidence room where it belonged. He was obviously saving it to drop on you when the time came."

"Jean-Marc, I'm sure a man with all your resources could get his hands on a fake report easily."

"I don't know what I can say to persuade you, except that you know how seriously I take my family. My father cared about you quite a bit. You were almost part of the family for a while there. You ate here, you slept here. My father was quite fond of you. We don't forget that kind of thing. We don't repay loyalty with betrayal."

My mind was racing. A dozen scenarios played out in my head in a matter of seconds. None of them was good. I looked at the gun once more and knew that one way or another, this was the end of things—either I took it and walked free or I took it and walked straight into a trap. My life was there on the table before me, mine to win or lose. It was as simple as that.

Still, it took a long time for me to come to a decision. And in the end it really wasn't much of one. I had no other choice but to take what they offered me and all the risks that came with it. I wanted my life in my hands, even if that meant letting it slip through my fingers and losing it forever. I wanted it in my hands again, even if only for a moment.

"Okay," I said. "Okay. I'll do what you want."

Long picked up the plastic baggy and put it back into the leather bag. Jean-Marc reached for his tall glass and took a long sip from it. I knew then that something had happened, that something had changed. But I had no way of knowing just what. Maybe it was just that business was over, that the meeting was done. Or maybe it was something more. Neither Jean-Marc nor Long looked at each other for a moment, as if any look between the two of them might give something away.

Jean-Marc returned his glass to the table and stood then. Long zipped shut the bag as he did the same. I was the last to rise. I watched them both. Vigilance was, as ever, all I had.

"Long'll take you back now. I'm sorry to rush you off, but with my father ill I have a lot of things I must take care of."

"I didn't know he was ill."

"The last few years have been rough on him. The doctors say he could go anytime now."

I remembered the old man. I remembered him making me feel at home. I remembered the money he gave me on my eleventh birthday. I remembered wanting to use it to run away from the family that had adopted me.

"I'm sorry to hear that," I said.

"I'll tell him I saw you. I'll tell him you were loyal to him to the end."

Jean-Marc led us across the patio and stopped at the back door. He extended his hand toward me. His eyes were steady and cold. I took his hand and we shook.

"I can count on your silence?" he said to me.

I said that he could. Long and I left then. He drove

us back toward the village, to my car behind the cinema. I could see more and more sunlight breaking out around us, like stilts in the sky. The brightness of it was hard on my eyes, but I didn't dare close them against it.

Long got out and opened the door for me. I got out and stood face to face with him.

"So now what?" I said.

"That's it, for you, anyway. Your part is done. Tonight we set a trap for Searls. You're welcome to come along with me if you want, see for yourself."

"No, thanks."

"You know, I could use you, MacManus. You could help flush out the Chief, you can help me get rid of him. You've got him frustrated, you won't come out in the open. Frustrated men do foolish things. What do you say?"

"I'm not interested."

"I'd think you'd be the first to jump at a chance to get him out."

"And when he's gone, who becomes chief? You? You obviously work for the Bishops. It would be more justice for the wealthy. No thanks."

"Look, I have no bone to pick with you, MacManus. The Chief's kid got what he deserved, in my opinion. His father kept cutting him slack, burying his 'mistakes.' We knew everything that boy did, and we couldn't do a damn thing to stop him. We were told to look the other way. There were threats of retribution if we didn't. I'm not the only one who wants him out. Not every cop in town is behind him. With people like Bishop out of his pocket, he can't last. Sometimes you've got to make a deal with the devil, you know what I mean?"

"I can't help you," I said.

"Just think about it. Think about it the next time you spot a cop car in your rearview mirror and you get that knot in your stomach, or when you're afraid to go for a walk for fear of being busted for jaywalking. With the Chief gone you can have your life back. I'd think after all this time you'd be eager for that. I'd think after all you've been through you'd do what has to be done to put an end to this bullshit."

I said nothing. I didn't even look at him.

Long waited, then nodded and said, "Yeah, well, you know where to find me, if you ever change your mind. Just think about it, okay? With you as bait we could draw him out and nail his ass good, once and for all. And then you could have that little girlfriend of yours over anytime you want."

I looked at him then. "Just find Searls and get him off the fucking street," I said.

Long nodded. "Take care of yourself, MacManus."

He got back into his car then and drove off, leaving me there holding that leather bag. Back in my apartment, I stashed the gun under a loose floorboard in my living room. Then I nailed the board back in place and went to my window and looked down on Elm Street. There was a part of me that wanted to believe this was, except for one detail, really over. But I knew it wasn't.

I called Augie. I didn't want to because I knew where it would go, but I had to. He had to know. The phone rang twice and then he answered it.

"They're supposed to bring him in tonight," I told him. "Searls. They're supposed to bring him in."

"So we just sit tight till then."

"Yeah."

"Did you find out how he got out?"

"The Chief sprang him, to work for a family named Bishop, not Welles."

"Now that's a family I've heard of. Any luck finding Scully?"

"No. It was a dead end."

"There'll be other nights. You're with me, right, Mac? You'll help me find him?"

I was tired but did what I could to not let Augie know that. "Of course."

"Let me know if you hear anything about our friend, okay?"

"We'll find him, Aug," I said.

He hung up. I stood there with the phone in my hand for a while before I dropped it onto its cradle.

Nine

I worked that afternoon, loading up the truck and delivering two pieces of restored furniture, first to a house in Hampton Bays and then later to a renovated potato barn out in the flat fields of Bridgehampton. My boss, the owner of the restoration business, wasn't around, just my supervisor, whom I could tell was pissed at me for the work I had missed. But there was nothing I could do about that. We avoided talking to each other when I was around the shop. But when I got back a little before five from Bridgehampton my boss's car was in the parking lot. I parked the truck out back and went inside to hand in the keys for the night. The owner took them and handed me a pay envelope. It wasn't payday. Before I could say anything he told me inside the envelope was what he owed me to date and that I was fired. I didn't put up a fight; I didn't see the point. I just took the envelope and left.

When I got back to my apartment I stretched out on my couch out of habit. I was beat. I fell asleep fast, and when I awoke night was all around me. A cool breeze was coming in through my windows. I was disoriented, confused. I had no idea what time it was or what day it was. For a moment I wasn't even sure where I was. It wasn't altogether frightening.

After a moment I heard a noise in my kitchen and got up and went out into the living room. I saw Tina then by my eating table, pouring cold tea from the container I kept in my refrigerator into a pint glass.

Sleep still had a hold on me. I tried to clear my head but there was no rushing it. I had no idea how long I had been out. I had awakened from nothingness into confusion. I checked my watch but couldn't make any sense of the tiny dial before me.

"Tina," I said. My voice sounded gravelly. My throat was painfully dry. My back had stiffened and gotten sore. "What are you doing?"

She returned the container to the refrigerator and closed the door, then stood in the kitchen door and looked at me. Her hands were empty. She had moved slowly, deliberately, and from across the small room I could smell her perfume.

"You okay?" she said.

"What time is it?"

"It's a little after nine. You were out like a light. I didn't wake you, did I?"

"Why aren't you home with Augie?"

"He sent me to Lizzie's."

"How did you get here? You shouldn't be walking around."

"I had your cab friend take me here."

"You shouldn't have come. It's not safe."

"I needed to see you."

"Don't."

She left the doorway then and took a few steps, stopping a few feet from me. I could smell a sharp sweetness on her breath. "I'm scared, Mac."

"Don't use that as an excuse."

"I only feel safe with you."

"You've been drinking."

"Just a little."

"You shouldn't drink, Tina. Your father will wring your neck if he finds out."

"It was the only way I could get the courage to come up here."

Now that my eyes had adjusted, the blue wash from the streetlights outside my windows was just enough to see her by. She was wearing hip-hugger jeans and a thin cotton half-shirt. The cool night air in my apartment told me that she was braless.

She wavered slightly. I didn't make a move toward her. My heart was beating to be soothed. We were in dangerous waters. I could smell her, I could smell the Southern Comfort on her breath, the shampoo in her hair, the perfume on her skin. She stared at me, her mouth opened slightly, her eyes drooping drowsily.

"You shouldn't be here."

"Augie shouldn't know that I've been drinking," she whispered. "We don't want him wringing my neck. I think I should stay here with you, don't you?"

"You'll sober up and I'll drive you back."

"I want to stay."

"What good would it do, Tina?"

"I just want to know what it's like. I want to find out with you. I want to be with you. All I want is to be with you. You make me feel safe."

"Tina."

"You love me, I know you do."

"You're a child, Tina."

"I don't want you to think of me that way anymore. I want to be close to you. It's all I think about."

"I'm sorry." Something was tightening around my throat from the inside. I couldn't breathe. Tina watched me closely. Then her hand came up slowly and lay across my chest. Her fingernails had been painted with red polish. I could feel her fingers tremble.

She leaned toward me then, bringing her face up to me. She stopped, her mouth just inches from my mouth. Her eyes sought out mine.

I placed my hands around her narrow waist and moved her gently back. Her breath was all around me, her face all I could see. The bones between my hands felt underdeveloped. They weren't the bones of an adult. I eased her back from me a little more still, as gently as I could.

"I have to go," I said.

"Where?"

"You can stay here till you're sober enough, then call Eddie and have him take you to Lizzie's. Tell him to come around tomorrow morning and I'll pay him the fare."

"Where are you going?"

"Out for a while."

"Just stay with me," she said. "I won't do anything. I promise."

"You should drink your tea. You won't be so hung over in the morning."

She said nothing to that.

"Call Eddie when you feel better," I told her.

She just stared at me. I left her then and went into the bathroom. I splashed cold water on my face and avoided my reflection in the smudged mirror over my sink. When I came out of the bathroom Tina wasn't in the living room. I looked toward the kitchen and she wasn't there, either. Then I looked into my bedroom.

She had taken off all her clothes and was standing beside my unmade bed. Naked like this her limbs looked to me even more awkward, more lanky than before. Her hands were hanging at her sides, against her thighs. She had tan lines. She stared at me, offering herself to me. I held her eyes for a moment and then just turned away and left her there in my bedroom.

I went downstairs and sat in my corner and got into some serious Beam action. It was a quiet night at the bar. At times there was no one around but me and George. I kept to myself and studied my tumbler. George got the hint soon enough that I wanted to be alone. Around midnight he went into the kitchen to close it up for the night. I looked up then and glanced at the mirror above the bar. I saw myself for the first time in a long time. I saw just what I expected to see. And then I saw something else, someone standing just inside the doorway to the bar, watching me with almost no expression on her face.

She came over to my corner finally and stood by the stool next to me. We were the only people in the bar.

She held her shoulders back like a cadet and her chin forward and up, like she always did, like she did as a child. It was hard to think of either of us as kids now. I looked for the changes in her face but gave up and remembered her smiling like an old friend at Long Beach. But there was no hint of that smile now, or much of anything else, for that matter, on her face. I could only assume that things were still in play between her and her brother. But I was out of that now. That deal was done. I was out of it and there were no two ways about that.

"If it isn't Marie Bishop," I said.

"I need your help." Her voice was still hoarse. But it sounded almost familiar to me, now.

I shook my head and took a sip of my Beam. "Sorry, Marie. I've made a better deal."

"It's important."

"I can't help you."

"You don't understand what's going on. If you knew, you wouldn't be sitting here, waiting for it to come up and hit you on the back of your head."

She was wearing jeans and a denim shirt. I tried to remember the way she looked as a girl, with those summer highlights in her hair, all those years ago. I could barely see in her now the child I once knew.

"I don't know what you're talking about, Marie."

"You're in danger."

"I'll worry about me. You worry about you."

"You saved my life once before. If you don't save me now, what was the point of what we both went through? You should have let me die back then."

"That was different."

"Actually, it's not different, not at all."

"I'm sorry, Marie. I can't help you."

"He got to you, didn't he? Jean-Marc got to you, just like he gets to everybody. Did he buy you off? Did he give you something you think you need?"

"It's family business, Marie. It has nothing to do with me."

"That's where you're wrong."

"He's just trying to protect you. You father's probably worried and wants to know that you're okay."

"Mac, my father's in a coma. Has been for the past month. He's dying. He's the one who told me to run, to hide from my brother."

"According to Jean-Marc your father's conscious."

"He lied to you."

I waited a minute, thinking about that, then said, "Why did your father tell you to go into hiding?"

"Because when he dies there will be nothing holding Jean-Marc back, and he knows that. Because when he dies all hell is going to break loose. All this, everything that's happened up till now, this is just the start."

"What do you mean, 'this is just the start'?"

"Does Jean-Marc know you met with me, that we talked?"

"Yes."

"Then your life is in danger, Mac."

"What are you talking about?"

"Whatever deal you made with him was for his benefit and his benefit alone."

I said nothing to that.

"If he knows you met with me, then it's possible I told you, too," Marie urged.

"Told me what?"

"What he doesn't want anyone to know. What people are getting killed over."

"What are you talking about, Marie?" I heard impatience in my voice, the beginnings of panic.

"Scully is missing."

His name caught me like a hook. I looked at Marie, holding my breath, waiting.

"What do you want from me?" I said finally.

"I want you to help me find him. Please. Just help me find him and I promise I'll tell you everything. I'm dead without him, Mac. Please."

I thought about a lot of things then, quickly, as quickly as I could. I thought about my deal with Jean-Marc, the gun hidden under my floorboards. I thought about Tina upstairs, about me having nowhere to go right now. But mostly I thought about Scully, out there somewhere, roaming free. I thought of Augie walking with his cane. I thought about the only promise I had made that really mattered to me.

The only sense I could imagine then was bringing Scully to Augie.

"Okay," I said to Marie. "Okay, I'll help you find him."

We drove to Montauk, to a cottage on the shore of Fort Pond Bay, not far from the train station at the edge of Montauk Village. Marie pulled to the side of the narrow road and parked on the edge of the yard. We sat together in silence, watching the side of the solitary cottage for a while. Its dark windows reflected the endless night around us, and a stillness hung over it that seemed almost unsettling, like maybe no one had been there for a very long time.

I could see the waves of the bay beyond the cottage moving toward shore. It was the only motion that my eye could see in the dark night.

Marie seemed preoccupied as she stared at the place. She had told me as we made the ride east that she had not heard from Scully since yesterday. She had driven by here several times but never saw any sign of him. She had a key but was afraid to go in by herself. She wanted me to check things out for her.

I sized the place up, then took the key from Marie and crossed the overgrown front lawn to the door. But before I was even halfway there something caught my eye.

Scully's pickup was parked in the driveway, on the other side of the cottage. I hadn't seen it from Marie's car. The truck's door was open, its interior light on and still burning brightly. I went around to the driveway and saw someone lying half in and half out of the truck door. Their legs were still in the cab and their torso was on the pavement. I looked back at Marie quickly, then rushed to the truck.

I saw the blood first, a pool of it. It was still spreading. Then I saw Scully's face. He was on his back. He had been beaten. His eyes were opened wide. He looked both weary and surprised. I could see two bullet holes in his head.

There was no point in taking his pulse. I knelt, though, and looked closely at him. Some of the cuts on his face looked as if they had begun to heal while others looked fresh. I thought about what Jean-Marc had said about negotiating with someone who could bring him to Marie. This, trying to beat it out of Scully, was clearly what he had meant. Scully was probably taking his licks while Bishop, Long, and I were having our chat on Bishop's back patio.

I looked at the blood and knew by the way it was still spreading that Scully's murder had occurred not long ago, maybe even just minutes. I knew, too, not to stand around there and try to make sense of all this. Scully was dead and I would tell Augie that and it would be done. With that clear in my mind, I stood fast and turned to leave.

But then something on the pavement caught my eye and I stopped dead.

It was almost directly below me, almost underfoot. I looked down at it for a long time, stunned, then finally moved in closer for a better look.

There were two bullet casings on the pavement. I knew just by looking at them that they were .32 caliber bullets. I studied both of them closely, then searched for more. But there were only the two. I hung there and thought about a lot of things before I finally picked them up with my shirt like a glove and stuffed them into my back pocket. Then I stood and turned again to leave.

This time I was stopped dead by the sight of Marie Bishop. She was standing just behind me, looking past me to the truck.

I knew that from where she was standing she couldn't see Scully's face. She took a few uncertain steps toward the truck, but I went to her quickly and stopped her. She looked at me without expression and said, "Is that him?"

"Yeah."

"Is he dead?"

"Yeah, Marie. He's dead."

She nodded at that but said nothing.

There wasn't time for any of this. We had to get out of there, fast. The killer could still be around.

"It's not safe for us here," I told her.

She looked at Scully's body, then back up at me.

"We need to go somewhere safe, Marie. Somewhere no one will find us."

"Okay" was all she said.

I led her across the lawn and back to her car. I drove, and it wasn't till we had pulled away and were heading back toward the village that I asked her where we were going.

She looked straight ahead, through the windshield. In a flat voice she gave me a Montauk address and asked me if I knew where that was.

"Yeah. But what's there?"

"My place. We'll be safe there."

Her apartment was a large studio above a pharmacy in the heart of Montauk Village. Her bed was on the far side of the room and stood between two floor-to-ceiling windows that overlooked Main Street. We entered and she went straight to her bed and sat on the side of it with her feet touching the bare wood floor. She looked out one of the windows and remained perfectly still, her hands folded together in her lap. She breathed gently, her back straight and shoulders back.

I stood by the door and watched her for a while, then eventually looked around the apartment. There was her bed and a bureau, a television, a small couch, and a steamer trunk. That was it, that was all she owned. The rest of the apartment was open space. There was a small walk-in kitchen and a bathroom by the door. The ceilings were high, and there were two ceiling fans mounted overhead, one over the bed, the other not far from where I was still standing by the door. Marie hadn't turned on any lights; she didn't need to. The red and blue neon glow of the pharmacy sign outside her windows filled the room with a kind of perpetual twilight.

Eventually I took a few steps toward Marie. She gave no indication as I approached her that she was aware of me. I didn't want to disturb her, but there were things that we needed to talk about. I was part of her business now. I needed to know some things, and time was ticking away.

I reached the foot of the bed and watched her for a minute, then looked past her bed to the nightstand on the other side of it. There was a clock on it, a half-filled glass of water, and a prescription bottle.

I looked back at her and tried to think of what to say. Despite my growing sense of urgency, I wasn't sure where to start. In the end it was she who spoke first.

Her voice was monotone, grave. She didn't take her eyes from the view outside her window as she spoke to me.

"You said it wasn't safe for us back there. Why?"

"I saw things I didn't like."

"What did you see?"

"Two .32 caliber bullet casings. The gun that killed Tim Carter was a .32. Your brother supposedly gave that gun to me as a show of good faith."

"But now you think otherwise."

"He gave me the gun this morning. Scully had been killed very recently."

"What did they do to him?" she said flatly.

I didn't answer.

"What did they do to him?" she repeated.

I told her that from what I could tell he had been shot twice in the head.

"Was he beat up?"

"Yeah," I said. "Yeah."

"Bad?"

I shrugged. "Yeah."

"Why would they do that?"

"If whoever did this worked for your brother, they

probably were trying to get him to tell them where you could be found."

"If he had told them, they would have been here by now, wouldn't they?"

"Probably, yeah."

"So that must mean he didn't tell them."

"Maybe. Yeah."

Marie nodded then in a way that made me think that she was convincing herself of something.

"So he died protecting me," she stated.

"I guess, yeah."

"It's important that we know that. It's important that we remember that. We're all that's left to remember these kinds of things. You and I are all that's left. It's important to keep these things straight, don't you agree?"

"I suppose." I took a step toward the corner of the bed and said to her, "What's going on, Marie? Why is Jean-Marc looking for you? Why is he killing everyone close to you?"

"Do I look anything like the girl you remember, Mac?"

I shrugged. "Maybe, a little. What does this have to do—"

"They had to rebuild my jaw. That was one surgery. Then later they had to rebuild my nose and one of my cheekbones. I look at pictures of me as a little girl and I don't see much of her in me now. It's like that little girl never grew up to be who she was supposed to be. It's funny, but I go out of my way to avoid my own reflection. I don't see me, just what I've become. I know that probably sounds crazy to you. It sounds crazy to me."

I said nothing to that.

"Anyway, my brother tells everyone it was my vanity, that that was why I had plastic surgery."

"But it wasn't."

"He doesn't like it when he's unable to control me. He never has."

"He hit you."

"For starters."

"Your father let this happen?"

"My father didn't know."

"How could he not?"

"He was away on business half the time. And, anyway, my brother knows how to keep his secrets."

"Why didn't you go to the cops?"

Marie laughed. "I can't believe of all people you're asking me that."

"Why didn't you leave?"

"Why didn't you? The things your adoptive father did to you. The way he treated you. You were more hired help than family. He was so cruel to you. You used to come over my house in tears. Why didn't you just leave, Mac?"

I said nothing. I could barely look at her.

"Most of the time I was afraid," Marie continued. "When I stopped finally being afraid and tried to leave, he convinced our father that I wasn't well and had me locked up in a hospital in Westchester. And if he finds me now, that's where I'll be headed."

"He can't just have you locked up. It's not like that anymore."

"He can't, but his doctors can. The thing of it is, he really thinks I'm crazy. He always has. Crazy and weak. He hates weak. He used to tease me when we were kids. He used to say that the dog that bit me had poisoned me and that's why I was crazy. To him anyone who doesn't do exactly what he tells them to do is crazy."

"He has doctors that will lie for him?"

"Of course. Christ, he tells doctors what to prescribe me, what drugs he thinks I need. He has a copy of the *PDR* by his bed. You should see the thing. It's had the shit read out of it. The doctors cut him all the scripts he tells them to."

"And your father knew of none of this?"

"My father has been ill for a long time. My brother runs everything. Everyone does what he says."

"Not everyone."

"I'm not going back to either place, Mac, that's all there is to it. I'm not going back to that house, and I'm not going back to that hospital. I just want to be left alone. I just want to live my life. You can understand that, can't you?"

"Yeah," I said. "I can."

"I have no one to help me now. I'm not very good on my own."

"What's behind all this, Marie?"

"What do you mean?"

"There's more you're not telling me. There's more going on than what I'm being told."

"Can't you just help, no questions asked?"

"I can't make any more bad deals on good faith. You're not telling me everything. Your brother is having people killed. The Chief got an animal out of jail and put him on your trail. I need to know what's going on."

"I can't tell you."

"Then I can't help you."

"Everyone I've told the truth to is dead. Carter, Scully, everyone. You're better off not knowing."

"Your brother is setting me up, Marie. One way or the other, my life is over. Telling me the truth can't make things any worse."

"I can't talk about it. Please. I can't."

"I can't help you then."

"Please, Mac."

"Why does your brother want to lock you up?"

"Please. I can't."

"You know something, is that it? You know something that could ruin him. You know something and he wants to keep you silent."

"You don't understand, Mac."

"Then make me understand."

"He doesn't think that what he did was wrong. He

doesn't think anything he could do is wrong. He's the crazy one. He's the sociopath. He can't see the wrong in anything he does. Anything."

"What did he do, Marie?"

"It was a long time ago."

"What did he do?"

"He used our father against me, to keep me quiet. He knew I would never tell anyone out of fear of it getting back to our father. I would never tell anyone what he did because I was too ashamed and I couldn't bear the thought of our father knowing about it, of him thinking of me in that way. So I kept it all in. I kept his secret. And when our father got sick and the doctors said it wouldn't be long, Jean-Marc realized that there would be nothing holding me back once he was dead. Jean-Marc knew all hell would break loose. I knew enough to get him sent to prison for a long time. He got nervous, he started acting strange. He took over everything. He took over the family business, he had the doctors confine my father and wouldn't allow any visitors. My father was helpless, and he saw for the first time the monster he had created. He wanted my brother to be a leader, a captain of industry. You saw how he treated my brother, you remember. It was just short of brainwashing. Anyway, that's when my father told me it wasn't safe, that my brother was dangerous. My father was right, but not for the reasons he thought. He thought my brother might have me killed so he wouldn't have to share the money. He didn't know the real reason why I was in danger."

"So you went into hiding."

"It was the only thing I could do. I cut all ties. I started going by all kinds of different names. I didn't want anyone to know who I was. After a while I think I started to forget what my real name was. I started to recognize my own reflection less and less."

"What was it that your brother did, Marie?

She shrugged, then stared at me for a long time before she finally spoke. I could hear the buzz of the neon lights beyond her windows.

"I was fifteen. I was pretty mixed up. I was running around with a thirty-four-year-old man, a bartender from a club in Westhampton Beach I used to get into with a fake ID. Of course nobody in my family knew about it. You learn to keep secrets well in that house. He was my boyfriend, or so I thought. He used to sneak onto our property at night and I'd meet him down by the water and let him do things to me. Then one night while he and I were together I realized that my brother was standing just a few feet from us. My boyfriend was on top of me, and all I remember was seeing my brother standing there, seeing the angry look on his face. Time just stopped. Then the next thing I knew was a sound. It came up so suddenly. It was the sound of a baseball bat crashing into my lover's skull. And it started time again. Just like that. My boyfriend slumped over on top of me and then just kind of rolled off me. My brother just kept hitting him. He hit him in the head maybe a dozen times. He just kept hitting him till he was dead, and then even after that. He kept hitting him till the bat cracked. And then he still kept on hitting. The sound was terrible. It was terrible. My brother was enraged, jealous. He dragged me back to the house by my hair and locked me up in my room. He wouldn't even let me get dressed. I was covered with dirt and blood. Our father was gone for the weekend, we were all alone. My brother nailed my door shut and then went away. Later on I saw him and another man down by the water. I knew who the other man was. He was an old family friend. I'd seen him around many times before. Together they wrapped the body in plastic and dumped it into a rowboat and went across the creek to the refuge. They had shovels with them, and flashlights. When they came back a few hours later it was just the two of them. They had buried the body somewhere in the refuge. They dropped the shovels in the water. Then the other man left and my brother stood alone in the backyard for a while, looking out over the water. Eventually he turned and looked up at me. After a few minutes he started toward the house. Then I heard him coming up the stairs. I could almost feel myself losing my mind, that's how scared I was. I could almost feel my sanity begin to slip."

She stopped there. I waited, then said, "What happened then?"

"He kept me prisoner in my room for three days. No food, no water, nothing. I had gotten dressed but was still covered in dirt and blood. Most of the time he was outside my door, threatening me, swearing me to secrecy, working on me. It was like the brainwashing my father had done to him. Sometimes he'd eat something and tell me all about it, what he was eating and what it was like. But he wouldn't ever give me any. Sometimes he'd pour water onto the floor so I could hear it, just to torment me. He hated me for being with someone else, he let me know that. He told me no one would ever touch me again. Finally he let me out before our father came home. He let me clean up, look pretty for Father. I was a wreck. I couldn't stop crying. I was exhausted. It was about a week after that that I was hospitalized. My father had no idea what was wrong with me. Jean-Marc visited me in the hospital two weeks after that. He tipped an orderly to give us privacy for an hour. I knew what he wanted."

I waited, saying nothing.

"He told me I couldn't say no. I believed him. He said he would tell Father what I was doing with men if I didn't let him do what he wanted."

"He raped you."

She shrugged. "That's where it started. I stayed in that hospital for close to a year. Jean-Marc visited every weekend. Every weekend he'd tip the same orderly to give us privacy."

"And when you got out of the hospital?"

"He'd come to my room at home during the night. When I went to Yale he came down from Harvard to visit me, at least a couple times a month. When I'd come home on vacations and in the summers he was there."

"You told Carter about all of this?"

"Tim was trying to use it to blackmail my brother. When I found out what he was up to, I left him. He was in over his head, it was only a matter of time before he turned up dead. I told him that."

"But he didn't listen."

"He wanted a big score. He never understood why I didn't want any of my father's money. He was a child. He said he'd put up with anything for half of a hundred and fifty million dollars. He said that with Jean-Marc in prison, all the money would be mine. There was nothing I could say to set him straight. He didn't know. He didn't know Jean-Marc."

"The man who helped your brother get rid of the body that night, who was he?"

"A family friend."

"I know that. But who was he?"

"Why do you want to know?"

"Just a hunch, that's all."

"What does your hunch tell you?"

"That maybe he was a cop."

"What else does it tell you?"

"That maybe his name was Miller."

"His name was Miller, yeah."

"The Chief," I said.

"He's chief now. He was just a cop then."

"And he helped your brother get rid of the body of a man your brother murdered in cold blood."

"Chief Miller was loyal to my father. My father helped him with his career. They met when you and I met, when that dog attacked us, when you came running to save me. Do you remember that?"

"Of course," I said.

"Chief Miller was the cop who shot the dog dead. He saved your life as you saved mine. You don't remember that, do you? You don't remember it was he who shot the dog."

"I didn't till now."

"I had them fix the scar on my leg, from where it bit me. You can still tell it's there, though. Sometimes I have dreams about that morning, vivid dreams. And I'll never forget the needles, those long needles they put in our stomachs because of the rabies. Do you have dreams about it?"

"Sometimes."

"I was scared that day. I didn't even know who you were, and there you were at my side. I'm as scared now as I was then. Maybe more. And here you are, beside me again. It's no accident, if you ask me."

"You should have told me who you were on the beach, Marie."

"I didn't know then if I could trust you. I didn't

know what the years had done to you, what kind of man that boy who had run to save me had become."

"None of us are who we expected to be when we were ten," I said. "Your brother isn't going to stop looking for you, Marie. You know that."

"I know."

"He hired a man to find you. He hired him through the Chief, who's obviously playing out his own agenda. It sounds to me like the Chief sent the man he sent on purpose, maybe to get rid of the lot of you."

"His loyalty was to my father. He hates Jean-Marc. He knows that with my father gone, there's no reason for me not to come forward with what I know."

"The Chief came to me and asked me to find you. I think that shows just how desperate he is right now."

"With my father gone, he'd have to take orders from my brother. I don't think he wants that."

"But would he kill you?"

"You better than anyone, Mac, should know that when it comes down to it, we're all pretty much capable of anything, if it means staying alive."

"So what are you capable of, Marie? What are you willing to do?"

"I used to have dreams about killing my brother, about stabbing him in the heart. I used to tell myself that it was a vision. I used to think it was going to come true someday."

I didn't say anything to that. Neither of us spoke for a while.

"Maybe it is time for me to go, Mac. Maybe it's time for me to leave the island."

"It would be dangerous for you to stay. This place is small."

"I grew up out here, that's the thing. It's home. I love this place. I'd rather not leave it if I can help it."

"He'll find you if you stay."

"So you think I should leave?"

"Yeah, I do."

"How soon?"

"As soon as possible."

"Scully took care of these kinds of things for me. I feel helpless without him."

"I'll help you get out. I'll help you now."

"Thanks, Mac. Thanks for everything."

"It's too late to leave tonight. We should rest. You don't want to be on any of the roads out here during the daytime. I guess that leaves tomorrow night then, after sundown. I'll ride with you as far as the expressway to make sure you get off the East End okay. From there on you shouldn't have any problems. Just follow the expressway to the bridge of your choice and you're off."

"How will you get back?"

"I'll hitch a ride home. Don't worry about me."

"Why are you so willing to risk your life for me? Are you in love with me or something?"

I smiled at that. So did she.

"Maybe I can save you the trouble I had to go through to get away from the people who raised me," I said.

"They were killed, weren't they? Your adoptive family."

"There was a boating accident. A fire. They went missing at sea."

"I remember that. I was at Yale. I remember your adoptive brother. Always getting into fights, you always bailing him out, running to his side. You two were inseparable."

"It was my job."

"You cared about him, though. I can tell."

"He was my brother."

"So what happened?"

I shrugged.

"You can't talk about it, can you? It's okay."

"There's nothing to talk about. It was a long time ago."

"And I bet you at times it feels like it was yesterday."

"Sometimes it feels like it's tomorrow. Sometimes it feels like tomorrow and I can't do a thing to stop it."

"I know that feeling."

"It's late. We should try to get some sleep."

"Okay, Mac."

We stayed dressed and lay side by side on her bed. The neon light outside made the room almost too bright to sleep in. I draped my forearm over my eyes, and that blocked much of the colored light. I could hear Marie breathing, I could feel her lying still beside me. We said nothing as time clicked away. I allowed myself to hope for a night of dreamless sleep, of unbroken unconsciousness. I allowed myself to hope, too, for a route out of town that didn't end badly for either of us.

Ten

At dawn I woke and stared at the ceiling above. I listened to the occasional car passing by below Marie's windows. My thoughts raced, and I could feel panic in my chest. I thought of Frank Gannon and the Chief. I thought of Jean-Marc Bishop and Searls. I thought of Tim Carter and Scully, of their violent deaths. There were still so many things I needed to know, so many ways that all this could fall in on me.

Eventually I got out of bed as carefully as I could and pulled on my boots. Marie was sound asleep. I slipped quietly out her apartment door. Then I crept down the stairs to the outer door and crossed the wide street. There was a sidewalk pay phone a few doors down and I went to it and inserted two quarters, then punched in Frank Gannon's pager number. I hung up and waited for him to call back. I wasn't really expecting him to call back. But I had to try.

It was a cool morning. The sky was clear, dark blue overhead but fainter along the horizon. There was a sharpness in the air that I could feel in my lungs. There were still a few stars to see in the lighter patch of sky just above the trees, pins of silver light that burned brightest in the minutes before they died.

Two minutes later the pay phone rang.

"Yeah."

"It's Mac."

"Where are you?"

"It doesn't matter."

"The prefix is Montauk. What are you doing there?"

"I don't have much time. You're a hard man to get hold of lately."

"I'm just cautious. A lot of big players on the field. Don't want to get crushed."

"So you put me out front to take the hits."

"What do you want, Mac?"

"I want some answers."

"What do you want to know?"

"I want you to tell me if anything happened in town last night."

"What do you mean?"

"That animal that jumped Augie, Searls, he was on the loose, in case you didn't know."

"I heard."

"But did you hear anything about the cops bringing him in last night?"

"No."

"Are you sure?"

"I would have heard about that. I understand through the grapevine that Bishop gave you a gun and a forensics report and a fairy-tale story and called it the Deal of the Century."

"You don't miss much, do you?"

"I'm not next door to Village Hall for nothing. It probably wasn't the smartest thing you've done."

"Just add it to the list."

"Sweep up your tracks and get out of there, Mac-Manus. I'll put some men on this, we'll figure out what's going on. I can protect you."

"Thanks, but no thanks, Frank. I need you to find out if Searls is still running wild. There's a dead body in Montauk that tells me he still is. If Searls hasn't been brought in yet, I want you to warn Augie. I want you to do what you can for him and Tina. This isn't a favor to me. Do you understand? Augie's your friend and you're going to make sure nothing happens to him. If something does I'm going to hold you responsible. Are we clear?"

"You sound to me like a man about to leave town."

"She wants to get free of him. I'm going to make sure that she does."

"You found the Bishop girl."

"She found me."

"It's all the same to me. Where is she?"

"That's the bad news, Frank. I'm getting her out of here. I'm going to see her on her way."

"We had a deal."

"Sue me. I don't care about the Chief anymore. I don't care about anything. I'm going to make sure she gets away once and for all."

"You don't want to cross Bishop, MacManus. Fucking me over is one thing, but fucking him is something else."

"I can't get much deeper than I already am, Frank. And, anyway, what's he going to do? Kill me twice?"

"Once should do it, I would think."

"Just take care of Augie. Understand me?"

"Yeah."

I hung up then. I looked around once, then headed back across the empty street toward Marie's apartment.

She was still asleep when I entered. I stretched out on her mattress without waking her. I lay there a while, thinking, and eventually fell into a shallow, turbulent sleep.

We were lying on our sides, facing each other, when we awoke together around noon. We looked at each other for a while without moving, then got up out of bed to begin her last day on the East End.

·　　·　　·

I was tired and moved slowly for the first hour after getting up. My back and joints were stiff, and I was groggy. Marie, as far as I knew, had slept straight through the night. But she didn't seem any better off than I. I watched her as she sat up in her bed and tilted two pills from the prescription bottle on the table into her palm. Then she tossed them into the back of her mouth and downed a long sip from the glass of water that sat next to the bottle.

Her back was to me as she did this. But she didn't seem to me to be making any effort to hide what it was she was doing. When she was done she replaced the prescription bottle and glass on the table, then turned her head and looked back over her shoulder at me for a moment before getting up and walking into the bathroom.

I heard shower water running and wrote her a note on the back of a paper towel telling her that I had gone to get us something to eat. Then I went downstairs to the street. I found a small market at the end of her block and bought fresh bagels and apples and prepackaged slices of watermelon. It was getting warm out, but the air was still pleasant. There was a sea breeze that brushed my skin like a kind hand.

Back upstairs, I set out the food while Marie dressed in the bathroom. She came out in jeans and a mannish shirt with her hair wet and uncombed. She looked younger that way. We sat on the foot of her unmade bed and ate off paper plates but didn't really talk. Her feet were bare and touched the wood floor. I stared at her small toes for a time. There was enough for both of us to think about, so that was what we did, we ate and thought and let each other be.

After breakfast Marie stood and picked up our plates. I caught then a glimpse of three long scars running up her left wrist, from the joint to midforearm. She carried the plates into the kitchen. I watched her as she went but said nothing. I wanted to say something to her about the scars, but there was just nothing to say, nothing anyway that wouldn't sound like some half-assed confession. We knew enough about each other already.

Later on Marie packed while I stood by her window and watched the traffic below. I looked for Searls, for Jean-Marc, for the Montauk police. The village was busy now. The angle of the sun cast a square of light against the wall beside me. I positioned myself so that I could stay clear of it and still manage to see a good part of what was going on outside. I felt drowsy, and my eyes ached. But I had nothing else to do but stand there and play lookout.

Marie put together a single suitcase in a half hour and set it by the door. That was it, she was ready to go. All we had to do was wait till sundown and make our run for Manorville and the Long Island Expressway. Before that the only roads for the most part were Sunrise and Montauk highways, two two-lane roads that cut through the heart of every village east of Southampton. It was on those roads that we were in the most danger of being caught.

At times that day there was no motion in the apartment at all, and no sound. That was all out there, beyond the open windows, in the air and on the street below. Sometimes as I stood there and looked out I felt that Marie and I were missing something, though I wasn't sure really what. But out of reflex I was quick to tell myself that it didn't matter. We were both lucky to be alive, she and I, if unlucky to have lived. All that mattered was peace, but, really, silence and stillness were close enough.

A little before six I went back downstairs to buy us dinner. It would blow my budget, but I didn't care. Marie would need all the money she had with her to start over, and I could miss a meal or two later on in the week for that.

I brought us back a pizza with feta cheese, sliced tomato, and black olives. We ate while sitting crosslegged on her floor, side by side, with our backs to a wall. I did my best not to see the scars on her wrist a second time. When we were done there were two slices left over. We wrapped them in aluminum foil to save for her to eat on the road later tonight, or for breakfast tomorrow. It was half-past six now, and you could feel night coming, you could see it influencing the sky, you could smell it in the air that flowed in over the low windowsills.

By eight the sky began to change more dramatically, and the same points of white light that had been the last to die this morning were the first to be reborn. I watched them grow sharper and sharper on the horizon, in a sky that seemed to drain of color by the minute.

It was twilight when I realized that Marie was standing at the window on the other side of her bed. She stood there watching the cooling sky for a while. I could tell that she was getting ready to say something. I looked at her and waited. Darkness was beginning to fill the corners of her apartment, shadows spreading out around us. When she spoke, the sound of her voice was like something new in an old world. It compelled me deeply. She stared out her window and I watched her and listened. There weren't many cars on the street below, so there were periods of time when all there was to hear was her voice, hoarse still but getting better.

"Maybe I should have done this a long time ago," she said. "Maybe I should have left this place far behind me and not clung onto it as desperately as I have. Maybe then things would have been different." She thought about something carefully. "My brother can have everything, the house, the money, I don't care about any of that. All I want is a job and a halfway decent apartment to be left alone in. I just want to find other people like me and find comfort in their presence."

I looked out the window at the darkening sky. I said nothing. Marie was still by the other window.

"How did you do it, Mac?"

"Do what?"

"How did you get away from your family?"

"You mean the family who adopted me?"

"Yeah."

"Why are you asking me that?"

"You said you wanted to save me from having to go through what you went through to get free. I was wondering what that was."

"It doesn't matter."

"Tell me anyway."

"I don't talk about it."

"You've never told anyone?"

"No."

"I'd like to know anyway. I want what you have now. I don't want any more than that. I want to do what you did. I want to turn my back on it all and just live my life. I want to know what you went through. I want to know if I could do no less than what you did."

"It's not something to be proud of, what I did."

"I don't care about that. I've told you mine. Now you have to tell me yours."

"Are we playing doctor here, Marie?"

"In a way, I guess, yeah. I want you to tell me what you did to get free. Please. I need to know."

"I've told you. We were sailing, my adoptive parents and brother. There was a fire."

"That's what happened. Now tell me what you did."

"That was the thing. I didn't do anything."

"What do you mean?"

"After the fire there was an explosion. They went overboard, his mother and father went overboard, and I did nothing."

"What do you mean?"

"I did nothing."

"What could you have done?"

"I could have thrown them a line. I could have sent over the emergency raft. I could have cut loose the dingy. I could have sent out an SOS, I could have called the Coast Guard. Their boat had every piece of radio equipment and safety gear there was. I knew what to do in an emergency. I just chose not to do it."

"You just left them in the water?"

"We were far out, you could barely see land. It was night. The boat was moving, we were under full sail. We were really moving. Even on fire it was moving, even after the explosion we were still moving. It didn't take much. It took just seconds, really. I did nothing, and I did it just long enough to where it was too late to do anything for them."

Marie said nothing, just looked out the window.

"I told you, it isn't something I'm all that proud of. There's a reason why I don't talk about it. I don't even let myself think about it."

"You were a kid."

"I was twenty. Old enough to know what I was doing."

"You wanted to get free of them. Remember, I knew them, I knew how they treated you. I knew the shit you had to put up with, the cruelty. My father knew it, even Jean-Marc knew it. You deserved better. You wanted a life of your own. They weren't about to let you have that. I can understand what you did."

"It doesn't make it right."

"Maybe not. But it was what you had to do. I remember when we were kids how you used to not want to go home. You used to linger in our yard, even after Jean-Marc and I went in, after our father called us in. You used to hang out in an opening in one of our hedges. I used to get ready for bed and then go to the window in the hall and see you there. You know, my father once offered to take you in. He invited your adoptive father over and told him that he wanted you to stay with us. Did you know that?"

"No."

"He turned my father down flat, said he had made a promise to your real father. But my father knew that wasn't true. He knew you were being mistreated. But there was nothing he could do, except make you feel welcome when you were at our house."

I felt a real sense of regret at hearing that. I couldn't help but wonder how many lives would be different right now had I come to their house to live all those years ago.

"And what about your brother?" Marie asked.

"The boat took on water and turned over. That put out the fire. We climbed up on it as far as we could and just waited. He just kept looking at me, like he knew what I did, like he knew the split-second decision I had made. It was late in the summer. The water and the night air were very cold. I passed out a lot. Each time I came to he was there, on the turned-over hull. Then one time I woke up and it was daylight and he was gone. I could see land then. We had drifted in. Eventually the Coast Guard came and picked me up."

"What did you do after that?"

"What do you mean?"

"You were free finally. What did you do?"

"I finished school. I lived with a woman for a while. My real father had been a cop and so I applied to the academy. I got in but didn't go."

"Why not?"

"I didn't have it in me."

Marie nodded at that and smiled, but I didn't ask her what the smile was for. Eventually she turned her head and looked at me. I kept my eyes fixed on Main Street.

"It must be hard for you to say no to people, Mac," she said. "It must be hard for you to see a person floundering and not want to jump in and help them. It must be hard for you to turn people away."

I said nothing to that. Several cars passed by below,

one right after the other. My thoughts were on our drive out of town. It was all I wanted to know about.

"Why don't you come with me, Mac?" she said then. "Maybe it's time for you to leave this place, too. Why don't you come away with me? My father I think would have been happy to know that we found each other again. He would have liked the idea of us looking after each other."

I didn't say anything to that.

"You're afraid, aren't you?" she said. "Just like me. You're afraid of leaving. This place is all you've ever known."

"It's not that."

"Then what is it?"

"A promise to a friend. If Searls is loose, I'll want to stick around and keep it."

"And if you didn't have a promise to keep?"

I didn't answer.

"Mac?"

I looked at her then.

"In a heartbeat," I said.

It wasn't long after that that the pharmacy sign outside the windows blinked on, and a blue and red light rushed over us and chased much of the dark from the corners. It was close to night now, near checkout time. We waited till nine, till dark had settled in completely. Then we got ready to leave her apartment. But before we did she went to her closet, opened it, and pulled something out. She turned and showed it to me. I recognized it at once. It was a denim jacket, like the one I used to wear, like the one I had put over Vogler all those months ago.

"Scully wanted me to give this to you." She handed it to me. I looked it over. There wasn't a spot of blood on it, but the third button from the top was missing. It was my jacket.

"What?"

"He told me the other day."

"How did he get this?"

"It was left on the street when they took Vogler's body away."

"What?"

"He said you didn't recognize him at the cottage. He was with Vogler when Vogler got shot. They were arguing. This was before Scully got all paranoid about being seen, before he shaved off all his beautiful hair, thinking people wouldn't recognize him so easily, thinking he looked meaner. He took the jacket and had it cleaned. He was a bit of a scavenger. He thought, after the cottage, that you should have it back. He thought it would be a gesture of good faith on our part. He wasn't a bad person, you know, despite what he did for a living. He was impressed by the fact that you tried to save Vogler. So was I. That's why I came to you that night."

"Wait a minute. Back up. You knew Vogler?"

"He was my boyfriend, before Carter. My brother paid him to stay away from me. He took the money and handed it all over to me. I didn't know where it came from at first. Anyway, that's why my brother had him killed, because he went back on their agreement."

"I saw that," I said. "My friend and I. We were there."

"I know. What my brother didn't know was that my father had already hired a private detective to rough Vogler up. The man he hired sent you. Without his knowing it, my father provided witnesses to a murder his own son arranged and paid for. That was when my brother decided to take control of things away from our father. That's when the shit really started to happen."

"Your brother was behind Vogler's murder?"

"Yeah."

"Who were the men he hired to kill Vogler?"

"I don't know their names. One disappeared afterward. He was beaten up pretty badly. I guess that was your doing? The other one has worked for my brother for years. He went away for a while but came back."

"What did he look like?"

"He was an ugly, pocked-face man, stubby. He used to be a boxer or something. I saw him a few times with my brother. He did bodyguard work when my brother traveled."

"Searls," I said.

"Like I said, I don't know their names."

"Wait a minute, you're saying your brother used this man, this ugly boxer with the scars on his face, a lot?"

"If it's the same man, yeah."

"Your brother told me different."

"What did he tell you?"

"He told me he asked the Chief for a man to find you, and the Chief sent Searls over. He made it sound like he'd never seen him before."

"Why would he say that?"

"Your enemy is my enemy," I muttered.

"What?"

"He's playing me and the Chief against each other."

"I don't understand."

"If Searls killed Vogler, then he's the one who killed that cop. The Chief released a fucking cop killer and didn't even know it."

"What are you talking about?"

"It's been your brother's show from day one. He's playing everyone against everyone. He orchestrated Vogler's murder. He leaned on the Chief and got Searls released from jail, then sent Searls to kill Carter and find out from Scully where you were hiding."

"You act like you don't know who my brother is, Mac, like this is news to you."

"But I don't understand something. How did Searls end up working for Scully?"

"What are you talking about?"

"Searls and Scully ambushed a friend of mine last May, over some photos my friend took. They put him in the hospital for three months."

"Searls never worked for Scully."

"No. Searls was with Scully when they broke into my friend's house. I saw him. It's what sent him to jail."

"I don't think so, Mac. Scully had help, yeah. But I've met them all. None of them looked like that man. None of them was named Searls."

"Then who was with Searls that night?" I said.

My thoughts raced then, in too many directions to follow. Images flew at me. I saw then in my mind the man wearing the baseball cap and hooded sweatshirt, the man who almost caught that second shell from Searls' shotgun, the man who bolted out of Augie's house when the shit hit.

That man wasn't the man we had been looking for. That man wasn't Scully. That man was someone else.

"Jesus Christ," I said.

Back at the phone booth, I dropped two quarters into the slot and punched in Augie's number. He answered on the second ring.

"Yeah."

"It's Mac."

"You okay?"

"It was Jean-Marc Bishop who sacked you."

"What?"

"The guy at your house last May wasn't Scully, it was Jean-Marc Bishop. The woman Frank sent me to find, Marie Bishop, Searls works for her brother. Searls was the one who killed Vogler. On Bishop's order. And the cop, too. We witnessed the hit, that's why they came after you."

"No, Mac, no. That was months later, remember?

Why on earth would they wait that long to come after me?"

"I don't know. It doesn't matter right now. All I know is Scully is dead and I'm pretty sure Searls killed him last night."

"Where are you?"

"Montauk. Did Frank call you?"

"Yeah."

"What did he have to say?"

"Searls was never picked up. He's not sure what happened, if the cops even tried. Apparently there's some shit going down over at the Village Hall, something to do with the Chief. Frank's temporarily out of the loop or something."

"Are you okay?"

"Frank put men outside my house. Two of them. They're just up the street, watching over me like I'm some old lady or something. But there's a bigger problem."

"What?"

"Tina's supposed to be with her girlfriend, Lizzie. But I just called there a little while ago and they said she and Lizzie took the car and went somewhere."

"Shit," I muttered. "Listen, call Eddie, have him swing by their house. Have him keep a lookout."

"I did that already."

"I'm heading back that way. I'll stop by my place and see if she's there. She might be waiting for me."

"I'd appreciate that, Mac. What's going on? You sound . . . funny."

"I'm just going to make a quick run somewhere. I'll be back in about two hours."

"What do you mean, a quick run?"

"Don't worry, I'm not going far. I'll come straight there when I'm done."

"Call me when you get to the Hansom House, though. Let me know if Tina's there."

"I will. I'll be there in forty-five minutes. I'll talk to you then."

"Hang on, there was something Frank wanted me to tell you in case you called."

"What?"

"He said the old man died today. Does that mean anything to you?"

I looked across the street and saw Marie waiting for me in her car. She was in the passenger seat, looking over a map. I noticed then that the black paint job looked new and cheap, too new and too cheap for the ten-year-old Saab.

I said, "Yeah, Aug. Yeah, it does."

"So do you want to fill me in?"

"It means all hell is about to break loose."

I said good-bye and hung up then. I walked back to Marie's Saab and got in behind the wheel. She folded the map and tossed it into her open glove compartment. I saw it land on top of a sheathed skin diver's knife. It covered the knife entirely. Then she swung the compartment door shut.

"Everything okay?" she said.

"We need to make a quick stop at my apartment."

"What's wrong, Mac? You look a little white."

I didn't know how else to do it, so I just came out and said, "I was just told on the phone. Your father died today. I'm sorry, Marie."

She considered that for a moment, staring at me blankly. Her eyes shifted thoughtfully; it was the only motion she made. I don't even think she breathed. Then she nodded once and turned her head and looked out the passenger door window. It was a little while after that that she said in her hoarse voice, "Get me out of here, Mac, while there's still time."

I shifted into gear and steered the Saab out onto the narrow two-lane road down which waited a darkness far greater than any night I have ever known.

I could see the Hansom House through the windshield of the Saab as we parked alongside the curb. I could see there was a light in my windows up on the third floor. I knew then that Tina was there, waiting for me. I undid my seat belt and looked over at Marie.

She seemed more preoccupied now than anything else, calm but not at all serene. There was something beneath her flat surface, I knew that. We hadn't spoken once during the entire drive in from Montauk.

"You okay?" I said.

Her eyes were fixed straight ahead, but not, I thought, on anything in particular. She nodded.

"I'm sorry about your father."

She shrugged, almost indifferently. "I said my good-bye to him weeks ago. I mourned him then, too. Let's just get out of here. Let's just go, okay?"

"I won't be long. If anything should happen to me, if someone starts toward the car, just drive away, okay? I won't let them follow, I promise that."

She nodded. I grabbed my denim jacket and got out. I followed the path to the front door and climbed the first flight, then the second. Then I walked down the dark hallway to my door. I inserted my key into the lock and turned the knob. I swung the door in and entered, closing the door behind me. I took a step into the living room and tossed the jacket onto my couch. I called Tina's name.

Then something told me to look to my left. I did, looking toward my bedroom. There she was, standing in the doorway. She was looking at me but in a strange way. I'd never seen this look on her face before. I stared at her for a moment, uncertain what to say. But by the time I realized what was going on, it was already too late.

He stepped out of the kitchen, slowly. I turned to my right then and saw him, saw his ugly, beaten face, his pockmarks and crooked nose. Then I heard a man's voice behind me. I turned toward it. Tina had moved out of the bedroom doorway and was standing in the living room now. The other one was beside, close to her, holding her by the arm.

"It looks like you like them kind of young, Mac," Jean-Marc said.

I wasn't at all happy to see him standing so close to Tina. I wanted him away from her, far away. I wanted it right now.

"Are you okay?" I asked her.

She nodded once, fast. She was frightened but looked unharmed. My heart grabbed at that like it was some kind of hope. She glanced from me toward Searls, then back to me. A look of confusion and alarm merged on her face.

"What do you want?" I said to Bishop.

"It's easy, MacManus. I want my sister."

"I have no idea where she is."

Jean-Marc nodded, then sighed as if approaching a tedious task and removed a long-barreled automatic from under his shirt. It was identical to the gun he and Long had given me. He grabbed Tina, pulled her even closer, and pressed the muzzle of the gun into her neck. He had cotton work gloves on, gardener gloves.

Tina winced at the sight of the gun and tightened suddenly, drawing a sharp breath. Her own reaction seemed to startle her as much as her captor's aggression. She rose up on her toes, as if to get away from the gun. She was unable to speak, her gray eyes wild and unfocused.

"It can be easy or it can be hard, Mac. It's all up to you."

"She's not a part of this," I said.

"Fine, hard it is," Jean-Marc said. He nodded toward Searls then. Searls moved in beside me fast and slapped a handcuff around my right wrist. There was nothing I could do. Then he attached the other cuff to his own left wrist. I heard the mechanism inside the cuff click. My heart slumped.

With his right hand Searls tossed a small pair of keys to Bishop, who snatched them out of the air and stuffed them into his jeans pocket. Then Bishop pulled Tina closer to him still, pressing the muzzle even deeper into her neck. She rose even higher up on her toes. I knew now she was trying to escape the pain the metal jamming into her thin neck caused.

Searls went straight for my Spyderco knife. He removed it from my pocket. As he did this his face entered my line of vision. I focused on it. I saw his slit eyes and pockmarked skin and scars. I could feel his breath, I could smell him. He smiled at me, his face turning even uglier. A tooth was missing.

"Twenty-five years of boxing," he hissed, "and I never got a tooth knocked out." He pointed to the empty space where one had once been. "This was you, last year. Remember?" He held my eyes for a moment, then leaned back and slid my knife into his own pocket. "You and me are going to have some fun, boy," he said. He tugged on the handcuff for emphasis. "You belong to me now. We're engaged."

I ignored that, or wanted to, and once Searls was

clear of my line of vision I looked again at Bishop and Tina. The sight of Jean-Marc's hand tight around Tina's upper arm pissed me off more than anything else. I did all I could to hide that from him.

"I don't have time to take the scenic route, Mac," Jean-Marc said. "As much as your friend would like the opportunity to persuade you to tell me what I want to know, I've got better things to do. I had a tap put on your friend's phone, the one you called from Montauk a little under an hour ago. That's how we knew to come here. Your other friend, the paranoid P.I. you work for, he uses the same pay phone on the corner of Main Street and Cameron every time he wants to make one of his secret calls, so that was easy enough. I heard your conversation with him this morning, I know you were with my sister, and I know she's with you now. I know exactly what you're up to. But it's not going to happen, do you understand me? I don't want it to happen, so it's not going to happen."

"You're too late, Bishop. She's already gone. I put her on a train a half hour ago. If you hurry maybe you and golden boy here can catch her at one of the twenty or so stops between here and New York."

"I don't believe you."

"Good, then while you're wasting time here, she gets farther and farther away."

"Just tell me where my sister is, Mac."

"She's waiting for me somewhere safe. You think I'm

stupid enough to bring her back here? Let the girl go and we'll talk."

"I don't like to be fucked with."

"I know what you like, Bishop."

"She's an unwell woman, MacManus. She talks, she makes thing up. You'd do well for yourself not to pay any attention to what she says."

"It's kind of hard not to."

"It's a simple dilemma before you, Mac. Who's worth more to you?"

He pressed the muzzle deeper into Tina's neck. She flinched and stiffened.

"My sister's a slut, Mac. She sleeps with men because she thinks they can help her. She goes to men and sleeps with them and tricks them into protecting her. It's the only skill she has. She lives off their money. She can't keep a job. She steals food, things from people's houses, people she knows. But she fools men into caring for her. She did it to Vogler. She did it to Scully. Fuck, she even tried it with you."

"You don't know what you're talking about, Bishop."

"So who's worth more to you? My slut sister or your little girlfriend here?"

"Why did you and Searls sack Augie last May?"

"That was that friend of my sister's idea."

"Which friend?"

"The scumbag drug dealer. Scully. We knew he knew my sister. We knew he was either hiding her or knew who was hiding her. We leaned on him and he gave us your friend's name, said he knew where she was. It wasn't till just before you came in that we figured out who he was, that we had been lied to."

"Why would Scully set Augie up like that?"

"The night before, your friend took pictures Scully didn't want taken. It was his way of getting us to do his dirty work for him."

"Why'd you tear the place apart then, like you were looking for something?"

"Searls here laid out your buddy with one punch before we had a chance to ask him where my sister was. I tore up the place looking for anything I could find. Searls stomped on your friend for a while for the exercise."

I glanced at Searls. His eyes were fixed on me. My heart was pounding.

"I know what you and the Chief did," I said. "I know everything. I've told Frank Gannon. Killing your sister or me won't help keep your secret."

"You're a liar, Mac. Remember, I heard your conversation with Gannon. You told him no such thing. Anyway, she's not a well woman. Don't believe everything she says."

"She's gone, Jean-Marc. Just face it. You lost. She's gone."

"If that's so, then that's very bad news for you and your friend here."

"Just let the girl go, Jean-Marc."

"I'm only going to ask one more time, Mac. And them I'm going to turn things over to your new best friend here. Where is . . . ?"

I saw his attention shift then, quickly, to something behind me.

"Rose-Marie," he muttered.

I turned and there she was, in the dark hallway just outside my door. She was looking at her brother, her face blank, her fists hanging clenched at her sides. She stared at him with her chin up and her shoulders back. A second later she turned and headed down the hallway.

Bishop released Tina. He called out again, "Rose-Marie." I had forgotten her full name, the name her father had called her all those years ago. Jean-Marc bolted full stride toward the door.

And then all hell broke loose.

I moved to intercept him, to check him into the wall as he ran past me. But Searls yanked on the cuffs, pulling me back. All I could do then was kick at Bishop's knee. I hit it, not hard, but enough to make him stumble and fall flat out on his face on my floor, enough to make him lose precious time, to further the lead Marie held. He pulled himself up quickly and scrambled out the door, just as Searls' big right hand came swinging down like a ball on a chain at my head.

There wasn't time to fuck with him. I stepped in

close, slipping under the overhand punch, and grabbed his balls with my right hand, my cuffed hand, while at the same time I grabbed the side of his head like it was a basketball with my left. Both his hands went down to grab my right forearm and pull it from his groin, and with my left hand undisturbed I sunk my thumb into his right eye, crushing it against the back of the socket. I felt the eyeball give like a soft-boiled egg.

He screamed out, and his hands came up then. My right hand came up with them. He grabbed for my left arm, freeing my right hand and allowing me to grab the left side of his head and sink my thumb into his other eye. It popped fast. Still holding onto his head, I lifted my knee sharply and thrust it into his groin. He folded at the waist then, his knees bending. I held his head between my forearms, my hands behind his head, my fingers linked, and landed one solid knee shot to his face, for Augie.

He collapsed then and dropped to the floor. He was barely conscious and his eye sockets were bloody. His face was broken.

I looked for Tina then but she wasn't to be seen. I heard her then on the phone in my bedroom, calling the cops. All I could think of was Frank Gannon telling me that Long was a good man to have as a friend. I hoped to hell that he was right.

There was no way to get the cuffs off, so I pulled Searls with me. I yanked on him with two hands and went out the door and down the hall. The stairs I thought would be easy, but halfway down he slid ahead of me and I lost my balance and tumbled down to the bottom with him. I landed hard on the floor with Searls on top of me. I scrambled out from under him, aching in a dozen places from the fall, and pulled him to the next flight of stairs.

This time I ran to keep ahead of him and made it to the bottom without a problem. Once I reached the ground floor I tugged Searls through the door and down the steps into the open night.

Bishop and Marie were at the end of the pathway, on the sidewalk, beside Marie's car. I saw that the passenger door was open. I saw that they were standing face to face near it, Bishop's back to me. I dragged Searls as quickly as I could behind me and hurried down the path toward them. But it was slow going. I knew that Bishop had the gun, but there was nothing more I could do but try to reach him before he could turn around and take a shot at me. My heart was racing not from exertion but in that way it used to race on dark nights when I wanted to fight back against my cruel adoptive father but couldn't.

Bishop was holding the sleeve of Marie's shirt with his left hand. They were arguing. But I couldn't hear what it was they were saying. Their voices were hushed, but the argument was at a pitch emotionally. Bishop was doing most of the talking, and Marie was looking at him and shaking her head stubbornly, her chin held high in defiance.

I continued toward them, Bishop's back as my target. I towed Searls as fast as I could. But I wasn't even halfway between the Hansom House and the sidewalk when Marie tried to get away from her brother. He held her shirt tight and pulled her back to him violently. He almost yanked her off her feet.

I could hear them now. I could hear him and his words. He shook her like an angry parent might shake a bad child.

"You're going to do what I say," he barked. "You're going to do what I say when I say it, understand? You're coming back home tonight, no more hide-and-seek, and no more games. I've got too much to do to waste time worrying who you're telling lies to now. Do you understand me? Do you understand?"

Marie struggled to break free, but Bishop held tight. The sleeve of her shirt started to rip then from the shoulder seam.

And this was all it took to send everything into high gear. Marie began to flail wildly with her arms and kick furiously at her brother's shins. One of her hands must have grazed his eye, because he flinched and leaned back suddenly. She broke free of his grip and dove for the passenger door of her Saab. But Jean-Marc recovered and caught her as she was bending forward, reaching into the car for something. He grabbed her around the waist with both arms and pulled her back. But she squirmed and fought him and bit his hand. He screamed out and let go of her again. Then she dove once more into the passenger seat of her car. He shook his injured hand and stomped his foot in anger, then went after her again. He leaned into her car, blocking my view of what was going on.

I heard her scream then, and I did what I could to run with Searls in tow behind me. I couldn't see what was going on, just Jean-Marc's back. He was leaning into the car, struggling with his sister.

I looked back at Searls quickly and saw that George and a few of the regulars were standing in the doorway. They were watching in total disbelief as I dragged the semiconscious body of a fifty-year-old toward the man and the woman grappling inside a black Saab parked at the curb.

I looked back at Bishop. I took a breath to prepare myself for the sprint the rest of the way to the sidewalk. But it was a breath I don't remember exhaling. Marie screamed loudly then, and I heard the condensed crack of gun going off inside a tight enclosure. It startled me. I crouched low out of reflex and froze in my tracks.

Then I saw the smoke rising out of the Saab and turned back to George and the others in the doorway and said, "Call an ambulance." George took a few tentative steps backward before bolting into the Hansom House.

I looked back toward the Saab and saw that

Jean-Marc was standing outside the car, the gun in his right hand. I could not see his face, but by the way he stood he seemed to be staring in disbelief at what was inside.

I pulled myself together and with a sudden burst of strength yanked Searls the rest of the way down the pathway. Jean-Marc heard me coming and turned around sharply. He raised the gun with one hand and leveled it at me. His hand was shaking, and his arm seemed rubbery. But his narrow eyes remained sharp and quick.

"She pulled a knife on me," he said to me. He was almost aghast at the idea. "She tried to stab me in the chest."

"Give me the keys," I said to him.

"She just grabbed the knife," he said without apology. "She tried to fucking stab me."

"Give me the fucking keys, Bishop."

He didn't move at first. Then he looked past me at the people standing in the doorway and, almost self-consciously, lowered the gun slowly. He dug into his pocket and pulled out the keys Searls had given him and tossed them to me. I let them land on the ground by my feet, then picked them up and unlocked the cuff and slipped my wrist free from it. I hurried past him then to the Saab.

I could see her from the curb. She was slumped over in the seat, her hands limp in her lap. The diver's knife was on the floor by the pedals. I took a step off the curb and leaned in and saw that her head was turned sharply. There was a bullet hole just above her right temple and blood down that side of her body. Bishop hadn't been struggling against a knife at the time he shot his sister because he had needed his left hand to press against her face and expose the right side of her head to the gun in his right hand. I leaned in for a closer look and saw that there were abrasions on her right jaw, and finger impressions.

Even though I already knew she was dead I searched her neck for a pulse. I found nothing but a fading warmth beneath the very tips of my fingers.

I closed my eyes. It didn't matter anyway if they were opened or closed. Either way all I saw was black. I leaned back out and turned and stood face to face with Bishop. The gun was still in his hand, the muzzle pointed toward the ground. I knew who he was and what he had done. I knew, too, that he was another creation of the Chief's, that he was just like the Chief's son, lofted by his own arrogance, unreachable even by his own conscience. But the actual son was nothing compared to Bishop. Bishop was the real beast. He had gotten away with murder before. He had gotten away with worse. And he clearly had no doubts that he would get away with this.

He had the connections and the money to pull it off, regardless of the witnesses, regardless of the evidence. No one knew better than I what the rich got away with in this town. I knew what to expect in the way of justice for someone like Jean-Marc Bishop.

I heard sirens coming from several different directions

then. They were off in the distance still but closing fast. Bishop casually tossed the gun past me and into the Saab. It landed on the floor by Marie's feet. He peeled off his gloves then and dropped them to the pavement.

I could feel my old anger mounting again. It was always just beneath everything. I could feel my heart pumping its poison through me. I could feel it rushing in the place of my blood.

Jean-Marc looked toward the sirens and listened without showing a hint of fear or even concern. I realized then that there was nothing I could do beyond the only thing there was for me to do.

The sirens were almost upon us. But I could barely hear them over the buzzing in my ears. I could barely think of anything past the fact that I was here all over again, that I was back in the dark night with the beast, that there was only one course of action left for me to take.

"You don't look so good, Mac," Bishop said. "You look like someone just shot your only friend. Trust me, buddy, she wasn't your friend. She wasn't anyone's friend. And, between you and me, didn't you find her a little less than enthusiastic in the sack—"

I exploded toward him then, snapping a double jab into his face. Then I ducked low and rushed him. I wrapped my arms around his waist and lifted him off the ground, then slammed him hard onto the sidewalk, landing on top of him with all my weight. I mounted him fast, both my knees on the pavement, my thighs locked tight around his ribs. His arms came up to defend himself and I slipped a lock around his left arm and twisted abruptly, breaking his elbow clean. He cried out and I repositioned the lock and twisted again, tearing the soft tissue in his shoulder. Then I abandoned that arm and sank my weight onto his chest and let go with a flurry of sharp punches to his face. Almost all of them connected and cut divots out of his skin. I heard voices calling me from somewhere but I ignored them and hit Bishop till my hands hurt. Then I leaned in and held myself over him with my left arm and threw a flurry of right-arm elbow shots into his head.

My rage was rushing through me steadily, like electricity. I heard more voices then. I heard people rushing toward me. I heard keys jingling on belts, I heard shoes on pavement. I noticed blue lights in the trees. I realized then that I was talking, ranting. But I had no idea what I was saying. And anyway I didn't really want to know. I was still working Jean-Marc when I felt hands on me, grabbing me and trying to pull me off him. I shrugged them away. But then more hands grabbed at me and pulled me off him and to my feet.

I struggled against the hands holding me, shoving people away. I knocked someone to the ground. Then someone else. I knew by then that they were cops but I couldn't stop myself. My rage wasn't done. I tried to break free. I wanted to throw myself back on Bishop.

But too many hands had me. Still, I managed somehow to twist free of some and to pull those clinging to me with me as I labored to get closer to Bishop. I managed to maneuver the pack and put myself in range and stomped hard on Bishop's head with the sole of my work boot.

And that's when the first nightstick came down on my head. The pack pulled me away again, and something jammed me hard in the ribs. I grunted and jerked my head in rebuttal, catching someone flush in the nose with the side of my skull. I knew then that after all I had done I was right where I wasn't supposed to be, in the hands of the Chief's boys, giving them the reason they needed to take me out.

The nightsticks all came out then, jamming me, banging me. I took a few glancing shots across the head, shots that stung me more than they rocked me. Most of the blows came to my body and legs. I wanted to fight back but my strength was close to gone. My wits weren't all that far behind.

I was determined not to fall, not to go to the ground with all of them over me. But my determination was weakening with each shot that came in. I felt my knees bending under the weight of their blows.

I was close to going down when suddenly I heard someone ordering "Enough! That's enough!"

But still more shots came, and I dropped down to one knee. The sticks were working my shoulders and upper back and arms then. There was nothing I could do. The swarm was too tight. There was nowhere to go, and no way out.

I dropped my other knee, then fell under all the blows down to my hands and knees. I took shots to the ribs, jabs that shifted my internal organs. I heard the same voice order with authority and anger, "That's enough, that's enough," and it wasn't long after that that the flurry of blows finally ceased and the swarm was no longer so tight around me. I realized then that I was on grass, on the lawn in front of the Hansom House. I looked up, laboring to breathe, and saw Augie pushing at cops with his cane, shoving them away. They didn't seem to know what to make of him. They looked to the Chief for his reaction. Then I saw Frank Gannon behind Augie. He too had his hands on a cop, on his shoulders, pushing him back. Between the two of them was the Chief. He just stood there in the middle of it all and looked down at me.

I bunched together what I had and got to my knees. From there I was able to stand. It took a minute but I did it. I stood face to face with the Chief.

There were patrol cars on the street behind him. EMT personnel were tending to the living, to Bishop and Searls, and cops were looking at Marie's body inside the Saab.

There were five uniformed cops scattered around us. Their sticks were still in their hands, their chests heaving.

I looked at the Chief. I was wavering like a drunk. He looked at me for a while, then looked at Augie. I wondered then if they knew each other. There was something in the way they stared at each other, a kind of brief recognition, that led me to believe so. Then the Chief looked away from Augie, almost quickly, as if to underplay the recognition, and turned to where Bishop lay on the sidewalk, not far from the Saab. He looked at him without expression. I watched the man's profile till he turned back to me. His eyes were hard.

He said to me, "You give a guy enough rope, and he'll hang himself with it eventually."

I didn't say anything to that. The Chief nodded toward the Saab and said, "Did you see this?"

I nodded. He gestured behind me, toward the doorway of the Hansom House and the people in it.

"Did they?"

"You'll have to ask them."

The Chief stared at me for a moment, then turned and waved a uniformed cop over. The cop rushed to the Chief. "Get statements from all these people over there," the Chief said. He raised his voice and announced to the other uniforms around him, "This is by the books, gentlemen. Do we understand this? This is by the books. Dot and cross."

The Chief took a step toward me. We locked eyes. His jaw was clenched shut.

"Get out of here," he muttered.

I stared at him dumbly and didn't move.

"Get out of here." His anger broke through the tight clamp he held over it. When I still didn't move he looked over my shoulder and yelled to someone there, "Please take your boyfriend and get him out of here."

I looked back. There was Tina standing on the lawn several feet behind me. She looked frightened, unable to move. She looked from me to the Chief and back.

The Chief regained his temper and said in a calmer voice, "Please, little girl, get him out of here."

She walked to me then, her eyes blinking, her mouth opened slightly. She came up beside me and propped herself against me like a crutch, wrapping her left arm around my waist and draping my right arm around her neck.

But I still didn't make a move to leave. I looked at the Chief as if the sight of him might help me understand.

He stared at me for a moment, breathing short breaths through his nose. His face was set in a wince, as though the sight of me caused him discomfort.

"You did me a favor," he said flatly, "and now I'm doing you one. Nothing has changed between us, nothing at all. Now get out of here, MacManus. Get out of my sight while I still have my dinner in me. Get out of my sight before I have a chance to change my mind."

I still didn't move. The Chief turned to Augie then and said, "Get this son of a bitch out of here."

Augie started toward me. I saw Frank behind him, slipping through the crowd of cops and into the night.

He didn't stick around. I didn't really expect or want him to.

Tina tugged on my arm, then, gently, and whispered, "C'mon, Mac." I had nothing with which to fight her. Augie came up on the other side, and together the three of us turned away from the Chief and headed across the lawn toward the Hansom House.

My legs were shaky, and my knees buckled with nearly each of the few steps I took. Tina held her hip tight against mine, bracing me, holding me up. Augie's arms were like tree limbs. It felt like there was something sharp caught between the ribs on my right side. The force with which Tina and Augie held me sent the sharpness deep into my insides.

I had to stop for a second, to catch my breath and work the pain from my cloudy mind. While I rested I heard a car door close on the street behind us. I turned and saw Officer Long walking from a patrol car through the maze of cop cars on the scene. He met the Chief. The Chief spoke to him for a moment, then walked past him. Long just stood there and did nothing. Then the Chief got into his Crown Victoria and left.

I looked for Marie then but couldn't see her through all the cops around the Saab. All I could think of then was that I wished there was a way that she could know how sorry I was. I wished there was a way I could tell her that now. But of course there wasn't. Of course she could never know.

"Mac," Tina said. "Mac, c'mon. Let's get you inside."

I maintained my morbid watch, hoping for one last look of Marie. But Tina tugged at me gently and I turned and looked at her.

"You've got blood on your hands, Mac," she said. "We should get you inside and wash it off."

Epilogue

There was an early autumn that year, the August nights for the most part unseasonably cool. Some mornings it was even cold in my apartment. During my free time I did little more than watch over Elm Street from my three front windows. I watched as the days passed. Eventually I found work at the Mexican restaurant next door to the Hansom House, washing dishes and cleaning up after the cooks. Weekends I worked double shifts, from seven in the morning to well after midnight. The money wasn't any better than what I was used to, but it was all I was willing to do. I didn't leave my block at the end of Elm Street much. Augie said there was shit coming down in town and I didn't want to know about it. I needed to play it safe. When I wasn't working I was home, at my windows; when I wasn't at my windows I was trying to sleep. This was as much life as I was allowed. I barely saw Augie. He made it clear enough right off that he was there for me if I needed him and then left me alone. I appreciated that more than anything. Augie knew the hurt I was in. He had been there when his wife was killed in Colombia.

Tina stopped coming around. School started, but of course it was more than that. We all knew that if it weren't for Tina, if I hadn't had to stop off at the Hansom House that night to look for her, Marie Bishop would be alive and long gone right now. Tina was a kid and I tried not to blame her for Marie's death. There was no way she could have known, there was no way she could have seen that coming. I knew that if she had, she would have done things differently. But what happened had happened, and it was because of this that Tina stayed clear of me.

Eventually after a few weeks of my self-imposed house arrest I did venture off my block and into town. I hadn't planned on it. It was my only day off from the restaurant and I stepped outside one afternoon and sensed a stillness in the air I hadn't known in a long time, since last spring, since that night I went down looking for Augie. It seemed, this stillness, to be coming from the heart of town. This was the kind of East End day we year rounders lived for, that day when the tourists are finally, completely gone and the town, which had vibrated all summer long with crazy energy, goes suddenly quiet, like a ringing tuning fork pinched into silence between two fingers. I put on my denim jacket with the missing third button and walked the length of North Main into the village.

I looked south, in the direction of Village Hall, but I didn't head toward that part of town. I had learned one thing, and that was that quiet didn't necessarily mean safe.

I walked west instead, past the IGA, walking with no real direction. A breeze brushed my unshaven face. The town was as silent as it was empty. Maybe it was this sense that led me to continue west. After a few minutes I was at the cinema, where Long had picked me up and taken me to the Bishop home. At this point I was aware that I was heading somewhere specific, though I still wouldn't admit to myself just where that was. I kept on, moving at a steady pace, heading into the breeze, deeper into the stillness. It wasn't till I turned from Hill Street onto Halsey Neck Lane that I finally admitted to myself where it was I was going.

The Bishop estate, behind its hedges and gate, looked all closed up, the way so many houses did here at the end of the season. The gate had been chained but there was enough slack in it for me to squeeze through. I walked the gravel drive to the front door. I remembered being told by Marie's father so long ago how that door, so heavy and ornate, had been rescued from a ruined church in France and brought over when the house was built in the 1920s. I remembered passing through it as a boy freely, how it was never closed to me. I remembered how I had felt inside that house, running down its long halls or feeling the sun on my skin as I ate meals with that family in what their father called the open room. I remembered how the sun was made even more intense by the thick glass it shone through, glass that ran in long, narrow lead-lined panes from ceiling to floor.

I walked around to the back of the house. I felt safe within my connection to this place. I was no trespasser. I walked confidently and stepped out onto the patio and looked across Taylor Creek to the Dupont Sanctuary.

I walked down the lawn to its edge. I thought of winter coming, of ice. I thought of the body buried there, of the man Jean-Marc Bishop had killed out of perverse jealousy, of year upon year of frozen ground tightening its hold on those forgotten bones.

Eventually I had enough of ghosts and memories, I had enough of this silence, so I turned to head back up to the house. But I was stopped short by the sight of someone standing on the patio. I looked at him for a while, then started back up the lawn. We stood on the slate and faced each other. There was a good ten feet between us.

He was in civilian clothes, slacks and a sport shirt and jacket. The shirt and jacket looked wrinkled. His face was like mine, unshaven, his eyes bloodshot and restless. Looking at him was nearly as difficult as looking at my own reflection. He looked to me precisely like what he was, a man who had lost it all.

"Came to savor the victory, MacManus?" he said.

"What are you doing here, Long?"

"I'm here to get a few things."

"Isn't it kind of late in the game to be tying up loose ends? Didn't the FBI tear this place apart already?"

"It's not loose ends I'm after today. So I take it you've heard. News travels fast in your neck of the woods."

"Heard what?"

"I mean, that's why you came here, isn't it, to savor the victory?"

"What victory?"

"Someone cut Bishop in prison this morning. Someone cut his throat."

"What?"

"Apparently he pissed off the wrong person. Can't say I'm all that surprised."

"He's dead?"

"They don't get any deader. Saves the state the cost of a trial. From what I heard Bishop had a shitload of doctors lined up. He was planning on claiming he was the victim of lifelong abuse at the hands of his father. Scum to the end."

"Jesus," I said.

"You don't look happy, MacManus. I thought of all people you'd be thrilled to hear that particular piece of news. Well, you and the Chief, anyway."

"Are you sure about this?" I said. I heard an almost desperate greed in my voice.

"Yeah. And your other friend, the one whose eyes you took out, they connected him to the cop who got killed last spring. They traced the badge and gun he sold to another leg breaker in New Jersey back to him. Automatic death penalty if he gets convicted, which I'm pretty sure he will."

I glanced across the water toward the refuge then. When I looked back at Long, his eyes were on me.

"I doubt it's still there," he said. "The Chief has been doing some pretty elaborate dance moves these last few weeks. I doubt digging up that body and moving it wasn't one of them."

"How'd you know?"

"Bishop."

"He trusted you that much?"

"No, he just wanted me to want the Chief out. He knew how to get to people, Bishop did. He knew how to get a person to do what he wanted them to do. You know that maybe better than anyone. You knew him the longest."

"Did you know the gun was a trick, that Searls had the real one still?"

Long nodded. "Yeah. Like I said, sometimes you

make a deal with the devil. It wasn't personal, Mac-Manus, you know that."

I looked back toward the refuge and thought about all that. I thought about the dead and about the injured, the maimed, the scarred. I thought about my own injuries, the ringing in my ears that started that night it rained nightsticks on me and hasn't gone away yet.

After a while I looked at Long and said, "So what are you going to do now?"

"That's the question, isn't it? That's what I'm trying to find out. Where do disgraced cops go?"

"Why did you do it, Long? Why did you care that the Chief was doing what he was doing? Why'd you risk everything and take him on?"

"I've got a daughter, MacManus. I've got a wife. We live in this town, or will anyway till the bank kicks us out of our home. I was supposed to make this town safe for them, for everyone, not just for a chosen few, not for the Chief's sociopath son and for rich scum like Bishop. I just couldn't sit around on my hands and watch anymore. It was getting harder and harder to look at myself in the mirror. It was getting harder and harder to see the reflection of my face in my daughter's glasses. Do you have any idea what kind of hell that is?"

I said nothing.

Long shrugged. "Anyway, they're proud of me. They don't care if we lose the house. As long as they don't learn the shit I did before my big brave stand, then maybe they'll stay proud."

"We've all done shit, Long," I said. "We're men, it's what we do."

Long waited a moment, then said, "I remember the morning I found you all shot up on the floor of that kitchen. You were in and out of consciousness, and you kept saying, over and over, 'I was too late. I was too late.' I find myself saying that a lot lately. Maybe there'd be a lot people still alive if I had done this sooner. You can drive yourself crazy just thinking about that."

I looked at Long and waited, saying nothing. I was back for a moment in the silence that had brought me here, brought me this far from my home.

"He's still out for you, MacManus," he said finally. "The Chief. You know that, right? He's out for you and for me both now. Hell, my name is probably right next to yours on his list. You know, I was thinking, we might want to keep in touch with each other, you and I, you know, in case some day one of us needs a friend."

I nodded. Over the flat water a hawk flew in a wide circle, hunting. There was no breeze here. The air seemed suddenly very cool, like a dead spot in a room.

"Yeah," I said. "Yeah, maybe that's a good idea."

"I don't know where we'll end up, my family and I, I mean. It's pretty clear we've got a transition ahead of us. I should have stashed some cash away, you know, when I started this whole thing. But you don't think that way, do you? You don't think that you can lose it all. If you did, you'd probably never do anything."

"Probably not."

"Anyway, you'll be around, right?"

"I'm not going anywhere, Long. You know where to find me."

Long looked at me for a long time then. I realized that he was holding a set of keys in his left hand.

"I'm sorry that she died, MacManus. From what I understand, you two had been through a lot together. Anyway, I'm sorry it turned out that way for her."

I said the only thing I could. "Me, too."

"I'd offer you a ride back to town, but I've got some things to do here."

"Don't worry about it, Long. Take it easy."

"You, too."

I left him then and walked around the house to the driveway. Long's car was parked by the front door. I saw that the gate was opened, the chain in a pile on the grass. I walked down the drive and passed through the gate but decided not to leave just yet. I had to confirm a realization that had come to me suddenly. I crossed the wide street and stood beside a tree at the curb and waited. It wasn't too long after that that I saw Long come through the front door. I watched him load his car with things that I recognized—Tiffany lamps, ornate wooden boxes that I knew contained silverware, gold candlestick holders, everything he could grab and sell for quick money. I just stood beside the tree and watched. It didn't matter to me one way or the other. After a few quick trips in and out of the house Long locked the door behind himself and got into his car and drove down the driveway. At the road he got out, swung the gate closed, and locked the shiny chain around it, then drove off.

I hid behind the tree as he went. I didn't care if he saw me. I just thought I'd spare him the embarrassment of being seen doing what he had to do for the sake of his family.

I retraced my steps back home that afternoon, avoiding that part of town where the Chief and Frank Gannon were. I craved my home suddenly, deeply. But when I got there I felt restless. I stood in the doorway of my bedroom and looked in at my unmade bed, at where we had come that night last spring, she and I, where I had held her in my arms, where she had told me her name was Rose and I was too drunk to know any different, and too drunk to act, not just in time but at all. I stood and watched the very spot where she had realized that I could not help her, that I wasn't the man she had hoped I was, where I had watched her dress and where she last stood before leaving me to continue on her search for someone who wouldn't betray her, who would die for her, who wouldn't ever let her down.

That night in my bed I searched for hours for sleep. When it finally came the last thing I was aware of was a smoky dawn outside my windows and the sound of a neighbor's dog barking in continuous warning a block away. I dreamed the dream again, of that long-ago morning when that rabid mastiff bore down on her, tearing into her and into me. The last thing I remember before coming to was the echo of the shots fired by the Chief cutting the summer air and Rose-Marie Bishop pulling me across the pavement slick with our blood toward her, pulling me away from the mouth of the beast that had tried to devour us, pulling me into her young, trembling arms.

About the Author

D. DANIEL JUDSON was born and raised in Connecticut. He writes full time from his home and is currently at work on another novel.